THE CONFESSIONS OF NIPPER MOONEY

D1220504

2-piece
set

Also by Ed Kavanagh

For Children
Amanda Greenleaf Visits a Distant Star—1986
Amanda Greenleaf and the Spell of the Water Witch—1987
Amanda Greenleaf and the Boy Magician—1991

Drama
*The Cat's Meow: The 'Longside Players Selected Plays,
1984-1989*—1990 (Co-author and editor)

The Confessions of Nipper Mooney

A NOVEL

ED KAVANAGH

Best wishes —
Ed Kavanagh

kiLLick press
an imprint of Creative Publishers

St. John's, Newfoundland
2001

© 2001, Ed Kavanagh

Le Conseil des Arts | The Canada Council
du Canada | for the Arts

We acknowledge the support of The Canada Council for the Arts for our
publishing program.

We acknowledge the financial support of the Department for Canadian
Heritage for our publishing program.

All rights reserved. No part of this work covered by the copyrights hereon may be
reproduced or used in any form or by any means — graphic, electronic or
mechanical — without the prior written permission of the publisher. Any
requests for photocopying, recording, taping or information storage and
retrieval systems of any part of this book shall be directed in writing to the
Canadian Reprography Collective, One Yonge Street, Suite 1900,
Toronto, Ontario M5E 1E5.

Lines from the poem "Sea-Gulls" (page 234) are taken from *Complete Poems/E.J.
Pratt,* edited by Sandra Djwa and R.G. Moyles, University of Toronto Press,
©1989, and are reprinted by permission of the publisher.

This is a work of fiction. The characters and incidents depicted are imaginary.
Any resemblance to real people and events is coincidental.

∞ Printed on acid-free paper

Published by
KILLICK PRESS
an imprint of CREATIVE BOOK PUBLISHING
a division of 10366 Newfoundland Limited
a Robinson-Blackmore Printing & Publishing associated company
P.O. Box 8660, St. John's, Newfoundland A1B 3T7

Third printing, July 2002
Typeset in 12 point Garamond

Printed in Canada by:
ROBINSON-BLACKMORE PRINTING & PUBLISHING

Canadian Cataloguing in Publication Data

Kavanagh, Ed, 1954-

The confessions of Nipper Mooney : a novel

ISBN 1-894294-28-9

I. Title

PS8571.A92C66   2001   C813'.54   C2001-900991-7
PR9199.3.K38C66   2001

LANL

To Theresa

and

In memory of Agnes and my parents

I have learned my songs from the music of many birds
and from the music of many waters.

—*The Kalevala*

THE CONFESSIONS OF NIPPER MOONEY

On the morning of August 15, 1962, the day his father passed away, Nipper Mooney was stolen by the fairies.

He had woken to the dull plod of cows shambling up the road to Tim's Meadow; he closed his eyes and listened to the brass tinkling of their bells. The cows passed so close he could hear the splatter of their droppings, the soft swish of Brendan's alder urging them on.

Nipper sat up. He parted the lace curtains and looked out. The sky was perfectly clear; the sun burned just above the tree line.

When the cows had passed, he dressed and went downstairs. His mother was out—probably having tea at Annie's. Nipper made a breakfast of corn flakes and milk. Then he put on his sneakers, pushed open the screen door, and stepped into the brilliant sunlight.

He crossed the oiled road and headed up the freshly cut hayfield to the pole line. At Wishing Rock he stopped and looked back toward his house. Through the shape-shifting light, he saw the figure of Brendan moving down the road, his alder switch drawing random patterns in the air. He plucked a straw and watched as the old man disappeared from sight.

Nipper wandered on and suddenly threw himself into a patch of soft grass. Scents of heather and juniper rose from the sun-soaked ground. He turned over on his back and looked up at the brightening sky. The air was perfectly calm. It was strangely quiet, the birds and insects hushed, dazed by the rising heat.

Nipper closed his eyes. He breathed deeply and listened to the muted drumming of his heart.

A shadow passed across his face. He got to his feet and wandered back down to the hayfield. When his house came into view, he stopped and looked up. The sky had clouded over, a freshened breeze ruffled the tops of the spruce and fir.

Aunt Mona was standing on the doorstep.

Even from such a distance, he could see that her face was swollen, distorted—like she'd been to the dentist. She knotted a red dishcloth, twisted it around her hands. She began to run across the road toward him.

Nipper stopped, amazed, and waited.

"Where have you been?" Mona said. She reached down and grabbed his hand. Nipper stared up at her wide, bruised eyes, the scarlet lipstick smudging her full lips. He had never noticed that her eyes were so blue.

"You had the life frightened out of me," Mona said, pulling him toward the house. "Where *were* you?"

"Nowhere. Just playing. Just up on the pole line. When did you get here?"

Mona opened the screen door. "Get in and get your supper. And not a word."

Nipper stepped into the vestibule. "What?"

"I said, go in and sit down to your supper. And no foolishness. The potatoes aren't fit for a dog."

Nipper pulled off his sneakers and stared at his aunt. "What are you talking about? I don't want any supper. Sure I just had breakfast."

Mona sighed. "Nipper—no foolishness. I'm not kidding. Not today."

"But why are you giving me supper?"

Mona snapped the dishcloth against her leg. "Why do you think? Because it's suppertime. Look at the clock."

The Timex above the oil stove showed only one hand. Then he saw that both hands were on the six. He looked out the kitchen window; creeping shadows darkened the barn door.

Nipper slumped into his chair. "But that can't be right. I just left the house a half an hour ago. It *can't* be suppertime."

"I said—give it up." Mona set a plate of sausages and boiled potatoes before him. "Eat."

Nipper stared at the food. "Where's Mom?"

His aunt turned back to the stove. "She's . . . at the hospital."

"Mona, what's wrong with your face?"

"Nothing."

"But—"

"I said, *eat.*"

The call came at seven o'clock. Mona listened silently, staring out the picture window, her face pale but calm. She passed the phone to Nipper. It was a bad line. His mother's voice sounded thin and metallic, as if it were coming from a great distance. She told him his father had gone to heaven. He was to obey his Aunt Mona. She would be home soon.

The first cars arrived twenty minutes later. By eight o'clock the driveway was blocked; pick-ups wound down the road, double-parked, hugging the drains and ditches.

Nipper sat in the living room and watched an assortment of legs pass before him. Everyone seemed to be moving in a continuous circle: kitchen, living room, dining room, kitchen, living room, dining room. Finally, a pair of legs stopped. A man crouched before him: Uncle Phonse. He always gave Nipper a dollar at Christmas. Phonse had a beer in his right hand; he laid the left on Nipper's shoulder and smiled. His uncle's eyes were a pale, watery blue; Nipper stared at their webs of veins and broken blood vessels.

Phonse pulled his tie away from his chapped neck and squeezed Nipper's shoulder. "You have to be the man of the house now," he said. Nipper smelled Phonse's beery breath. He wondered if he was supposed to say something. Phonse finished his beer and looked at Nipper intently. "Did your mom talk to you?"

"Yeah."

"What did she say?"

"All about heaven and stuff."

Phonse nodded. "That's where he is now. He was a good man, your father."

"I know."

"Are you all right?"

Nipper shrugged. "I . . . "

"Yes," Phonse said. He glanced at the floor, then back at Nipper. "Listen, I know it's hard for you to understand. But it's better this way. He'd been in a lot of pain. It was all very peaceful in the end. He just . . . passed peacefully away." Nipper remained silent. "Do you understand?" Phonse said. "He wasn't going to get well—"

"I *know*," Nipper said, surprised at the irritation in his voice. He stared over his uncle's shoulder at the carousel of passing bodies. "I know."

Phonse stroked his chin and placed his empty beer bottle on the end table.

"Phonse?"

"Yeah?"

"Something kind of weird happened today."

"It's been a hard day for everyone."

"No, not that . . . something else."

Phonse shifted his weight painfully. "What?"

4

"Well," Nipper said, rocking back and forth on the chester-field, "I was . . . I was playing up on the pole line this morning and . . . "

"Yeah?"

"And I was walking up by Wishing Rock and . . . "

"Go on."

"And . . . well . . . " Nipper stopped rocking. He looked down at the floor. "Nothing," he said. "It was probably nothing."

His uncle patted Nipper's knee. "You're sure?"

"Yeah."

"Well, all right, then."

Phonse reached inside his jacket, hesitated, then withdrew his hand. He squeezed Nipper's shoulder and went out to the kitchen.

The living room was thick with cigarette smoke. Nipper got up and threaded his way through a tangle of arms and legs. Hands attached to murmuring voices caressed his head and shoulders. His mother was standing near the television. She wore a string of pearls and a blue-black dress he had never seen before. Her face was as pale as her pearls; her eyes, always dark, seemed almost black. It struck Nipper that his mother was strangely beautiful. She stirred, felt someone looking at her. He watched as her eyes scanned the room, her gaze, finally, coming to rest on him. She smiled weakly and nodded.

Nipper went upstairs. He threw himself face down on the bed and closed his eyes. *You have to be the man of the house now.* He turned over on his back and stared up at the ceiling. The man of the house. That worried him. Phonse had sounded like he really meant it.

Nipper got up and looked out the window; it was getting dark. He heard the grating of a bicycle chain, and in the half-light he saw Brendan Flynn pedalling slowly up the road. He stopped in front of the house and got off. Brendan was wearing a rumpled white shirt and a bow tie. He leaned the Raleigh against the fence and carefully patted down his shirt and pant legs. He went to the gate, lifted the latch, and pushed the gate open.

Brendan hesitated.

He reached in, swung the gate closed, and went back to his bike. Then he wheeled around and set off down the road, the fenders of the ancient Raleigh jangling with the dip of every rut and pothole.

ONE

1

*P*atrick Mooney leaned forward and peered into the glowing incubator. The infant clenched his eyes and quivered, his red, wrinkled limbs folding and unfolding like the tendrils of some exotic plant.

Patrick looked up. "He's a little nipper, isn't he?"

The doctor smiled. "It's all relative," he said. "Four pounds six ounces isn't too bad." He gestured around the room with his clipboard. "There are two or three here even smaller. Compared to them, this fellow is quite large."

Patrick glanced at the doctor sideways. "Large?" he said. "Sure the cat could go off with something the size o' that."

The doctor laughed. "Don't worry. His breathing is much better and his heart rate is excellent." He laid a hand on Patrick's forearm. "He'll be fine."

That afternoon Patrick looked out the window of his wife's hospital room and studied the traffic passing along St. Clare Avenue. "I hope that doctor is right," he said. "There's certainly not much to our little Nipper—not yet anyway."

Sharon sat up in bed and jabbed a finger at her husband. "Oh no," she said. "Don't get started. You're not calling him that."

"Calling him what?"

"I mean it, Pat. I know you." She turned and pounded her pillows. "He's got a lovely name. I don't want you ruining it."

For months Sharon had agonized over a proper Christian name for her first child. A girl, she'd decided, would be called Peg—after her favourite aunt; a boy, Nicholas—a name which in her mind bore just the right combination of dignity and flair: a name befitting a businessman or politician, even a movie star or a priest. She had no intention of letting Nicholas be usurped by a nickname—especially something as silly as Nipper. Patrick pointed out that if their son ever did don the clerical collar he would rarely be called by his first name anyway, just "Father Mooney"; so what difference did it make? "Besides," he added, "how are you going to feel if the child grows up fat, with a cherry nose, wearing a red suit and handing out presents to every Tom, Dick and Harry? He'll have us bankrupt in no time."

Sharon was not amused. "The child's name is Nicholas," she said, savouring the word on her tongue. She settled into her pillows and glared at her husband. "*Nich-o-las*," she repeated, drawing out each syllable. "Or," she added, lightly tapping her chin, "Nick." Sharon clasped her hands in her lap and lowered her eyes. "It's one or the other, okay?"

But Patrick persisted.

It had seemed natural for him to call the child Nipper; as far as he was concerned, that should be his name. And despite his wife's protestations, that's what he continued to call him. Soon, even the doctors and nurses were referring to the Mooney baby as Nipper.

Weeks later, then, when the child was carefully bundled up for the journey home to Kildura, neighbours and relatives prepared for the homecoming of Nipper—not Nicholas—Mooney. And throughout his childhood and teenage years, only a handful of people ever called him by his Christian name.

The first Kildura Mooney was an Irish servant who had jumped ship at St. John's in the late eighteenth century. This was the opinion of Kevin Mooney, Nipper's grandfather. Something of a local historian, he occasionally visited the archives in St.

John's. One day he came upon a notice in the *Royal Gazette*, which he promptly copied into his scribbler:

> Deserted:
> From the Service of Thomas Bulley & Co. on Saturday last the 21st instant:
> William Mulves—23 years of age, fair complexion, brown hair, 5 feet 4 inches tall—a native of Ireland.
> John Mooney—24 years of age, fair complexion, dark hair, with foxy whiskers, 6 feet high—a native of Ireland.
> The above Deserters, arrived here in the Brig Thomas, Thomas Bulley, Master, from Waterford. A reward of Three Pounds for each man, is hereby offered to any person or persons who will apprehend the above named deserters, or either of them, or give such information as will lead to their apprehension.
>
> Masters of vessels and others are hereby cautioned not to harbour, conceal, or carry off the above named deserters, as they will be prosecuted to the utmost rigour of the law.
>
> St. John's, 26th May, 1796

Nipper's grandfather was convinced that John Mooney had made his way to Kildura—was, in fact, his ancestor. When it was pointed out that, if the Mooney deserter had come to Kildura, he probably would have changed his name, Kevin shrugged it off. "A Mooney would never give up his name," he said. "Not forever, anyway."

Other Kildura families, the Murphys and Walshes in particular, also claimed deserter lineage. Ship-jumping had been common in St. John's in the eighteenth century, and in the early part of the nineteenth, it increased. Kildura was well known as a deserter enclave. Most eventually moved on, wanting to put as much distance between themselves and the scene of their desertion as possible, but others—perhaps John Mooney among them—stayed, cleared the forests, and farmed some of the best land on the Avalon Peninsula.

By the late nineteenth century Kildura was a thriving farming community. Perhaps because so many early Kildurans had assumed aliases, naming, both of people and places, had become something of a local art form. Some of the names were purely utilitarian—Beaver Pond, Rocky Pond, Three Island Pond (this for a pond that could legitimately claim but two islands, one long submerged and now visible only in years of drought)—but most of Kildura's woods, rivers, meadows and marshes seemed to have been christened by poets or painters: the Fairy Woods, Table and Chair Mountain, Shalloway Pond, the Damsel's Eye, Heart Lake, Bitter Cherry Orchard, the Roundabout. Two parallel, finger-like ponds were known as the Devil's Darning Needles, in deference to the hordes of dragonflies that crowded their rushes and reeds. And yet, while every gully, valley or body of water big enough for people to drown themselves in had been named, when it came to the roads of the community, the imaginative quirks of the early settlers had deserted them, and the three main arteries were dubbed the Upper Road, the Lower Road, and the Old Road. It was to a house on the Upper Road that Nipper Mooney was brought after his premature birth and prolonged stay in St. Clare's Mercy Hospital.

The Old Road, merely an extension of the Upper Road, led west from Kildura—not much more than a woods road really, and often no more than a muddy path that meandered through ten miles of woods and barrens. At the five-mile point, near the Darning Needles, the road crested, offering up, in varying shades of blue or grey, an ever-changing vista of the Atlantic. At times the water was indistinct or completely lost in mist, fog or snow; at other times it shimmered, sparkling blue, flecked with the white of distant icebergs or pricked by ships which lay below the horizon like markers on a map.

From here the road descended through five miles of barrens and tuckamore to the fishing community of Deep Harbour, the first of many small communities that stretched down the jagged coast. Deep Harbour was only ten miles away, but it might just as well have been a thousand, for the ocean was not a sight which many Kildurans ever saw or cared to see, and even the most ardent walkers rarely travelled that far.

In a photograph of Nipper Mooney taken when he was three years old, he is standing on the shore of the Damsel's Eye holding a plastic fishing pole. Patrick, tanned, and with a twisted roll-up dangling from his mouth, grins into the camera, one arm wrapped around Nipper, the other shielding his eyes from the sun. A cork bobber floats a few feet offshore; Nipper stares at it intently, as if wondering what it might possibly be.

Numerous paths branched out from Kildura's Old Road, and it seemed to Nipper that he had always known them. The paths led everywhere and nowhere: to logging woods of spruce and fir; to cow pastures thick with thistle and clover and rimmed with whitening windfall; to brackish ponds framed by wild raisin and purple chokeberry; to stands of bright birch, the bark of the young trees as smooth and shiny as a child's face; to marshes and bogs peppered with red, rubbery pitcher plants; to fields of blueberries and partridgeberries; and to yellow carpets of pungent chanterelles.

Nipper always wondered why so many paths criss-crossed the Old Road. It seemed that Kildura's early settlers had rarely worked together when choosing a route. Everyone had their own way of getting somewhere, and while some of the lesser trails had been lost to encroaching woods, their shadowy outlines still remained, visible only when the sun hit the trees at a certain angle or when a wet fog hung low over the brush; then, like a watermark when paper is held to the light, long-forgotten paths would emerge into spectral silhouettes.

Along the Old Road, a wanderer could see rabbits, fox, muskrat, snipe, weasel and black duck; a partridge might whir up from a gully, its wings ruffling like the motor of an electric fan. Beavers were rare, but their ancient houses still existed, stone-grey and crumbling, looming out of the fog like archaeological ruins. Juncos, jays and robins skittered through the trees and sky. And always, the herring gulls wheeled and soared, a reminder that the freezing Atlantic was only miles away.

Kildura's distance from the sea and its devotion to farming made it something of an anomaly in eastern Newfoundland. It was also singular in that, while the whole coast was Irish Catholic, Kildura was the only community named for a saint—albeit, indirectly—for Kildura translates from the Gaelic as "church of the oak," a reference to St. Brigid, a fifth-century Irish saint who had started her first abbey near an oak in what is now County Kildare. Few Kildurans were aware of the complete legend, but the original settlers, more connected to their Irish roots, knew that St. Brigid was the patron saint of farmers, as she was of smiths, healers, learning and poets. She was Brigid the all-provider, the nurturer, symbolized by her cow that always gave milk. A perfect saint for a dairy farming community. And so the early settlers had named their town Kildura, and their church, St. Brigid's.

St. Brigid's emblem was fire. It is said that when she took her vows a flame issued from her forehead. After her death, the sisters of her order kept a fire burning in her honour for over six hundred years. Perhaps the local bishop knew of St. Brigid's affinity with fire, for when Kildura's church burned to the ground in 1906, he decreed that the new church would be renamed for St. Christopher—Brigid not even warranting a stained glass window. St. Christopher, as far as anyone in Kildura knew, had never been to Ireland, and while he was, as Nipper's Grandfather Kevin put it, "a good hand in the water," he apparently knew nothing about farming. Kildurans worried that no good would come of this change, but their importunities to the bishop were in vain. Kevin Mooney was so incensed at the dethroning of St. Brigid that he put on his best suit and, in a driving rain, walked all the way to St. John's. He rapped on the bishop's door and insisted on seeing him. When the bishop finally appeared, Kevin came straight to the point.

"I'm telling you, sir, that if the name of Kildura's church is not changed back to St. Brigid's, I'll never step inside those doors."

The bishop regarded Kevin coolly. "Maybe not," he said, closing his own door. "But someday you'll be *carried* in."

Neither was Monsignor Murphy, Kildura's parish priest when Nipper was growing up, a devotee of St. Brigid. He never mentioned her in his services and St. Christopher rarely. Still, over the years, she survived in collective memory, and, in the 1920s, when a new school was built, the people would not be denied: it was named for St. Brigid.

As a Christian name, Brigid was rare in Kildura, although there were some older ladies named from the derivative—Bride or Bridey. Nipper himself had a rather prickly great-aunt named Biddy Mooney. "Your Aunt Biddy is coming for supper to-night," his mother would say. "So I don't want to hear a peep out of you." But for a long time, even after the christening of the new school, there was only one little girl in all of Kildura named Brigid.

2

*L*ike the ancient paths of the Old Road, Nipper Mooney's first Kildura memory was shadowy—some of its edges clear, others rounded and soft.

It was the day of the Garden Party, and he stood outside the Parish Hall holding his mother's hand and clutching a glass-eyed teddy bear. He was tired from wandering the grounds, and, despite cotton candy and a bag of chips, hungry and looking forward to the turkey tea. It was a sultry evening; although a fine, even rain hissed steadily on the front steps, the huge hall doors were thrown wide open.

His mother rummaged in her purse, pressed a two-dollar bill into his hand, and nudged him forward.

"Pay Mr. Keough."

Nipper offered the bill to a man sitting in the cramped ticket office, and he and his mother passed into the crowded hall.

They found places at a long, paper-covered table. Nipper sat, legs dangling, looking in wonder at the assortment of salads, hams, pies and cookies spread before him. Five or six places to his right, Brigid Flynn sat with her Uncle Brendan. At a table below the stage, he saw Ronnie Sheehan. Nipper knew Brigid and Ronnie; they lived just down the road from him.

His mother stabbed turkey, scooped potato salad, and passed him a plate. Aproned women wandered up and down the aisle bending low to his ear.

"Got enough, my duckie?"

"Anything else, my love?"

Nipper noticed that the stage curtains were open. At a table set stage right, two men dressed in black sat eating. He tugged at his mother's elbow.

"Who are they?"

"That's the priest—Monsignor Murphy," she said, raising her tea cup. "Sure you knows him. You sees him every Sunday."

"Oh yeah," Nipper said. "He looks different. Why is he all dressed in black?"

"Because he hasn't got his vestments on—his church clothes. That's his everyday clothes."

Why would a priest wear black? Nipper had thought that only wicked people wore black—like the bad guys in the Saturday Westerns.

"Who's the other one?"

"That's the bishop."

"What's a bishop?"

"Well, he's a priest, too—but higher up. He's Monsignor Murphy's boss."

Old Monsignor Murphy had a boss? Nipper could not picture anyone telling him what to do—not even God.

"Why are they up there?"

Nipper's mother cradled her chin on her hands and looked up at the stage. "I suppose it's just so they'll have more room. So they can spread out. You see, they're special guests—especially the bishop."

Nipper studied them again. They were digging into their food as if they hadn't had a meal in weeks. Being a priest must be hungry work. They looked funny all by themselves. As he watched, a woman approached them with a teapot and carefully poured into their delicate china cups.

His mother pushed her plate away and turned to him. "I'm going to help out in the kitchen for a bit. You stay there and finish your supper."

Nipper nodded. As he reached for a date crumble, he felt

someone looking at him, or perhaps someone had called his name. He scanned the bustling hall, listening over the clatter of cutlery, the scrape of chairs on the wooden floor. He glanced toward the open doors; people were still lining up to pay the admission, taking off caps, and shaking rain from their clothes.

Just outside the doors, peering around the corner, stood a boy Nipper had never seen before, a shock of red hair rain-plastered to his forehead.

Nipper's first thought was that the boy needed a haircut. He peered into the hall, his hands jammed into his pockets, his shoulders hunched slightly forward. He stared at Nipper, who was munching on his date crumble, crumbs spilling down his chin.

The boy wore a white, long-sleeved shirt. Nipper wondered why he was wearing a shirt like that when it was still summer. When the boy's turn came, he pushed the hair out of his eyes and approached Mr. Keough. He said something and listened to the reply. Then he hovered momentarily near the wicket, turned, and disappeared around the side of the building.

Nipper smelled perfume and coffee at his shoulder, and a warm voice asked, "Had enough, my love?"

He put the half-eaten date crumble back on his plate and nodded. As the woman passed by, he looked again toward the doors. The boy was nowhere to be seen, but now a rain-slicked spaniel had crept to the entrance. The dog tilted its nose and sniffled, scuffling forward until a man hissed and stamped his foot. The spaniel retreated a few yards and circled the steps. It flopped on its belly and began to inch forward once again.

The boy did not reappear.

In Nipper's memory of the Garden Party, some things were etched clearly: the sweetness of the date crumble, the way Monsignor Murphy and the bishop leaned over their food, the creeping of the soaked spaniel. But the face of the boy in the rain was a blur.

Sometimes Nipper wondered if he had really been there at all.

3

St. Brigid's School was a single storey, long and low, with doors at each end like a railway car. To the south, flowed the Waterford River. The front of the school faced the road, and the back, atop a sloping hill, allowed for a half-basement. Even in the spring and early fall, the building was damp and cool, its radiators perpetually bubbling and hissing. The wooden desks, their black wrought-iron legs fixed to the floor, still smelled of the nineteenth century. There was no lunchroom, no library, no gym. The school consisted of six classrooms, a cramped principal's office, two chilly bathrooms, and a janitor's cubby-hole crowded with mops and shovels, wax and disinfectant. In a corner of the foyer, perched on a chipped, marble pedestal, stood a statue of St. Brigid, a cluster of plastic flowers curling at her painted feet.

On Nipper Mooney's first day of school, the principal, Sister Mary Ignatius, visited his classroom. Her speech, which he would hear every September, varied little from year to year.

"As you know, our parish church just down the road is named for St. Christopher—the Christ Bearer. Long ago St. Christopher carried the Baby Jesus across a raging river—a river, I would assume, not unlike our own. The farther St. Christopher went into that river, the heavier the Baby Jesus became. Because you see, boys and girls, the Baby Jesus was carrying the weight of all the world's sins. And that great weight passed onto the shoulders of poor St. Christopher. But he persevered and brought Our Lord and Saviour safely to shore. For that brave and selfless deed, he was made a saint.

"Now, I am a great admirer of St. Christopher. But I would prefer that he not have to come out of retirement and save one of *you* little boys and girls if you play too near the river and end up falling in. It has happened in the past. I do *not* want it to happen again." She buried each hand in its opposite sleeve and lowered her pale eyes. "Do I make myself clear?"

And Nipper Mooney, along with the rest of his classmates, answered with the phrase he would repeat thousands of times over the next five years.

"Yes, Sister."

Sister Mary Ignatius was the most colourless person Nipper had ever seen. The only parts of her that were not black or white were her washed-out blue eyes and her antique, gold-rimmed glasses. She was skinny and tall—well over six feet. The skirt of her habit rode high above her ankles; it was easy to see her scuffed, black leather shoes.

She taught, like most of the nuns, by filling the blackboard with endless lines of numbers and letters that the children copied down, attempted to memorize, and were later quizzed on. During some of those writing marathons, Nipper often thought that all the colour had been drained from the world. Black and white—everything was black and white. He marvelled at how well the nuns blended in with the blackboard: the white of the chalk and the black of the board merged mystically with their black-and-white habits, and, in the case of Sister Mary Ignatius, with her pasty-white complexion. When Nipper looked up from the drudgery and glanced outside, the maples along the river burned such a shimmering, fiery green they almost hurt his eyes.

The nuns' habits covered every inch of their bodies except for their faces and hands. Sister Mary Ignatius didn't even like bare hands, and she often pulled them up inside her sleeves.

Nipper thought it was funny that the nuns were so covered up, when Jesus, nailed to the wooden crosses hanging on their chests, was just about naked.

One Christmas, as the nuns filed silently into the first row of St. Christopher's and kneeled—heads bowed, hands full of Rosary beads—Patrick Mooney winked at Nipper. "They puts me in mind of a line of turrs perched on a cliff," he said.

"Pat, give it up," Nipper's mother whispered. "That's a mortal sin for you. It's Christmas, for God's sake."

But Nipper knew what his father meant. The nuns *did* look like birds—especially when three or four, their long skirts floating and twirling, bustled around the Kildura Parish Hall, setting up the chairs for bingo. When Sister Mary Ignatius was at the blackboard, her bony hand wrapped firmly around a tiny chalk-end, she reminded Nipper of a crow scratching in the dirt.

When the students had finished with the material on the blackboard, Sister Mary Ignatius would come around to check their work. As she leaned over Nipper's desk, he was overcome by that unique nun smell: a combination of chalk, powder and the stifling, mothballed odour of her habit. He wondered how often the nuns washed them. Did they wash them themselves? How many habits did they own?

The only thing that fascinated him more than their habits was their hair. Was it short? Long? Put up in a bun? Did they have any hair at all, or were their heads completely shaved? And if so, who shaved them?

Sister Bernadette was reading the class Bible stories. Nipper liked Sister Bernadette. Sister Bernadette arranged the flowers at the feet of St. Brigid every morning. She spoke softly and hummed to herself when she printed things on the blackboard. Her skin was pale—almost as pale as Sister Mary Ignatius's. Nipper thought this was because she prayed all the time and never got any sun. Sister Bernadette was the holiest nun in all of St. Brigid's—perhaps in the whole world.

She closed the book.

"For the rest of class we will have reflection. You may read quietly in your catechism or put your head down on your desk and meditate."

Ronnie Sheehan put up his hand. "What does 'meditate' mean, Sister?"

"It means 'think,' Ronnie."

"What are we supposed to think about?"

"That's up to you. You could, for example, think about the great love borne to you by Our Lord and Saviour, Jesus Christ."

"Oh," Ronnie said, putting his head down.

Nipper liked reflection. Most of the children just went to sleep, but he always looked in the catechism. The cover of the catechism was a deep sky-blue—so vivid he wondered it didn't stain his fingers. Enclosed in an oval, the Virgin Mary clasped her hands in prayer and gazed at the Baby Jesus lying in His crib. Somehow her hands looked too small—the hands of a young child attached to a woman's body. A golden light glowed around the infant. He gazed heavenwards with wide, piercing blue eyes.

The pages of the catechism were glossy white, the questions printed in stark, black bold:

> **Who made us?**
> God made us.
>
> **Who is God?**
> God is the Supreme Being, infinitely perfect, who made all things and keeps them in existence.

Nipper reached into his desk for a pencil. Then he bent down and peered inside. He slid out of his seat and raised his hand.

"Sister?"

No answer; his voice was too low.

"Sister?"

Sister Bernadette looked up, offered Nipper raised eyebrows and a questioning twitch across her full lips.

"Sister, there's a mouse in my desk."

Behind him, Violet Dobbin screamed and jumped up on her seat. Some of the other children bounded into the aisles.

"There's a . . . *what* in your desk, Nipper?" Sister Bernadette asked.

"A mouse, Sister."

"Go way," Ronnie Sheehan said, coming to look.

"Ronnie, stay where you are," Sister Bernadette said. "Everyone, back in your seats." She raised a hand to her throat and looked Nipper in the eye. "Are you absolutely . . . sure?"

"Oh yes, Sister. Look!" Nipper reached into his desk for the evidence.

"No, don't!" Violet said, struggling to keep her balance. But Nipper was already holding up the mouse by its tail.

"Jeez," Ronnie sniffed. "It's dead."

"Yeah, I never said it wasn't dead."

"Well, that's no fun if it's *dead.*"

Sister Bernadette looked at Nipper. "Is the beast dead?"

Nipper shook the mouse and nodded. "It's dead."

"Then take it and put it in the garbage—no, bring it to Mr. Meaney. He'll know what to do with it. And Nipper . . . "

He turned to her.

"Wash your hands."

"Yes, Sister."

"You can get down now, Violet," Sister Bernadette said.

"Don't like mice, do you, Violet?" Ronnie asked. "Sure they won't hurt you—especially the dead ones."

Sister Bernadette shook her head and sighed. "The next

time, Nipper, say right away whether or not the beast is dead, will you?"

"Yes, Sister."

Nipper dropped the small grey corpse on his speller and grinned around the room. Holding the book before him, he headed for the door. From their seats the boys strained to look; the girls sat tightly, a mixture of fear and disgust on their faces.

"There better not be no mouse in my desk," Violet said, peering around.

"No, you probably got a rat in your desk," Ronnie said. "A great big black— "

"Oh, Sister, tell him to stop!"

"Now, class, that's enough excitement for one day," Sister Bernadette said. "No, you may not leave the room, Ronnie," she added, anticipating his waving arm.

Once more the class settled down. As Nipper was leaving, he saw Brigid Flynn look up from her book. She sat in the first desk by the door. She'd been the only one in the class who hadn't seemed the least bit interested in the mouse. Nipper paused and then shoved it under her nose. Brigid glanced at it and rolled her eyes. She shook her head and settled back to her book.

"God Love 'im Roy Driscoll" sat behind Brigid Flynn. He was older than everyone else. Nipper wasn't sure how much older he was, but he was awfully big to be in grade one.

Roy Driscoll got his nickname because he was simple. People were always saying, "Poor Roy, God love 'im. Yes, he's a bit off, but sure he's as good as gold. He's not harmin' anyone." Nipper's mother said it. So did Annie who lived next door. And then they'd ruffle his hair or give him a quarter and send him on a message down to Blake's Groc. and Conf.

God Love 'im's printing and numbers always looked backwards and jumbled. The nuns hardly ever asked him a question; they knew he'd never get the right answer. He didn't even have to memorize the catechism; Sister Bernadette just got him to repeat everything after her. God Love 'im only put up his hand when he wanted to go to the bathroom. He hardly ever talked to anyone except Brigid; sometimes he tapped her on the shoulder and asked when recess or lunch was.

Nipper had heard that simple people always went to heaven. He wondered about that, didn't think it was fair. Nipper might not be as good as gold, but sure he wasn't harmin' anyone, either. But if *he* wanted to go to heaven, he had to learn his catechism and arithmetic. God Love 'im Roy Driscoll didn't have to do any of that, but Jesus watched over him just the same.

Nipper knew why grown-ups treated Roy Driscoll the way they did. There wasn't any harm in him—him with that dopey grin plastered on his face. Always on his way down to Blake's or coming back with a pack of Export "A" or a half-dozen Coke for someone. Sure he was as good as gold—not a bit of harm in him.

Nipper discovered that God Love 'im Roy Driscoll wasn't all there on the very first day of school. Just before recess God Love 'im put up his hand.

"Yes, Roy?" Sister Bernadette said.

"Can I go to the bat'room, Missus?"

Missus—not even Miss. Everybody laughed, including God Love 'im, but Sister Bernadette just smiled and said he should call her Sister. And he did after that—most of the time. Sometimes he'd forget or he'd catch himself and say, "Yes, Missus—*Sister.*" And everyone would laugh. But sure what odds if people laughed at you if you had a free ticket into heaven? God Love 'im would have the last laugh, wouldn't he?

Nipper sometimes wondered what Roy would do when he

got to heaven. He'd probably hang around with all the other simple people—all of them as good as gold, sitting around on clouds and not harmin' anyone. Or maybe God would take away his simpleness, and he'd finally get to be an ordinary person. But sure he still wouldn't have to do any work—he'd be in heaven. Nipper knew envy was a sin, but sometimes he was envious of God Love 'im Roy Driscoll. It might be all right being simple.

God Love 'im liked Brigid Flynn because she sat in front of him and never made fun and always shared her bars and chips. Not like Barry Gallagher, who sat behind, and was always pucking him on the arm or poking him with a ruler. Lots of other people gave him a hard time, too.

One morning Nipper saw God Love 'im Roy Driscoll surrounded by a bunch of older kids—Mikey Sinnott, Randy Harding, Betty Bragg. They were trying to get his recess money. Roy still smiled his dopey smile, but his eyes were all hurt and confused. He tried to break through their circle, but they kept pushing him back. They kept saying, "Come on, b'y. Sure it's only a quarter. Don't be so mean." God Love 'im grew more and more flustered. He even stopped smiling his dopey smile. Finally, he just hunched down on the ground and clamped his hands over his ears.

And then Brigid Flynn pushed through the crowd. "Can't you just leave him alone?" she said. "Huh? Can't you? He's not hurtin' you."

"What's wrong, Bridgie?" Harding said. "Stickin' up for your boyfriend, are you?"

Brigid slapped her hands on her hips like a gunslinger on the Saturday Westerns. Her lower lip quivered and curled. "Just . . . leave him alone."

"Oh, go lie down out of it, you little jackatar," Mikey Sinnott said.

Betty Bragg sneered. "Jackatar."

Brigid's eyes flamed. She charged Mikey, swinging her bookbag and aiming a wild kick at his shin. But Mikey just grabbed her by the wrist and held her at arm's-length.

And then someone appeared at Mikey's side: Paddy Dunne. He pushed his red hair out of his eyes. "Let her go."

Mikey looked at Paddy. "Shag off. We're only having a bit of fun."

Paddy reached over and grabbed Mikey's free arm. "I said ... let her go."

Brigid broke free. She took one last whack at Mikey with her bookbag, then ran over and helped Roy up. She took him by the sleeve and led him into the school.

"Let go of my arm," Mikey said. But Paddy just stared at him as if he hadn't heard. And then Nipper saw Mikey's face screw up tight, and he knew that Paddy was squeezing his arm. Hard. Mikey's face grew red and puffy. He tried to pull away, but Paddy adjusted his grip and kept on squeezing.

The west door banged open. Sister Mary Ignatius charged out, her heavy Rosary beads swinging, her habit billowing behind her.

"What are ye youngsters up to? Get in the school. Now."

Paddy looked at Sister Mary Ignatius. He gave Mikey's arm one last squeeze and pushed him away.

"That was Paddy, Sister," Mikey said, shaking out his arm. "He was pickin' on us. We were just—"

"I said—*in the school.*"

Jackatar. What did that mean? Nipper knew what tar was. There were broken tar barrels up by his house where there used to be a quarry. Some of it had spilled out. In the summertime, the tar got hot and sticky, and Nipper had seen dead robins and sparrows stuck in it. Once, even a gull. His mother was always telling him to stay away from the bloody tar. "It'll ruin your clothes," she said. "There's no way you can get tar out. I'll have to put 'em in the garbage."

Tar.

Jackatar.

And then Nipper knew.

It was because Brigid was dark. Because her eyes were black. Because her long hair was as black and shiny as fresh tar.

Danny and Jack, Brigid's older brothers, were dark, too. But not like Brigid. Nobody in the whole school was as dark as Brigid.

That morning, during reflection, Nipper watched her. She sat quietly. Too quietly. Sometimes she rubbed her eyes with the back of her hand. She didn't read or meditate on the great love borne to her by her Lord and Saviour, Jesus Christ. She just sat.

During recess Nipper went over and dropped into the seat next to her. Her eyes were moist and red.

"Hey, Brigid, you want some Cheezies?"

"No, thank you."

"How about a cookie?"

"No . . . what kind?"

"Chocolate chip."

"All right." She took the cookie and slipped it into her brown-paper lunch bag.

Nipper looked around the classroom. Ronnie Sheehan was leaning up against the radiator, eating an apple. He stared at Nipper, then turned and headed out the door.

"Hey, Brigid, how come you're not drinking your Pepsi?" Nipper asked.

"I hates it."

"You hates *Pepsi*?"

"Uh-huh."

"I'll trade you my chocolate milk for it?"

"All right."

The exchange was made, and they sat drinking chocolate milk and Pepsi and not saying anything.

Every recess Brigid and Nipper traded drinks. But it was tough being friends with a girl. Ronnie Sheehan didn't know what to make of it. "Just because you trade drinks it don't mean you have to sit with her all the time."

"Yeah, well it don't mean I can't, either."

Ronnie shook his head. Nipper knew it wasn't that he didn't like Brigid. Brigid was all right. She'd even take a swing at Mikey Sinnott. And Ronnie didn't mind playing with her on the Upper Road. But why hang around with a girl in school when there were lots of boys to play with?

Nipper continued to sit with Brigid. One day he said, "Hey, Brigid, how come you weren't scared of the mouse that time?"

"Sure it was only an old mouse."

"Yeah, but Violet was frightened right to death. They don't bother you?"

"Why should they? I'm after seeing thousands of them. We got 'em home. There's tons in the barn. Father sets traps for 'em and catches 'em. Violet was cracked to go hoppin' up on her desk like that."

"Yeah," Nipper said. "Know what my dad said when I told him about it?"

"What?"

"He said it was just as well the mouse was dead 'cause he probably would've died laughing at her."

Brigid smiled. "I'm not saying now that I *likes* mice, but there's lots worse things to be scared of than an old mouse."

Nipper nodded. Yes, he thought. There certainly are.

4

*N*ipper stirred fitfully in his sleep. He sat up and peered out the window into the murky half-light. From downstairs came the rumble of a boiling kettle, the scrape of a knife on toast. He heard his parents moving about the kitchen, talking softly, murmuring. Why were they up? It was too early for breakfast. Nipper sank back into bed. Was it a school day? No, it was Saturday. He was going to hike out to Shalloway Pond with Ronnie. Nipper closed his eyes and drifted back to sleep.

The bed dipped, creaking the springs. He turned and saw his father silhouetted in the thin light. His hair was slicked back; he wore a jacket and tie. Nipper smelled his aftershave: Old Spice.

"Wake up," his father said softly.

Nipper yawned and put his arms under his head. "I am awake. Why are you dressed up? It's not Sunday."

His father tucked the bedclothes up to Nipper's chin. "I know," he said. "I got a job. I have to go away for a while."

"Far?" Nipper asked, wondering what kind of job required a jacket and tie.

"Cape Breton," his father said. "Nova Scotia. Pretty far."

Nipper rubbed his eyes and blinked. "What are you gonna do up there?"

"It's in a mine," his father said. "I got a job in a mine."

A mine. Nipper didn't like mines. Once he saw a movie on TV about miners. They had black faces and white eyes. They rode down underground in an elevator that looked like a cage. Just thinking about mines made Nipper queasy. Working in a mine must be like being buried alive.

"Why didn't you tell me before?"

"They just called last night."

"How come a mine?"

His father shrugged. "It's a good job," he said. "Pays good."

"Yeah, but—"

"I got to go now. I just came to say good-bye."

Nipper sat up. "When you coming back?"

His father got to his feet and brushed down the sides of his jacket. "Probably not until Christmas."

"Christmas! Christmas is years away."

His father grinned. "It's not that long." He kissed Nipper on the forehead. "I'll bring you back something nice." He went to the doorway and stopped. "You be a good boy for your mother."

"I'm getting up," Nipper said, throwing aside the covers.

"No, it's too early. It's not morning yet. Go back to sleep."

The door closed and his father was gone.

Nipper did not sleep. He turned on his side and watched the light changing in the window. The road, the trees, Annie's fence and shed next door—everything was slowly taking its shape.

A truck pulled up in front of the house—Francis Hartery's by the sound of the muffler. Nipper heard the door slam, the clatter of chains, the grating of the dropping tailgate. The screen door opened, the hinges whining and creaking, then snapped closed.

It wasn't until the truck had pulled away and he heard his mother's soft step on the stairs when he finally fell back to sleep.

How his father made a living had always been a mystery to Nipper. Whenever he was asked about it at school, he was at a loss to say. As near as he could figure it, he did a bit of everything. Once, when they were playing catch, Ronnie Sheehan suddenly said, "What does your father do?"

"Do?" Nipper said. "He . . . he works. What do you think?"

"Yeah, but what at? He don't farm like we do."

Nipper shrugged and tossed Ronnie the softball. "Business."

Ronnie frowned. "What does that mean?"

"Business, b'y. Business. Don't you know what business is?"

Ronnie tossed the ball back to Nipper. "Sure," he said. "I knows."

"Well, that's what he does. Business."

Ronnie nodded slowly. "Oh."

At least now Nipper could say something everyone would understand: *My dad's a miner up in Nova Scotia.*

With his father gone, the house felt different—empty. It wasn't that he'd ever spent much time indoors. He always seemed to be outside—fixing a tractor or working on a car up on blocks. Sometimes he drove over to Deep Harbour, and once he took Nipper with him. But all he did there was talk to some fishermen. Still, the house wasn't the same. It smelled different, too: no cigarette smoke, no Old Spice in the bathroom.

Not long after Nipper's father had left for Nova Scotia, his mother got a job in Blake's Groc. & Conf. "It's only part-time," he heard her tell Annie. "Just a few bucks to tide us over until Pat gets straightened away."

When Ronnie Sheehan walked into Blake's and saw Mrs. Mooney behind the counter, he biked up to Nipper's house and rapped on the door.

"Does she bring you home stuff?" he asked.

"No . . . what kind of stuff?"

"Chips, b'y, and bars. Stuff like that."

Nipper shook his head.

"Go way. She must. She works in a *shop*. She must get all that stuff free."

"Yeah?"

"Yes, b'y. Everyone knows that."

"Well, she don't bring home nothin' to me." And it was true. All Nipper ever saw were the usual things: bologna and Carnation milk and Lemon Cream crackers.

Ronnie didn't believe him. "I bet you're keeping all that candy for yourself. Don't be so greedy."

"Honest to God," Nipper said. "She don't bring home no candy. Sure ask her yourself."

The next day, Ronnie did just that. Nipper's mother rolled her eyes. "Ronnie, go lie down out of it. There's nothing free in this world."

Ronnie shook his head. "What's the point of workin' in a shop if you can't even get any free candy?"

Nipper's mother told him that if he ever got home from school and she wasn't there, he could go over to Annie's. Sometimes Nipper did that—especially if it was raining. Annie always had cookies, and the picture on her TV was a lot better than theirs, which blinked half the time no matter how much you twisted the rabbit ears. But usually he played down on Sheehan's farm or wandered up the Old Road. He visited the places his father had taken him. Nipper wondered about him up in Nova Scotia working under the ground. He looked out over the rolling barrens, and when he thought of his father with a black face crouching in a tunnel, or going down in the grimy cage, he got dizzy. He looked up at the sky and breathed long deep breaths. Why would anyone want to be buried alive instead of milking cows and seeing to the hay and vegetables? How could you work with tons of rock piled on top of you?

Nipper wondered if miners had a patron saint—someone to

watch out for them like St. Brigid did for farmers. He made a note to ask Sister Bernadette. Nuns knew all about that kind of thing.

5

Nipper Mooney reached into his chipped, wooden pencil box and took out a ruler, eraser and freshly sharpened HB pencil. He opened his new arithmetic scribbler to the first page and drew a two-inch line through the middle of the top margin.

He carefully inscribed "JMJ" above it. Jesus, Mary and Joseph.

Nipper sat back and sized up the letters. The flowery swirls and curls of the script never seemed quite right; the letters leaned too far to the left, like a line of Irish dancers caught by a camera, frozen in mid-kick. Script. Cursive script. That's what Sister Bernadette had called it. Script. Cursive. Curse. That's what you did if you spoke those words in anger: cursed. That was a sin. Nipper remembered that from his catechism:

What is the second commandment of God?
The second commandment of God is: Thou shalt
not take the name of the Lord thy God in vain.

If you put "JMJ" at the top of each page, then the grace of Jesus, Mary and Joseph would fly down from heaven and help you with your schoolwork. That's what Sister Bernadette had said. And it did help. Sometimes. But not with arithmetic. Perhaps Jesus, Mary and Joseph didn't like arithmetic. Perhaps for something as hard as arithmetic the letters weren't enough. Nipper leaned back and straightened his legs. Perhaps these things worked like Indulgences. Sister Bernadette had said that every time you blessed yourself you got a one-hundred-day

Indulgence. If you used holy water, it was three hundred days. Maybe he should spell the words out. Nipper took his pencil, printed "Jesus, Mary and Joseph," and tapped out the letters: eighteen. Or maybe it was only fifteen. Maybe the "and" didn't count. Still, fifteen letters would surely be better than just three.

Nipper turned to a fresh page in his scribbler and drew a new line. He lowered his head close to the desk and wrote out "Jesus, Mary and Joseph" in his lopsided cursive script.

He would need all the spiritual help he could get to pass arithmetic.

For as long as he could remember, the last words Nipper Mooney heard at night were, *Say an Act of Contrition before you close your eyes.* When he was very young, his mother whispered it as she tucked him in; then, later, she said it while she stood in the doorway or at the foot of his bed. Even if he'd been sent to bed early because he was sick or bad, she would still call up the stairs, "Nicky, say an Act of Contrition before you close your eyes." Nipper would pull the blankets up to his chin and recite: *O my God, I am heartily sorry for having offended Thee, and I detest all my sins, because of Thy just punishments, but most of all because they offend Thee, my God, who art all-good and deserving of all my love . . .* The reason you said an Act of Contrition before you closed your eyes was because if the house burned down, or the heathen Russians dropped the atomic bomb and you died in your bed in the middle of the night, you'd be all right. You'd go straight to heaven. The Act of Contrition wasn't as good as confession, but you'd still be all right. The only problem was that all the time Nipper was saying it he was wondering if he really *would* die in the middle of the night. Maybe the Russians would drop the atomic bomb. Maybe the house really would burn down.

There were nights he said the Act of Contrition twice.

. . .

Sometimes Sister Mary Ignatius dropped into Nipper's class to give arithmetic bees and spelling bees. He could tell that Sister Bernadette didn't like this, but she was young and pretty and Sister Mary Ignatius was old and she was the principal. If the principal wanted to barge into class and interrupt phonics or religion or vocabulary and give an arithmetic bee, that's exactly what she was going to do. She could probably put Sister Bernadette in the arithmetic bee if she really wanted to. So Sister Bernadette just smiled tightly and put away her books and watched as Sister Mary Ignatius lined the children up around the classroom. She gave each student a word to spell or a sum to do. If you gave the wrong answer, she rapped you across the knuckles with her pointer: hard. Nipper was a good speller, but he hated the sums; he hardly ever got the sums right.

Billy Abbott stood just across from Nipper under the painting of the Sacred Heart. Billy Abbott was smart. He never gave a wrong answer. But Sister Mary Ignatius made him nervous. He kept his eyes on her pointer; he fidgeted and shuffled his feet and bit his lips. And one day, between bites, Nipper noticed something: Billy Abbott mouthed the answers to himself. *Everybody's* answer. So when Sister Mary Ignatius gave Nipper a hard sum, he glanced at Billy Abbott and saw "sixteen" form on his lips.

"Sixteen, Sister," Nipper said.

Sister Mary Ignatius stepped back and looked at him. He had never answered so quickly. "Very good. You're getting better."

She turned to Ronnie Sheehan.

Nipper wondered if watching Billy Abbott's mouth was a sin. If he forgot to say the Act of Contrition some night and the Russians dropped the atomic bomb, would he go to hell? Was he cheating? Was watching someone's mouth the same as copying? It wasn't his fault that Billy Abbott moved his lips, was it?

One day Nipper noticed that Barb Cleary was looking at Billy Abbott's mouth, and so was Alice Dillon. And then even God Love 'im Roy Driscoll got the right answer to a sum, and Nipper knew *he'd* been looking at Billy Abbott's mouth, too.

Sister Mary Ignatius knew something was going on.

Nipper saw her eyes squinting behind her glasses and her nose twitching just like Blackie's, Ronnie Sheehan's setter. He could tell what she was thinking: Had the Holy Ghost descended upon the children with all the right answers? And why had Nipper Mooney improved so much in the arithmetic bees, but he nearly always failed the written tests? Sister Mary Ignatius asked Sister Bernadette about that, but Sister Bernadette just smiled her pretty smile and shrugged. So Sister Mary Ignatius turned to Nipper.

"Well, young man?"

Nipper looked down at his shoes. "I . . . I guess I just think better standing up."

Then the thing that Nipper Mooney hoped would never happen, but knew *would* happen, *had* to happen, finally happened.

Billy Abbott didn't come to school.

Billy Abbott had to get his tonsils out. And the next day Sister Mary Ignatius swept into the class and announced a surprise arithmetic bee. Now it was Nipper who was fidgeting and shuffling. And so were Barb Cleary and Alice Dillon and God only knew who else.

Sister Mary Ignatius gave Nipper his sum.

He blinked and looked at her.

She gave him the sum again, but Nipper couldn't concentrate; it was all gobbledegook. Sister Mary Ignatius sounded like Monsignor Murphy speaking Latin. And it was hard to think when everyone in the whole class was looking at you—everyone except Billy Abbott, who was home hove off on his chesterfield watching the cartoons and probably eating tons of ice cream because when you got your tonsils out you couldn't eat real food. And when Sister Mary Ignatius gave him the sum a *third* time, Nipper said, "I don't know, Sister."

Sister Mary Ignatius flicked her pointer under his chin. "I don't know? Was that what you said, *I don't know?*"

"Yes, Sister."

"I don't know," Sister Mary Ignatius said, "is not an answer. That's something little boys and girls who don't go to school would say—boys and girls who don't have the privilege of going to school, like the little boys and girls over in China and Africa. If someone gives *them* a sum, they have the right to say, 'I don't know, Sister.' But you're not a little Chinese boy, are you?"

"No, Sister."

"And are you a little African boy?"

"No, Sister."

"That's right. You're a little *Newfoundland* boy who has the *privilege* of going to St. Brigid's so he can learn his sums and not grow up ignorant. Correct?"

"Yes, Sister."

"Well, then. What is the answer to the sum? Concentrate."

Nipper stared into Sister Mary Ignatius's pale eyes; the light reflected off her gold-rimmed glasses. He felt dizzy. He clenched his jaw and prayed for the Holy Ghost to fly down from heaven with the right answer.

Nothing happened.

Nipper knew he wasn't a little Chinese boy or a little African boy, but he said again, "I don't know, Sister. I don't know." Even as he said this, he saw Sister Bernadette get up from her desk and come toward him. She stood behind Sister Mary Ignatius and looked at him over the principal's shoulder.

Her mouth moved silently.

"Twelve," Nipper said. "The answer is twelve."

Sister Mary Ignatius smacked her lips in satisfaction. "Right," she said. "Twelve." She spun around and brandished her pointer at the class. "See what happens when you concentrate?"

The children shuffled their feet and nodded.

Oh yes, Sister. We see. We see.

6

*N*ipper's mother had been after him for weeks to help her clean out the barn, but he didn't want to. Their barn wasn't like the Sheehans' or the Flynns'; it was a dead place. It had been years, back in his grandfather's time, since it had housed any animals other than dogs or an occasional litter of kittens. It wasn't really a barn at all anymore—just a storage shed full of old harnesses, wagon parts, woodhorses, cowbells, rotten feed sacks, barrels of rusty nails, bent bicycle tires, an old catamaran, and a wooden hay rake jammed between the rafters. It still smelled like a barn, though, especially when it rained. Then the wooden walls gave off a dull, sour scent of feed and manure. It seemed that the air itself was years and years old. Nipper thought it was probably the same air Grandfather Kevin had breathed when he worked milking the cows or feeding the horses and chickens. Nipper tried to picture the barn filled with animals, imagined the stamping of their hooves in the broken stalls. But it was useless. This wasn't a barn; it was a junk shop. His grandfather would hardly recognize it.

Nipper liked barns. *Real* barns. He liked the smells and the steaming heat. He liked the sound of hot milk streaming into galvanized buckets. He liked the way the patient cows and horses looked at him with their brown, liquid eyes.

He especially liked the haylofts. When Nipper climbed the splintered ladder leading up to Sheehan's hayloft, it was like entering a different world—a world of secrets and shadows. Ribbons of light streamed through cracks and seams, lighting up specks of straw that hung on the dark air like dust. Sounds were different in the loft: his voice sounded hollow and muffled, as if it belonged to someone else.

In Sheehan's loft, hay bales, some neatly stacked, others jumbled every which way, pressed from floor to ceiling. On the south wall, shutters opened to the potato fields and beyond to the bald hills, the sweeping line of woods and bog.

One morning Nipper raised the trap door to Sheehan's loft and poked his head through. Low laughter and the thump of hay bales hitting the floor: Ronnie and his little brother, Gerard, building tunnels. Every year when the hay came in, it was the same. They were the master builders of the hayloft, their tunnels, some up to fifty feet long, criss-crossing in a vast maze of darkness and straw.

Nipper heard their grunts, the snap of heavy hay rope. He pulled himself up through the trap door.

Gerard dragged a hay bale into a corner and glanced at him.

"We're building a tunnel out to the south shutter. Wanna help?"

"Well . . ."

Ronnie grunted. "*He's* not gonna help. Sure he won't even stick his head inside a tunnel. Afraid it's gonna cave in. Like a tunnel *I* built would ever cave in."

It was true. The moment Nipper put his head inside a tunnel, waves of nausea, as thick and hot as lava, engulfed him. Once, taunted to the point of distraction by Ronnie and Gerard, he had suddenly plunged into the nearest tunnel and dragged himself twenty feet to the first breathing nook. He pulled his knees to his chest, gulping the dry air, pricked by the hot, leaning hay bales, fighting a surge of vomit. The low ceiling contracted and expanded, pushed down with the force of an avalanche. Suddenly, Nipper darted back the way he had come, back into the blackness, scuttling along the shrinking, stifling burrow, the sick rising in his gullet, praying *Oh God, oh Jesus, oh Blessed Mary, don't let Ronnie and Gerard block this tunnel.* That would be their idea of a joke: a hay bale stuffed into the entrance and the two of them sitting on top, holding their sides, breaking up with laughter. Or worse, following after him, pushing him backwards, forcing him even farther under. *Oh please, Blessed Mary, oh please, St. Brigid, I'll make novenas, I'll say the Rosary every night for a year, but let the entrance be clear, let Ronnie and Gerard be gone—doing the milking or shovelling shit—anything, but don't let the entrance be blocked.*

On that day, St. Brigid had been with him. The entrance was open, Ronnie and Gerard gone. Nipper collapsed on the floor and sucked air into his pinched, burning lungs.

He had vowed never to set foot inside a tunnel again.

Nipper liked Sheehan's loft. It was so still, lulling, as quiet as a chapel. Only the faintest shuffling of the cows below, the occasional dark notes of their lowing.

Yes, he liked the loft.

It was only the tunnels he hated.

7

*I*t was a special day in religion class—so special that Sister Bernadette sat at her desk with her book closed, and it was Sister Mary Ignatius who paced before the students, her black catechism clutched behind her back.

Nipper Mooney was learning to confess his sins.

The grade ones had already begun this with Sister Bernadette, but it was such an important matter that the principal had come to help.

Sister Mary Ignatius wheeled around and faced the class. "It is of the utmost importance that we make a *good* confession," she said. "What does making a good confession mean?"

Pauly Mackey put up his hand. "It means that you confess all your sins and that you are truly and heartily sorry."

Nipper looked at Brigid and rolled his eyes. Pauly Mackey lived a little farther down the Upper Road from him and Brigid. He loved religion. He wanted to be an altar boy, and he always carried a copy of the *Altar Boy's Ceremonial* in his bookbag—even though he couldn't even read it yet. He was going to be a priest when he grew up.

"That's right, Pauly," Sister Mary Ignatius said. "All your sins. Truly and heartily sorry. That is a good confession. Class, what do we say at the beginning of our confession?"

"Bless me, Father, for I have sinned," the class chimed in ragged unison.

"And then?"

Pauly's hand went up again. "Then we say how long it's been since our last confession."

"That's right," Sister Mary Ignatius said. "You don't have to worry about that on Friday because that will be your *first* confession. So you will simply say, 'This is my first confession.' But in the future you will have to say how long it has been. While you're at St. Brigid's, you'll be going every week." Sister Mary Ignatius regarded the class through her gold-rimmed glasses. "And how should we . . . speak in the confessional?"

"In English?" Ronnie Sheehan said.

Sister Bernadette laughed and quickly raised a hand to her lips. Sister Mary Ignatius turned to her, frowning. "Of course, *in English*," she said, turning back to Ronnie. "But in what tone? How should we speak?"

"Politely?" Alice Dillon said.

Sister Mary Ignatius sighed and opened her catechism. " 'When in the confessional we should use a distinct whisper loud enough to be heard by the priest, but not so loud as to be heard by others; we should neither mumble nor speak too fast.' " She fixed her gaze on Ronnie Sheehan. "Did you get that, Ronnie? A distinct *whisper*. On Friday I don't want to be hearing your big voice booming through the whole church enlightening all of Kildura about your latest shenanigans. Not too fast, not too loud. And don't mumble. You know Monsignor Murphy doesn't hear all that well. Understand?"

"Yes, Sister."

"Good. Now—"

Ronnie's hand flew up.

"Yes, Ronnie?"

"What does distinct mean?"

"It means *clear*, Ronnie. Clear. Speak in a clear whisper."

"Yes, Sister."

"Good, now—"

Ronnie's hand flew up again.

"Yes, Ronnie?"

"What sins do we give first, Sister? Mortal or venial?"

Sister Mary Ignatius held up the catechism. "I was getting to that." She leaned against the blackboard and read. " 'After telling the time of our last confession, if we have committed any mortal sins since that time, we must confess them and also any that we may have forgotten in previous confessions, telling the nature and number of each. We may also confess any venial sins we wish to mention.' So," she said, "mortal first, venial second."

Again Ronnie's hand flew up.

Sister Mary Ignatius closed the catechism and looked at him. "What?"

"Sister, what do we do if we don't have any sins?"

A titter ran through the class.

"What do you mean, if you don't have any sins? Do you mean, if you don't have any mortal sins?"

"No, if we don't have any sins at all."

Sister Bernadette looked down at her desk and smiled. "Well, Ronnie," Sister Mary Ignatius said, "I don't think that's something *you* need worry about. But, if the occasion ever arises, give an old sin you've already confessed. That way the priest can give you absolution. Do you think you'll at least have some old sins?"

"Oh yes, Sister."

"Yes, I'm sure you will. And if you can't think of any, just come to me or Sister Bernadette, and we'll remind you."

Nipper looked out the window. There didn't seem to be anything hard about confession. Not hard like arithmetic was hard. He knew what to do and say. But it would be easier if he didn't have to confess to Monsignor Murphy. Why couldn't he just tell his sins to God? God would know if he was truly and heartily sorry. But no. It had to be Monsignor Murphy. That was the law of the church. Nipper thought about their parish priest. Maybe that was why he always looked so mean—because he knew the sins of everyone in all of Kildura. Well, except for the people who didn't go to church—like Brigid's Uncle Brendan. He didn't go to church or confession. That's what Nipper's mother had said. Nipper started and sat up. Monsignor Murphy even knew his *mother's* sins. Even Sister Bernadette's—although she couldn't have that many and they were probably all venial. Make no wonder he looked so vexed all the time. He was like St. Christopher carrying the Baby Jesus across the raging river, weighted down with the sins of the whole world. What did he think, sitting up on the stage at the Garden Party with the bishop, looking down on the people and knowing all the bad things everyone had been up to? You'd think it would put him right off his potato salad. It didn't, though. He always ate everything on his plate and then asked for more. The bishop, too.

On Friday morning the class was marched over to St. Christopher's. Nipper had two sins for Monsignor Murphy. They were the same as Ronnie's: he said a bad word; he disobeyed his mother. He had asked Brigid what her sins were, but she wouldn't tell him. That was okay. Nipper was nervous, but it probably wouldn't be too bad. At least Monsignor Murphy wasn't going to give him a sum.

When Nipper's turn came, Sister Bernadette smiled at him. He stepped into the confessional.

Instantly, the world changed.

No one had told him the confession box was so small.

So dark.

It wasn't that he was afraid of the dark. He wasn't like Pauly Mackey, who needed a night light or he couldn't get to sleep. Once, when his father was back from the mines, they had been walking home along the Old Road late at night. There were no stars and not the tiniest piece of moon. It was so black that sometimes you couldn't even tell where the road was, and he still wasn't scared.

But the confessional was more than dark.

It smelled like it had been waxed with incense and candle smoke. It smelled like a dusty trunk full of someone's old mothballed winter coats. Nipper's throat dried up and coiled into a knot. Monsignor Murphy was hearing Barb Cleary's confession on the other side. As he waited, Nipper tried to practice.

But the walls pressed in on him.

He felt like he was down in a mine.

He tried to speak but could manage only a croaking whisper. He knew his whisper was not distinct. He knew Monsignor Murphy was old and hard of hearing and—oh, my God, what would he say when he discovered that Nipper Mooney, a big boy in grade one, couldn't even talk? How would the priest know what his sins were?

Monsignor Murphy drew back the separating panel, the wood creaking harshly on the runner.

Nipper tried to swallow. "Bless me father . . . *his stomach muscles clenched and turned . . .* for I have sinned . . . *a dizzying, piercing light exploded behind his eyes . . .* this is my first . . . *his throat felt rimmed with barbed wire . . .* confession."

He moved his dry lips but nothing more came.

"Speak up, boy," Monsignor Murphy said.

But Nipper could not speak up.

As his eyes adjusted to the light, he saw a shadowy Monsignor Murphy behind the latticed partition, his head nodding and bobbing. The old priest breathed heavily. A bead of sweat hung from the tip of his nose, which, in the light of day, Nipper knew was red and pitted and had hairy nostrils like old Brendan's. Monsignor Murphy raised a Rosary-entwined hand and brushed the sweat away.

Nipper felt the ceiling push down on him.

The walls pushed in.

The confessional was like the tunnels in Sheehan's hayloft.

It was like a coffin turned on its end.

Nipper had to get out. What if the door was locked and he couldn't get out? Monsignor Murphy turned slowly to look at him. Nipper clasped his palms together, bowed his head, and he'd just managed to croak out that he had disobeyed his mother when he heard Monsignor Murphy sigh and give him the absolution.

That wasn't supposed to happen yet.

But it was happening.

"For your penance say two Hail Marys, one Our Father and a Glory Be," Monsignor Murphy said.

He blessed Nipper and pulled the shutter closed.

Nipper reached for the brass knob. He stumbled, blinking, into the church. Everyone in the class looked at him. They turned to each other and giggled—even Brigid giggled. They thought Monsignor Murphy must have bawled him out or he forgot what he was supposed to say. Nipper's face and neck blushed scarlet. Sister Bernadette looked troubled. Sister Mary Ignatius glared.

But despite his burning face, Nipper felt better: his throat relaxed; the dizziness passed; his lungs filled up with the warm, humid church air. He slid in next to Brigid and Ronnie and thought, My God, do I have to do this *every* week?

Nipper knew he had not made a good confession. He wondered if he ever would.

8

*E*very Sunday on the way to mass at St. Christopher's, Nipper and his mother drove past the Dunnes'. That's what everybody called both house and family. It was never "the Dunnes' house" or "Paddy's house" or "Rosarie's house." Just *the Dunnes'*—as if the building didn't deserve to be called a house; as if it were impossible to separate the people from the glass and clapboard surrounding them.

The Dunnes' was unlike any other house in Kildura. It lay at the top of a rutted lane surrounded by stunted firs and black spruce. It was a tiny house, not much taller than a man; a big man like Francis Hartery could probably rest his elbows on the roof. A rusting oil tank, clinging to the back wall like some metallic growth, seemed to be nudging the house down the lane. Nipper wondered why they needed such a huge tank—until he realized it wasn't that the tank was so big, but that the house was so small.

"Why is the Dunnes' so tiny?" he asked his mother one Sunday morning.

Sharon shrugged and kept her eyes on the road. "I don't know, duckie. It's probably all they can afford."

"What does Mr. Dunne do?"

"He collects the garbage—sure you knows that."

"Yeah, but is that all?"

"No, no. He does different things. Odd jobs."

"Are the Dunnes poor?"

Sharon sighed and gripped the wheel. "I expect so."

"Poorer than us?"

Sharon glared at Nipper. "Sacred Heart! What are you gettin' on with? We're not poor."

"We're not rich—not like Mr. Blake who owns the store."

"Well, we're not poor, either. You get that notion right out of your head."

"What kind of house is the Dunnes'? Is it a cabin?"

Sharon wrinkled her brow and glanced at Nipper. "No, it's a regular house. It's . . . it's just *the Dunnes'*. Not everyone has got to have the same kind of house, you know."

Maybe not, but Nipper had never seen anything like the Dunnes' before—not a real house anyway. It looked like something from a storybook—a dwarf's house or the hut of some poor woodcutter.

Nothing seemed right about the Dunnes'. The sunken roof—missing shingles, tarpaper flapping in the breeze—looked as if it might collapse with the next snowfall. Neither was the house quite level: it seemed crumpled somehow, splayed out at the corners, as if the cable on a crane lowering it to its site had snapped at the last moment, smashing it into the ground. For such a small house, it had a lot of windows—four on the front alone, with an extra one in the door. The windows were always tightly closed, the curtains always drawn. The house seemed abandoned, forgotten: as if it had been washed up after a flood.

The Dunnes' wasn't a saltbox or a bungalow or a farmhouse; it wasn't a barn or a shed or any other kind of building Nipper knew about. And although he had never seen a real one, he knew it wasn't a cottage like they had in England, like the houses in his school reader. Those were neat and pretty and had picket fences and window boxes full of daisies and geraniums. Nipper could not picture a window box gracing the Dunnes'.

Then one morning Sister Bernadette opened her tattered

copy of *Grimms' Fairy Tales* and read aloud "The Fisherman and His Wife":

There was once a fisherman who lived with his wife in an old rundown shack by the sea . . .

And instantly Nipper knew: that's what the Dunnes' was—a shack—a shack not much better than the ones his father slept in when he was away hunting or fishing.

Nipper had never been inside the Dunnes'; neither had his mother nor any of his friends. That was strange for Kildura: the children were always in and out of one another's houses. When he went next door to Annie's to watch TV or wait for his mother to come home from Blake's, he didn't even knock. Annie would have laughed at him if he did.

The Dunnes' was a silent place; whatever secrets it had, it kept to itself. Despite the oil tank, both summer and winter cigarette-blue woodsmoke wafted from a red brick chimney—for some reason the only thing always freshly painted. Three people lived there: Paddy Dunne, his little sister, Rosarie, and their father, Stephen. Nipper wondered how many rooms there were. The house was so small it seemed there could only be one or two. But there must be at least three. There'd have to be a bathroom and a separate bedroom for Rosarie.

As he always did when they drove past the Dunnes', Nipper pressed his nose against the window and scanned the backyard. No, there was no sign of an outhouse. Surely to God there must be a bathroom.

Coming back from mass, Nipper saw Paddy Dunne crouched Indian-fashion by the side of the Lower Road. Rosarie stood behind him, lining up cans with her feet. Paddy had picked his spot carefully—a long, straight stretch just across from the cemetery, where he could be easily seen, and there was lots of room for cars to pull in. His advertisement, daubed in black paint on a jagged piece of plywood and jammed between two rocks, read simply: WORMS. When a car approached, he stood up and held out the sign—unless the car was driven by a woman, something Paddy could tell from five hundred yards. Even as Nipper and his mother drove by, he remained on his haunches, staring at them passively.

The captive worms were imprisoned in an assortment of Campbell's soup tins—Tomato, Cream of Mushroom, Chicken Noodle—as if the worms themselves came in different flavours. Nipper pictured a fisherman standing by Shalloway Pond, changing worms the way fly fishermen change flies. *Well, I'm not having much luck with the Tomato. Guess I'll try the Chicken Noodle. It just looks like a Chicken Noodle kind of day.* Nipper could see himself sitting by the side of the road selling vegetables or hubcaps or even the sugary Freshie his mother made in the summer. He'd spend the money on candy down at Blake's. But he could not see himself sitting in the dust, jumping up like a jack-in-the-box at each passing car, holding up soup tins full of worms. Or, if he had to, he would at least take the time to peel off the labels. And when a car stopped, he wouldn't run up to it; no, by God, he'd sit there and let the car back up to him.

Nipper wondered how Paddy could do it: hours on end, day after day, his hands trailing in the dirt, Rosarie sitting next to him playing alleys, hoping he would let her take the money or at least pass the worms to the next customer. Didn't he get bored? Why didn't he bring a transistor radio or a comic? But Paddy seemed content to crouch with his sign, peering up and down the road, a miniature city of soup tins crowding his muddy boots.

Sometimes, in the early morning, Nipper saw foxes up on the Old Road. There was something of the fox about Paddy Dunne.

Not in his build, for Paddy was broad-shouldered and squat: blocky, Ronnie Sheehan's father would say. *That fella's right blocky.* Nor was it in his step, which wasn't exactly slow, but rather measured and determined. No, the fox was in his colouring: oily, cowlicked red hair—thick, unruly hair that looked as if it had been cut by a kitchen knife; and rather startling green eyes—eyes flecked with beads of rust and framed by pale, delicate lashes.

His clothes were a mystery. Like Brigid's Uncle Brendan, he seemed to dress almost entirely in someone's discarded dress clothes: white fancy shirts (in later years a crumpled package of Drum tobacco peeking over the edge of the breast pocket), and black or grey flannel trousers, the frayed ends bunched over the tops of oversized work boots. In the spring and fall, he often wore a black sports jacket patched at the elbows.

Paddy Dunne knew the Old Road even better than Nipper. When he wasn't in school or selling worms or helping Stephen on the garbage truck, he wandered the Old Road with his bamboo fishing pole. Sometimes Rosarie tagged along, but not often; she was too young and always looked pale and tired. Nipper knew that even he would have trouble keeping up, for Paddy often tramped miles over the springy barrens in search of just the right pond. In the same way he knew if a distant car was driven by a woman, he knew the ponds where the big trout would be biting that day, and he didn't mind walking to get to them.

Sometimes on his rambles Nipper came upon Paddy fishing in secluded coves on the Damsel's Eye or Shalloway Pond. He would hide in the thick spruce or behind a lichen-stained boulder and watch. Paddy was the best fisherman Nipper had ever seen—even better than his father. When he cast out, he drew the bamboo lightly over his shoulder, dropping the cork bobber with a delicate splash, exactly, you knew, where he had intended. He showed infinite patience, his eyes never leaving the water, both hands wrapped firmly around the pole, departing only to brush away a mosquito or light a cigarette. Again and again the supple bamboo arced wand-like over the pond, enticing muds and browns from the murky bottom. They darted upward and one by one were pulled to shore, twisting and curling across the clear water. Paddy knocked them out with one swift crack on the edge of a rock—something Nipper could never do cleanly. His trout always struggled, slipping out of his hands, requiring weak blow after weak blow until he became disgusted with himself, felt he was torturing the poor creatures. If, as sometimes happened, a trout wriggled off Paddy's line, he gave no grimace or oath, just re-baited, and then another soft cast dropped the bobber to where he knew more trout lay waiting.

Nipper's father had given him a new fibreglass fishing pole and a Daiwa spinning reel for Christmas, and he had a forest-green case full of bait spinners and Red Devils and clutches of hooks and flies, yet the fish were reluctant to take his bait; they seemed too aware, bumping his hook doubtfully, jumping over his Silver Doctor or Black Gnat. But Paddy Dunne was a magician, his supple pole as true as a divining rod, casting spells over the still pools and gurgling streams, believing that, sooner or later, the dazed, spell-struck fish would rise to his bait.

As they always did.

9

One morning during arithmetic, Nipper noticed Brigid Flynn looking at him curiously from across the classroom.

"What?" he said, when he joined her for recess.

"How come you always look so . . . white when you comes out of the confessional?"

Nipper sat up. "Do I?"

"Uh-huh. Just like a ghost."

Nipper glanced quickly around the room. "It makes me sick," he said, blushing.

"Confession makes you sick?"

"Yeah."

"Why?"

"Don't know."

"Is it Monsignor Murphy? Are you scared of him?"

"*No.* I'm not scared of him."

"Are you sure? I am. Kind of. Sometimes."

Nipper shook his head. He looked around the room again. "It's not him so much," he whispered. "It's . . . it's the *box.* I don't like places like that. I gets all sweaty and clammy. I feels like it's going to cave in on top of me."

"Why?"

"Don't know."

Brigid nodded slowly.

The next day, when she was handing her Pepsi to Nipper, she said, "You know what you need?"

"What?"

"A plan."

"What kind of plan?"

"A plan so you can get in and out of the confession box really fast. That way you won't have time to get sick."

Nipper stared at her. "How do I do that?"

Brigid had already thought about it. Over the next few days, they came up with a set of guidelines.

(1) Never have more than three sins.

(2) Make your sins short: I told a lie; I wouldn't let my friend use my baseball bat.

(3) Always give the number of sins because if you don't Monsignor Murphy may ask. You don't want that. You don't want to get into a conversation with Monsignor Murphy.

(4) If possible, position yourself in the church so you can go first; that way you won't have as much time to worry.

(5) If you have to wait while Monsignor Murphy is busy with the person on the other side, close your eyes and take slow, deep breaths and imagine you're up on the Old Road hiking in over the barrens with your fishing pole.

(6) Never, ever, *ever* give a sin you don't understand. Even if you think you're boring Monsignor Murphy to death with the same old stuff every week about lying and baseball bats and bad words, and any minute you're expecting him to say, "What in the name of our Blessed Saviour is wrong with you? You didn't lend your friend your baseball bat *again*?" don't bother changing. You'll just get into trouble.

Soon Nipper was the fastest in the confessional of anyone in his whole class. One day when he came out, Sister Mary Ignatius took him aside. "You were awfully quick," she said. "If I didn't know any better, I'd say you didn't have anything to confess." She poked him in the chest with her pointer. "The confessional is a holy place. Don't be in there racing through your sins."

"Yes, Sister—I mean, no, Sister."

Nipper learned rule six the hard way. One Friday morning when he went into the confessional, Monsignor Murphy was waiting. "I told two lies . . . "

"Uh-huh . . . " from Monsignor Murphy.

"I hit my friend . . . umm *once.*"

"Uh-huh . . . " from Monsignor Murphy.

"And I had bad thoughts."

When Nipper uttered his last sin, the priest turned to look at him so quickly that he struck his bulbous nose on the wooden partition.

"You had . . . *what?*"

"I . . . I had bad thoughts."

Monsignor Murphy rubbed the tip of his nose. "What kind of bad thoughts did you have?"

"I . . . I . . . don't remember!"

"You had bad thoughts, and you don't remember what they were?"

"No, Monsignor, I . . . " Nipper wasn't even sure what he had confessed. He had overheard the expression "bad thoughts" out on the school playground.

"If you had bad thoughts, they must have been about something," Monsignor Murphy said. "What were you thinking about? Stealing?"

"No."

"Goin' on the pip?"

"No—"

"Well, *what* then?"

"I . . . I don't remember. Really, I don't."

Monsignor Murphy sighed. He sat back and resumed his profile. "Well," he said, "I guess they couldn't have been that bad if you can't even remember what they were." He turned and peered at Nipper through the window. "Tell me, now," he said a little softer, "did you *really* have bad thoughts?"

"No, Monsignor. I didn't have bad thoughts."

"Then what did you say you did for?"

A fair enough question. His sense of the dramatic? His concern that he was boring the old priest to death? Then Monsignor Murphy's eyes lit up, and a knowing smile twisted his face. "Now listen here, young man. You came in here today, into this sacred place, and told me that you had told two lies. Correct?"

"Yes, Monsignor."

"That was the first thing you confessed?"

"Yes, Monsignor."

"*Two* lies?"

"Yes, Monsignor."

"But it wasn't two at all, was it?" he said with the tone of someone imparting a great secret. "It was *three!* You lied when you told me you had bad thoughts, didn't you?" Nipper was beyond answering. "You see the trouble this kind of behaviour can get you into?"

"Oh yes, Monsignor, I see!" Nipper said. "I won't lie any more. If I tell you I've had bad thoughts, I promise I'll really have them!"

Monsignor Murphy shook his head and sighed. He raised his beads to his lips and mumbled the absolution. Then he turned to Nipper. "For your penance, young man, say two Hail Marys, an Our Father and . . . the Stations of the Cross."

The Stations of the Cross. That was about the worst penance anyone ever got. It took about an hour to get through the Stations of the Cross.

"Yes, Monsignor."

Nipper blessed himself and turned to leave. As he opened

the door, Monsignor Murphy rapped on the partition. "And in future, don't be coming in here making up your sins!"

Nipper learned the lesson: stick to bad words and baseball bats.

10

*M*onday morning, just after prayers, Sister Mary Ignatius knocked on the classroom door. It was easy to know it was her: she always rapped on the glass four times—sharply, quickly, rat-a-tat-tat, the sound Ronnie Sheehan made with his stick machine gun. Without waiting for Sister Bernadette to answer, she pushed the door open and came into the classroom. She was not alone: she was followed by Paddy Dunne.

Nipper's first thought was that something heavy needed to be moved, and Sister Mary Ignatius had brought Paddy to help. He looked toward the door to see if Mr. Meaney, the janitor, was coming as well, but no one else entered. Then Nipper noticed that Paddy was holding schoolbooks and scribblers; his face and lips were tight, and his fox eyes were hard and narrowed. For once, Sister Mary Ignatius didn't say anything, just nodded at Sister Bernadette, and, as abruptly as she had entered, she turned and left. Paddy watched the door close, then moved down the aisle to the last place in the window row. He dumped his books on the floor and slumped heavily into the seat.

Sister Bernadette watched him and smiled. "Yes, Paddy," she said, "you can sit there."

Paddy didn't say anything.

Nipper glanced at Brigid and Ronnie. What was Paddy Dunne doing in their class? He was supposed to be with Sister Annunciata. He was too old to be in this class—like God Love 'im Roy Driscoll. But everyone knew God Love 'im was simple.

Sister Bernadette pushed back her chair and stood up.

"Yes," she said, "we have a new student. Paddy will be joining us. Now, open your readers to page 20."

During recess Sister Bernadette called Paddy up to her desk. As Nipper walked by, he saw him nodding and heard Sister Bernadette say, ". . . help you with your reading . . . " Nipper sat next to Brigid. She looked up at Paddy and shook her head. "It must be awful to get put back," she whispered. "I hope it never happens to me."

Nipper nodded. "Yeah," he said, passing Brigid his chocolate milk. "Me, too."

The next day Sister Mary Ignatius knocked on the door again, then swept into the room flourishing her pointer. She nodded at Sister Bernadette, pulled a tissue from the sleeve of her habit, and polished her glasses. She settled them on her nose and peered at the class. "Tomorrow," she said, strolling down the aisle to where Nipper Mooney was sitting in the third desk with his speller out and open, "tomorrow St. Brigid's is privileged to have a visitor. A very interesting visitor."

Nipper sat up straight. A visitor? Besides the teachers and the janitor, the only people he'd ever seen in St. Brigid's were Monsignor Murphy and the school board superintendent. But they usually turned up unannounced. Sister Mary Ignatius went to the blackboard. She took the chalk and drew a rough map of North and South America. Next to it, in block letters, she printed:

THE MISSIONS

She turned to the class. "The Missions," she said. "Now, you boys and girls know about the Missions—we collect for them in school, don't we?"

"Yes, Sister."

"Yes, of course we do. Brigid Flynn, why do we collect for the Missions?"

Brigid pushed her hair back from her dark forehead. "We collect for the Missions so the people in all the poor countries will have enough food to eat and . . . "

"Yes?"

" . . . enough food to eat and . . . and so they can have schools and churches."

"Correct. Very good. We collect for the Missions so we can help the poor, educate them, and bring them the word of God." Sister Mary Ignatius measured the length of her pointer. "Well, tomorrow we are privileged to have a visit from a Sister who works for the Missions—a missionary. Sister Francesca de Palma."

"Who?" piped up Ronnie Sheehan.

"Sister Francesca de Palma."

Ronnie snickered. "That's a funny name. I never heard of a name like that before."

"It is a Spanish name, Ronnie. Sister Francesca is Spanish. She has come to Newfoundland all the way from Monsefu, Peru, where she has worked for the past two years. Now, does anyone know where Peru is?"

"South America?" Brigid said.

"That's right," Sister Mary Ignatius said. "South America. A long, long ways from here." She went to the front of the class and tapped on the blackboard with her pointer. "South America . . . Peru . . . Monsefu . . . Newfoundland. Approximately, of course." Sister Mary Ignatius leaned against the blackboard and splayed the pointer against her thighs. "Sister Francesca will tell us about her work in Peru. She has slides to show you, and you may ask questions. Now, what would you like to ask Sister Francesca?"

Silence.

"Surely, there must be *something* you'd like to ask?"

Silence.

"Nothing? You're all experts on Peru, are you?"

Silence.

Sister Mary Ignatius sighed. "Nipper Mooney, what would you like to ask Sister Francesca?"

Nipper shrunk into his seat. "Umm . . . well . . . maybe . . . maybe I could ask her about . . . about the animals in Peru?"

Sister Mary Ignatius slid the pointer under her arm and took off her glasses. "The animals. Yes, I suppose you could ask about the animals. That would be very enlightening, I'm sure. What else?"

Silence.

"Well, wouldn't you like to know if it's at all *interesting* to be a missionary?" Sister Mary Ignatius said, looking at Pauly Mackey.

"Oh—yes, Sister," Pauly said.

"Good. That will be your question, Pauly. Get out your scribbler and copy down it down so you won't forget."

Ronnie Sheehan put up his hand.

"Yes, Ronnie?"

"How much money does a missionary make? Can I ask her that?"

"No, Ronnie, you may not. We may not ask any personal questions. But wouldn't you like to know what happens to the money for the Missions that we collect in class every week?"

Ronnie shrugged.

Sister Mary Ignatius looked at Alice Dillon. "Alice, wouldn't you like to know?"

"Yes, Sister."

"Good. You will ask Sister Francesca tomorrow. Copy down the question." Sister Mary Ignatius smiled. "That's two good questions."

Brigid put up her hand.

"Yes, Brigid?"

"Three questions, Sister. Three. Nipper's going to ask about the animals."

"That's right. The animals. We mustn't forget the animals."

The next morning, at the stroke of nine, there was a soft knock on the door, and a young nun in a white habit pushed a slide projector into the classroom. The children could not even pretend to be quiet. Sister Francesca may have been a nun, but she wasn't like the nuns at St. Brigid's. Besides her white habit, she was wearing sunglasses—little green sunglasses. And she had a suntan even though it was February. She didn't blend in with the blackboard; she looked like she shouldn't even be indoors. Nipper had never imagined that a nun could wear sunglasses or have a suntan. Could Sister Bernadette—pale Sister Bernadette—ever have a suntan like that?

Sister Francesca's habit was not just white—it was blinding white. When she stood next to Sister Mary Ignatius, Nipper was reminded of the albinos he'd seen once on a science special. And her veil—well, there was hardly anything to her veil. You could even see her hair.

Sister Francesca had a sweet smile and the whitest teeth Nipper had ever seen and a dimple like his Aunt Mona's. Her habit was made out of some kind of thin material, almost like a dress his mother would wear. It clung to her body very tightly. Nipper could see more of Sister Francesca than of any nun he'd ever come across.

When Sister Francesca had positioned the projector and plugged it in, she turned to the class and smiled. "Good morning, boys and girls."

"Good morning, Sister."

Nipper liked her voice. She had a nice accent—like music, even though she pronounced her words in a funny way.

After Sister Mary Ignatius had welcomed the visitor to the class, the lights were switched off and the slides flickered against the blackboard. The pictures weren't just from Peru; some were from Malaysia and Africa and other places where Sister Francesca had worked.

Black and brown boys and girls smiled shyly at the camera. It looked so pretty and hot and green, but now there were pictures of people lying in hospital beds made out of bamboo like Paddy Dunne's fishing pole; you could see right through the walls in the hospital. And, my God, weren't the nuns *hot* in those long, white habits when everyone else had hardly anything on at all? And what did the natives think of Sister Francesca and the other missionaries? They were probably happy to see them coming with food and money all the way from Newfoundland. But, still, they must have thought the nuns were awfully silly to dress up like that when it was about a hundred and fifty degrees out. And everyone seemed very skinny. There didn't seem to be a single fat person in any of those poor countries, which made sense, because that was why you gave to the Missions in the first place—to buy food for them. Maybe one of those countries was where Tarzan and Bomba the Jungle Boy lived. Well, he knew they were just made-up characters on TV—but they could live there if they were real. The slides flickered more and more quickly, and Sister Francesca talked in her pretty accent over the hum of the projector about leprosy and smallpox and a lot of other diseases. Sometimes Nipper missed what she was saying, but not very often. And then the lights came on and the slide show was over.

Nipper rubbed his eyes.

Sister Francesca moved to the front of the class. "Any questions?"

Sister Mary Ignatius smiled and pointed at Alice Dillon. "Alice, I believe you have a question for Sister Francesca?"

Alice stumbled out of her seat. She grinned shyly at Sister Francesca and squinted at her scribbler.

"Sister Francesca, how does—"

"Louder, Alice, so Sister can hear you," Sister Mary Ignatius said.

Alice cleared her throat.

SisterFrancescahowdoesthemoneywecollectinschoolfortheMissionshelp thepoorunfortunatenativesofAfricaandSouthAmericaastheywallowin squalorinthedepthsofdespairwithoutadequatefoodclothingorshelter?

Alice inhaled loudly and flopped into her seat.

"Jumpins, Alice," Ronnie Sheehan said, "what are you tryin' to do? Win a race?"

Sister Mary Ignatius glowered at Alice and Ronnie. Sister Francesca smiled. "Well, Aleese," she said, christening Alice with the nickname that stuck to her for the rest of that year, "every penny helps. And Our Lord knows what great hardships you good children go through in order to donate to the Missions. He smiles on you for it." Sister Francesca folded her arms and beamed her own radiant smile around the room.

There was suddenly a voice from the back of the class.

A low voice that did not stumble or stutter but growled its question through a veil of sarcasm.

"Then why don't God smile on them people down there and give 'em some food and houses and stuff in the first place?"

Nipper had never heard such an outburst before—certainly not with an important guest in the room. Everyone swivelled in their seats and stared at the speaker. In the last desk in the window row, Paddy Dunne sat slumped, his eyes fixed on Sister Francesca, a pencil shoved firmly between his teeth. Sister Mary Ignatius was so shocked she couldn't speak, just stared at Paddy as if wondering, Who is this person and how did he get into my classroom? Some giggling snapped her out of her trance. She silenced it with a glare.

"Paddy Dunne, you know better than to speak out of turn—"

"It's all right," Sister Francesca said, nodding and laying her hand on her colleague's forearm. "It's an excellent question." As she gathered herself to answer, Paddy swept the pencil out of his mouth and gestured around the room with it.

"I mean, like it's no hardship for most of the crowd here to give twenty-five cents to the Missions every week. They just goes without a bag o' chips or a bar or somethin'. Sure half of 'em don't even do that—they just gets an extra quarter from their mother."

Nipper hung his head. He remembered the time his mother had given him a quarter for the Missions and he'd spent it on a Puff Bar and jujubes.

Paddy leaned forward. "That crowd in the pictures you showed us—sure they probably never even seen a Pepsi or a bag o' chips, did they?"

Paddy's speech had left everyone a little breathless. Nipper found himself nodding. Of course, they'd never seen a Pepsi. How could they when the world was filled with sinners like him who weren't content with their good fortune and *stole* from them? From all of those poor little boys and girls he'd just seen in the slides.

Sister Mary Ignatius shook her head and swayed slightly on the balls of her feet. She stared at Paddy Dunne the way Nipper stared at really hard arithmetic sums.

But Sister Francesca just smiled. "No," she said, "I wouldn't say that many of them have seen a Pepsi."

"I mean, like it seems to me," Paddy said, "that all of them poor people in them hot countries got nothin' not because of what they *done* or anything, but just because of where they lives. Don't seem fair. They never asked to be born down there."

"Yeah, well at least they haven't got to shovel snow in the winter, do they?" piped up Wally Coady, who lived at the top of Kenny's Hill.

"Sure who cares about that?" Violet Dobbin said. "I'd rather have to shovel snow and not be hungry than not to and be starved half to death all the time."

"At least we haven't got *hurricanes*," Alice Dillon said. "And *earthquakes*."

"Or *leprosy*," Pauly Mackey said, shivering with disgust. "Parts of your arms and legs rottin' and fallin' off—"

"Enough," Sister Mary Ignatius said. She paused and took a deep breath. "It is not our place to question the will of God."

"I'm not saying that the Sister there is not doing a good job or nothin'," Paddy said, sitting up. "I just can't understand what God has got against them people, that's all."

"God hasn't got anything *against* them," Sister Mary Ignatius said. "God loves us all equally. Doesn't He, Sister?" She looked to her colleague for support.

Sister Francesca nodded and opened her mouth to speak.

"He got an awful queer way of showin' it, then," Paddy said. "Look at them pictures she just showed us—"

"*She* has got a name," Sister Mary Ignatius said. "It's Sister Francesca. Please be so kind as to use it."

"Sister Francesca showed us," Paddy continued. "Sure my Uncle Frank got a old huntin' shack up on the Witless Bay Line that's ten times better than their houses. And he don't go to church, he drinks like a fish, he got about seven youngsters even though he was never married—"

"*Enough!*" Sister Mary Ignatius said through clenched teeth. She glanced apologetically at Sister Francesca.

Paddy leaned back in his seat and examined the point of his

pencil. "Yeah, well, I'm just saying it don't seem fair to me, that's all," he said quietly. He shoved the pencil back in his mouth and stared out the window.

"What was your name again, young man?" Sister Francesca asked.

"Paddy."

"Paddy what?" Sister Mary Ignatius said. "Take that pencil out of your mouth and look at Sister when she's talking to you."

"Paddy Dunne," he said, shifting in his seat.

"Yes, Paddy, you're right," Sister Francesca said. "It doesn't seem fair. But, as Sister Mary Ignatius has pointed out, the ways of God are not always ours to understand. We must have faith that the Lord knows what is best. You see, in this world there are many mysteries . . . "

She talked until the end of class, all about the Mysteries—Joyful, Sorrowful, Glorious—that the children had studied with Sister Bernadette in religion. But Nipper could tell that Paddy had stopped listening. It was funny. Sister Francesca was a nice woman, and he knew she really wanted to help those poor people. And she was very pretty, with her suntan and green-tinted glasses and gleaming white habit. But after a while Nipper stopped listening, too.

Paddy's excellent question earned him three straps on each hand and a week's detention. And something strange happened. Nipper had never seen him give to the Missions before, but now he began to contribute five or ten cents a week. When Sister Bernadette asked him about it, he shrugged. "I don't know much about God's ways and faith and all that stuff," he said, "but the shacks them black people lives in makes my house look like a mansion."

11

*N*ipper stood high on the pedals and steered his bike through a maze of oozing potholes. It had rained all night. Twice he heard his mother getting up to empty the bucket beneath the bathroom leak. But in the morning the weather had cleared, and now the sun shone in a cloudless sky.

Opposite Flynn's meadow the back tire blew out. Nipper got off and kicked at it in disgust. He looked up the meadow and saw Francis Hartery and Mick plowing the steep incline of the potato field. Mick's shaggy, tangled mane swayed in the sun. Nipper pushed the bike to the side of the road and laid it down. Then he jumped the gushing drain and bolted up the meadow, pausing in mid-stride to swing at hay and red clover.

He was just about to call out to Francis when he saw Mick stumble—almost as if he were slipping on ice. His front legs pawed the uneven ground delicately, almost prettily—the practised move of a plumed circus horse; then he lurched forward and collapsed on bended knees, tangled in the traces as if genuflecting.

Nipper froze. He waited for Mick to get to his feet, but the horse did not move. Francis stared straight ahead, his hands still glued to the plough. He seemed unaware of Nipper. Finally, he let go of the handles and stepped around the furrow. He took off his sweat-stained ball cap and gave Nipper a bewildered look. "Jesus Christ, if that don't . . . " Francis laid a hand on Mick's back and went around to his drooping head. Mick's tongue lolled like a Newfoundland dog's. Francis slipped his fingers inside the harness and shook the horse's head. He pressed his ear against the wet nostrils. "Jesus Christ," he said softly. He untied the reins and traces; Mick slid gently forward, his hooves jutting sideways. Francis slipped off the harness and pulled back the plough. He shook his head. "The poor bastard. Jesus, I wasn't working him hard. I was just lettin' him go at his own pace."

One of Mick's eyes was closed, the other completely open. There was no doubt in Nipper's mind that the horse was dead. No chance that the closed eye would suddenly flicker to life, and Mick would struggle to his feet and carry on up the meadow.

Mick was gone—gone to wherever dead horses go.

Nipper's throat ached dryly. "What happened to him?"

Francis shrugged. "Jesus, I don't know. That's the first time I ever saw the like o' that. The poor frigger . . . It was his heart, I suppose. He was goin' along fine and then he just . . . stopped. Gave up."

"What'll happen to him now?"

Francis stared at Mick. "Huh? What? Jesus, bloody good question. I'll have to get Densmore's tractor up here—and the sled. Sure as hell can't leave 'im in the middle of the friggin' potato field. Jesus *Christ*. And where the hell am I goin' to get another horse?"

Francis pulled his cap down to his eyebrows and stumbled up the meadow. Nipper looked at Mick; somehow he seemed incredibly small. He gazed down the meadow. Everything was sharply etched: the sun glinted on the fenders of his bicycle; a flock of black ducks flew north, quacking loudly; a pair of gulls wheeled in lazy circles.

Nipper crouched by Mick and watched Francis talking to old Brendan by the dairy, gesturing frantically. Brendan headed down the meadow, picking his steps, his hands deep in his jacket pockets.

Brendan said nothing—just looked at Mick and nodded at

Nipper knowingly, as if a dead horse in the middle of the field was something to be expected. He knelt at Mick's head. A dragonfly pitched on the horse's open eye. Brendan stared at Mick for what seemed like a long time. Then he stood up and laid a hand on Nipper's shoulder.

"Brendan, how come Mick looks so small?"

Brendan pulled out a handkerchief and mopped his forehead. "Because his soul has fled his body," he said. "There's less of 'im now. I've always noticed that about the dead—how small they look. Animals and people."

"Horses got souls?"

"Sure they do. And now it's freed. So of course he'd have to look smaller. Only makes sense."

Nipper considered this, looked again at Mick. "Where's his soul gone?"

Brendan shrugged. "God only knows. But it's not here anymore, that's for sure." He knelt and brushed a hand along Mick's back. "His soul has fled. That's just his body now." Brendan shook his head. "Poor thing. Died in the harness. Not much of a life, was it?"

"What'll . . . what'll happen to him now?"

"We'll get a bunch of men and bring him down to the gulch."

Nipper's stomach heaved. That's where they threw all the dead animals. There were slimy white bones there, and the skins of the cows and horses blew around the bones. The skins looked like old, thrown-out carpet.

"God, not the gulch. It *stinks* down there."

"It don't matter where he goes, Nicky," Brendan said. "It's not him anymore. It's his soul that's important. Now Mick will have his rest. God knows he worked enough for it."

Flies began to pitch on the warm body: on Mick's mane and nose, even on his thick tongue. Where did they come from so quickly? What drew them? Nipper swung at the flies with his hand, but more kept coming.

He pictured Mick in the horse barn, remembered the clump of his shod feet shuffling. Horses had always struck Nipper as living in some kind of magical, secret world. Owls, too, although he'd only ever seen a live owl once. He'd been cutting a Christmas tree with his father, and he looked up to see a snowy owl shoot him a fierce, yellow-eyed glare and then swoop off through the snow-laden treetops. Nipper often wondered what owls and horses thought about. What had Mick thought about, standing in the horse barn for hours on end, scarcely moving; or in the meadow, his head drooping over the spruce fence, rubbing his rough neck, his tangled tail swishing at flies? He had to be thinking about *something*, didn't he? Dreaming something, lost in whatever dreams horses had. Sometimes Nipper used to feed him carrots, Mick nuzzling him, pushing his head into Nipper's chest, pulling back his upper lip, showing off his stained-green teeth. Nipper would stare into Mick's brown eyes, wondering what lay behind them. Brigid had told him once that on Old Christmas Day, at midnight, the animals spoke. He didn't know whether to believe that or not, but he wanted to believe. What would Mick—standing quietly under the high moon, his steaming breath smoking the frosty air—have to say?

A burst of shrill, bird-like cries floated up the meadow. Nipper looked to see a gaggle of children running hard: Brigid, Pauly, Ronnie and Gerard. Rosarie Dunne, following behind, stopped well back and watched. The others gathered around the fallen horse. Ronnie made as if to speak, then fell silent. Pauly raised a hand to his mouth and began to cry softly, but no one else made a sound. They stared at Mick as if seeing him for the first time, which Nipper thought funny, considering he wasn't even there.

12

There didn't seem to be much to Holy Communion: you just stuck out your tongue. You didn't even have to talk to Monsignor Murphy. "It's as easy as hops," Ronnie Sheehan whispered to Nipper as Sister Bernadette printed on the blackboard. "All you got to do is stick out your tongue." Nipper thought Ronnie wouldn't have much trouble at all. Half the time he looked at him, Ronnie had his tongue stuck out.

"You will kneel at the altar rail," Sister Bernadette said. "When Monsignor Murphy stands before you, he will say, 'Corpus Christi.' Who remembers what Corpus Christi means?"

Pauly Mackey waved his arm.

"Someone else?"

"Body of Christ, Sister," Barb Cleary said.

"That's right. Body of Christ. Then you put out your tongue, and Monsignor Murphy will give you the host. Don't chew it, just swallow. Bow your head respectfully, bless yourself, and go back to your seat."

That didn't seem too hard. Nothing to memorize. Nothing to say. Even God Love 'im Roy Driscoll would probably get it right.

Nipper discovered that a big difference between confession and communion was that people wanted to see you make your First Holy Communion. No one had seemed very interested in his First Confession. But Annie from next door said she was going to be there—wouldn't miss it—and Aunt Mona and Uncle Derm were coming in from St. John's. And then, one morning at breakfast, his mother gave him a letter with a silver dollar in it all the way from Nova Scotia.

Nipper's hair was already short, but his mother took him for a haircut anyway. She bought him a new navy blue blazer. On the morning of the big day, a white satin ribbon was tied in a bow around his upper arm, a corsage pinned to his breast.

Nipper walked up the aisle and knelt at the rail. He wasn't nervous; a little excited, but not nervous. And sure there was nothing to worry about: all you had to do was stick out your tongue. "Corpus Christi," Monsignor Murphy intoned in his gravelly voice. Nipper stuck out his tongue, received the host, and bowed his head. The old priest moved on to Violet Dobbin.

Afterwards, in the bright sunlight, the children were lined up on the church steps for pictures. Nipper squeezed in next to Brigid and Ronnie. Cameras clicked. When the picture-taking was finished, Annie went up to Nipper and patted him on the head. "My God, you're gorgeous." She opened her purse and pulled out a dollar bill. "There," she said, poking the bill into his blazer pocket. "It's not every day you makes your First Holy Communion."

"Nicky," his mother called, "come over and get your picture taken with Brigid."

There's no end to this, Nipper thought. But there didn't seem to be any end to the money, either. "Good for you," Brigid's mother said when the picture had been taken. Suddenly, there was a second dollar bill in his blazer pocket. And then Francis Hartery gave him one and Mr. Sheehan, too. Nipper grinned and thought, This isn't too bad. My soul is filled up with the Body of Christ, and now my pockets are filling up with money. And I didn't even have to talk to Monsignor Murphy.

Not bad for just sticking out your tongue.

When the communion bell rang on the following Sunday, his mother nodded at Nipper. He slid out of the pew and stepped briskly up the aisle. He knelt at the rail. From the corner of his eye he saw Monsignor Murphy to his right, murmuring "Corpus Christi," his gnarled, knobby hand dipping rhythmically into the ciborium.

And then he was standing before Nipper. "Corpus Christi," Monsignor Murphy said, laying a host on Nipper's tongue. Nipper bowed his head and waited for the priest to move on.

But Monsignor Murphy did not move on.

He gasped and remained standing in front of Nipper. Then, under his breath, he said something that sounded remarkably like . . . *shit.* Nipper raised his eyes. Monsignor Murphy looked very upset. He snapped something at the altar boy, who scurried off in the direction of the sacristy.

Nipper's body froze. But his mind raced through a hundred reasons why the priest had stopped: he was a bad child who threw stones at frogs and disobeyed his mother; he rested his tailbone on the pew during the Good Friday service instead of kneeling properly; he sometimes kept the money his mother had given him for the Missions. Did priests automatically know things like that? And then Nipper thought, Oh, my God! Maybe he remembers me from my First Confession, when I couldn't speak. Sister Mary Ignatius was right. How can a priest give Holy Communion to a little boy who didn't make a good confession?

Nipper felt the eyes of everyone in the church boring into his back. They had to be wondering what awful thing he could have done to make the priest stop the church service. Nipper began to tremble. It wasn't his fault if he couldn't talk inside the confessional. He tried, didn't he? Brigid and him had even made up a set of rules. What was Monsignor Murphy going to do? Why wasn't he saying anything? The host Nipper had taken was stuck to the roof of his dry mouth. Then he was struck with a horrible thought.

My God. Maybe he wants it back! Maybe he's waiting.

Should he swallow it anyway? Spit it out?

A hand gripped Nipper's shoulder. He moaned and slumped over the altar rail. It was the devil come to lead him down to hell.

"What is going on?" his mother hissed.

Nipper couldn't speak. She took him by the elbow and led him down the aisle. It seemed like miles. He moved like a zombie. The congregation stared suspiciously.

As they squeezed into their pew, Aunt Mona leaned over to Nipper's mother. "He dropped it," she whispered.

"I did not!" Nipper said. He could afford to be self-righteous: the proof was still stuck to the roof of his mouth.

"Not you," Mona said. "Monsignor Murphy. He must have dropped a host. Look."

Nipper peered over the shoulder of the man sitting in front of him. The altar boy was handing Monsignor Murphy a crystal decanter. The priest took the bottle and dropped painfully to one knee. Then, slowly, he picked something up from the floor. He poured from the decanter and wiped the spot with a clean white cloth.

"I thought it was me," Nipper said as they drove home. "I thought I'd done something wrong."

Sharon laughed. "Sure what could you do wrong? All you got to do is put out your tongue."

Nipper could barely touch his Sunday dinner; he even pushed away the apple pie. Mona reached over and squeezed his arm. "Don't worry about it. We've all had our run-ins with Monsignor Murphy."

"Well, you did anyway," Sharon said. "I'd say it's just as well you're living in St. John's now, or you'd probably be excommunicated."

Mona laughed. "Probably."

"What are you talking about?" Nipper asked. "What kind of run-in did you have?"

"Oh, that's ancient history now," Mona said, digging into her pie.

"Tell me."

Sharon got up from the table and filled the kettle. "It was years ago. You weren't even born yet."

"Weren't even thought of," Mona said. "You know, I never liked that Monsignor Murphy. I remember the first time I saw him when I was a youngster. I said to myself, My God, where did they dig that up? I mean, he looked as old as the hills even then. He must have been in his seventies. I thought he should have been retired."

"Some joke," Sharon said. "Remember Mildred Pike? You know, who used to keep house for him? According to Mildred, the bishops were always after him to retire. He wouldn't hear of it. And you know, most of those bishops are dead now, and here's old Monsignor Murphy still going strong."

Nipper got up and leaned against the kitchen counter. "Yeah, but what kind of run-in did Mona have with him?"

His mother grinned. "Well, Monsignor Murphy was saying mass down to St. Christopher's this Sunday morning, and Mona burst out laughing at him."

"I didn't *burst out* laughing," Mona said through a mouthful of pie. "And I wasn't laughing at him. I was laughing at his singing. My God, his voice . . . " She turned to Nipper. "You know how he got that gravelly old voice on 'im. Well, he'd just started in sounding like that. I don't know why—old age, I suppose. Or maybe it was that pipe he always had stuck in his face. Anyway, he sounded just like someone shaking up an old Pepsi bottle filled with rocks. And—I don't know—it just struck me right funny. I felt awful about laughing—"

"You had this big wad of tissue stuffed halfway down your

throat," Sharon said. "And then you started biting on your purse."

Mona nodded. "It was shockin'. And you know how it is when you're trying to stop from laughing—the more you try to stop, the more you wants to laugh? And then I looked at Sharon—"

"I was mortified," Sharon said. "*Mortified.* And sure I wasn't the only one. Half the church was turned around looking at her."

Mona giggled. "They were. Old Mrs. Quigley. My God, her eyes were shootin' the daggers right into me. And sure that only made it worse—made me laugh even more."

"So what did you do?" Nipper asked.

"Well, when I got home I put my foot down. I made up my mind that I was going to stop," Mona said. "I mean, I had to do something. I felt pure awful about it."

"And on top of that," Sharon said, "she was frightened to death because she thought it was a sin."

"I'm sure it was a sin," Mona said. "Laughing at the priest. In church. During mass. That's sacrilege."

"So what did you *do?*" Nipper asked.

"Like I said, I just told myself, That's it. I'm not going to laugh anymore. I resigned myself to it."

"But the next Sunday she was worse than the first time," Sharon said.

"I was. I thought I was going to have to leave the church."

Sharon got up and shifted the kettle. "And then Lent came up."

"Lent came up. So I figured I'd make a vow for Lent—a vow that I wouldn't laugh at Monsignor Murphy's singing anymore. And, you know, I really thought I was going to get it under control."

"But you didn't?" Nipper said.

Sharon laughed. "That's what she never. Sure she was worse than ever."

"More fool me," Mona said. "It was Lent, for God's sake. So there was more singing during mass than ever."

"And she burst out *again*," Sharon said.

Mona shook her head. "I felt terrible. I was after laughing at the priest, oh, I don't know how many times. I was after breaking my Lenten vow—"

"So she figured she had to confess," Sharon said.

Nipper dropped into his chair. "Confess? To *Monsignor Murphy*?"

"I had to," Mona said. "I couldn't very well make my Easter duty unless I went to confession. So I decided to tell him."

"You didn't," Nipper said.

"I did. The next Saturday evening I went down to St. Christopher's. And my God—nervous? You don't know how nervous I was. Anyway, I went into the confessional and started in with all the usual rigmarole. Then I rhymed off all my regular sins. But old Monsignor Murphy knew I had something on my mind. I mean, after my last sin I made this big pause, right? And he says, right suspicious-like, 'Is there anything else?' And I says, 'Well, yes, Monsignor, there is.' I don't know what he thought I was going to say—probably that I was after murdering somebody or I was pregnant—"

"Mona!" Sharon said.

"Anyway, he perked right up. 'Carry on,' he said. 'There's no sin so terrible that Our Lord cannot find it in his Sacred Heart to forgive you.' I'll always remember that. Those were his very words. And I thought to myself, I hope to God you're right. Anyway, I took a deep breath. 'Well, Monsignor,' I said, 'you see ... it's just that ... well ... I ... I've been laughing at your singing during Sunday mass!' I finally blurted it out, just like that."

Nipper's eyes widened. "My God. What did he do?"

Mona got up and took the kettle off the burner. "Well, first he didn't do anything—didn't say a word. There was just this ... icy silence in the confessional. I thought he was after taking a stroke or something. And then he says in that gruff old voice, 'I see.' I was frightened to death. I started babbling away to him. I told him I knew it was wrong, but I just couldn't help it. Then he says, 'Well, my dear'—you know that superior way he got of talking?—'well, my dear, how much money did you put in the collection plate last Sunday?' I didn't know *what* he was getting on with. But I says, 'Twenty-five cents, Monsignor. Just like I always do.' Then he shifts in the box and looks at me. 'Well, what did you expect for twenty-five cents?' he says. 'Bing Crosby?' Well, I was that shocked I couldn't even laugh."

"What penance did he give you?" Nipper asked.

"Oh, I don't remember now. But it wasn't too bad. I thought he was going to give me a hundred turns of the Stations of the Cross or make me scrub the church floors with a toothbrush. But he just gave me the regular penance."

"Did you keep laughing at his singing?"

"No," Mona said. "I managed to give it up. Took awhile, though."

"You'd still crack a smile every now and then," Sharon said.

"Oh yes. Every now and then. But sure a smile's nothing. I don't suppose it's a sin to smile. Even in our church."

13

The only books in the Mooney house, other than schoolbooks and Sunday missals, were the *Family Catechism*, *Butler's Lives of the Saints*, a spine-shattered Bible, *A Pictorial Medical Guide* (by Forty Specialists), *Irish Saints and Martyrs* and two water-stained volumes of *Reader's Digest Condensed Books*. All had been inherited from Grandfather Kevin. But there was also a ten-volume *Universal World Reference Encyclopedia*. Sharon often told how they got it.

"We had no money, God knows—us just married and Pat with no job and not the one bit of interest in farming. Anyway, I was washing up the breakfast dishes one morning when there came a knock on the door. I thought it might be that fella Sparkes from Deep Harbour sellin' fish. I got my purse and went out, planning on buying a couple of pounds of fresh fish, and there was this man—young man he was, nice-looking—standing there all dolled off in a jacket and tie, carrying a suitcase and sweatin' like ten workhorses. And, of course, the first thing I thinks is: Jehovah's Witness. I opened the door wondering how I was going to get rid of him—not that I got anything against the Jehovah's Witnesses, but if you starts talkin' to 'em, my dear, they'll *wear* you right out. Well, sure enough, the door was hardly cracked when he started in giving his spiel. But he wasn't a Jehovah's Witness at all. He was a salesman. Selling encyclopedias. I was so relieved he wasn't a Jehovah's Witness I just let him talk. He asked me if I had any children and of course I said yes, and he said, well, this was my lucky day because the encyclopedia would be a *wonderful* educational tool for the child—keep his school marks way above everyone else's. I was just about to tell him that Nicky was only a little baby and we wouldn't be wanting anything like that for years and years, when he was in the door and sittin' at the kitchen table with one of the books out showing me some picture in it—I don't know what it was now—some tropical place—Africa, I believe. Well, he had me right bewildered. It was like I was glamoured by the fairies. And he kept on yakking away until by the end of it I believe I would've bought *two* sets of the bloody books just to get rid of 'im. And Pat? Well, you can imagine. 'You bought *what*? How much? For a set of *books*?' He was that upset, and sure I couldn't blame him. I felt awful about it—offered to cancel the order. But he said, 'No, no. You bought 'em, we'll keep 'em.' Proud, see. Anyway, we got the encyclopedias. And what use they are, I don't know. I never looked at 'em and neither did Pat. I don't know whatever happened to that salesman—became a politician, I suppose."

Like the silverware and the good china, the encyclopedia was something fragile, grand and best left untouched. Nipper's father made a walnut case, and there the books stayed—always dusted but never opened since the day of their delivery. Until Nipper suddenly had need of them.

Nipper Mooney woke at dawn. His head was throbbing, his skin on fire. He sat up in bed and stripped off his pajama top. He was covered in itching sores running with yellow pus and the pus had soaked into his singlet. Nipper yelled for his mother. She came into the room and switched on the light. Nipper was trying to take off his singlet, but everywhere the cloth was stuck to his body.

"No!" Sharon said. "Leave it alone."

But Nipper was already peeling off the singlet, and as it came he felt his skin coming with it. Now there was pus and blood. He cried and cried and his mother took his head in her hands and soothed him. Nipper's body felt like someone else's body—someone else's sickly, stinky body. He didn't want this body; he wanted his old body back.

His mother bathed his sores and dressed him in clean pajamas. She made a bed for him on the chesterfield so he wouldn't have to stay in the bedroom all by himself.

It felt funny not to have to go to school. Nipper asked what Sister Mary Ignatius and Sister Bernadette would think.

"Don't you worry. I called St. Brigid's and told them you have the chicken pox."

The chicken pox. Why did they call it chicken pox?

Nipper lay on the chesterfield and tried not to scratch. His mother had said that scratching was bad. If you scratched you'd have scars for the rest of your life. But the itching was so bad. Nipper tossed and turned.

"Do you want to watch TV?" Sharon asked. And for a while Nipper did. But morning TV was boring. The shows were either for babies or grown-ups: shows with people sitting around smoking cigarettes and talking about the government.

Nipper lay on his back and tried not to scratch. He looked up through the picture window at the fluffy clouds. There were faces in the clouds: people faces, animal faces . . . *boring* faces. Nipper didn't know how long he could stay on the chesterfield before he went crazy—even if he didn't have to go to school and his mother brought him anything he wanted.

His gaze fell on the corner bookcase, the gold-embossed spines of the encyclopedias.

When Sharon brought him a mug of cocoa he said, "Mom, can I look at the encyclopedias?"

She looked puzzled. "I believe you're a bit young for those books yet. What do you want with them?"

Nipper shrugged and tried not to scratch. "Just something to do."

Sharon went and knelt before the bookcase. She reached in, then looked back over her shoulder. "Which one?"

"It don't matter."

Sharon plucked a book, brought it over and handed it to him.

"Now don't you get that dirty. They cost a fortune, those books. They're not playthings."

Nipper ran his fingers over the wine cover. The corners were adorned with figures: Saturn surrounded by stars; a goose quill and inkwell; an Indian elephant; an old-fashioned microscope. Nipper opened the book. It had never been opened before and it creaked. It still smelled new, and as he flipped the pages a yeasty paper smell blew around him. On the first page was a quote from someone named Samuel Johnson:

> Knowledge Is Of Two Kinds:
> We Know A Subject Ourselves,
> Or We Know Where We Can Find
> Information Upon It.

Nipper spent the morning going through the encyclopedia. He read about the Pharaohs, Original Sin, Napoleon—even Newfoundland, which he learned was the tenth largest island in the world. There were photographs and drawings of famous people: Queen Victoria, George Washington; there were paintings and sculptures: the Mona Lisa, Romulus and Remus, the naked David. One volume had a colourful children's section with "A Selection of Fairy Tales." Nipper's favourite part was "Life in Prehistoric Time," which showed a caveman discovering fire by putting a branch into a glowing lava stream, and a Cro-Magnon man in a cave painting a picture of a deer. There were drawings of hairy mammoths, sabre-toothed tigers and dinosaurs. One caption read: *A Neanderthal man offers battle for the protection of his home.* Nipper's favourite illustration was of two feathered hunters spearing a gigantic, stumbling bison with a sadly bewildered expression on his black face.

When Nipper looked up it was dinnertime. His sores began to itch again. Sharon looked at him curiously. "Don't you find those too hard? They're not storybooks."

"No," Nipper said, "they're not hard. There's lots of pictures."

The next morning Nipper woke from a nap to see Annie standing before him. She clutched a bundle of books to her huge bosom. "Your mom said you were reading the encyclopedia," she said, dumping the books at his feet. "I brought these over. Charlie had 'em when he was a youngster. I was going to send them up to the grandchildren in Ontario, but it costs a fortune. You can have 'em if you want. Probably better than a boring old encyclopedia."

"Thanks," Nipper said. He sorted through the books. Some were stained or had torn or missing pages. But most were in good condition. *The Adventures of Tom Sawyer. The Adventures of Huckleberry Finn. Tarzan. The Bobbsey Twins at the Seashore. The Famous Five on a Treasure Island.*

He began to read.

Nipper got to stay home for a whole week. But he wasn't really home because he was reading *Huckleberry Finn* and *Tom Sawyer.* He was no longer scarred by chicken pox and lying on a chesterfield in Kildura. He was drifting down the Mississippi; he was lost in the black caves with Tom Sawyer and Becky Thatcher and a rapidly dying candle; he was flying through the sweltering jungle with Tarzan.

Nipper was more fevered by the books than he was by the

chicken pox. Over the next few weeks he began all of Annie's books. He dipped into all the volumes of the encyclopedia.

He even began to look at the religious books.

These were kept in a small cherry bookcase with glass doors. *Butler's Lives of the Saints* was the best—nice and gory. It had lots of pictures and detailed descriptions of the martyrs' agonies as they were brutally crucified or torn apart and eaten by wild beasts. *Irish Saints and Martyrs* was duller, full of information about the founding of monasteries, with endless lists of each saint's good works. The only things Nipper found interesting were the miracles.

He read about St. Brigid.

One time, the servant of a rich and powerful nobleman accidentally killed his master's favourite dog, mistaking it for a wolf. The nobleman was so outraged he decided to put the servant to death. In the meantime, his friends sent for St. Brigid. When she arrived, the nobleman was away. They told her what their master was planning to do. Brigid noticed two harps hanging on the wall. "When your master comes into the room," she told them, "take down the harps and play for him." The men told her they couldn't play; they had no skill. She smiled and told them to trust her. When the nobleman came home he barged into the room and immediately ordered the head of his servant. But the man's friends did as they were told. They took down the harps, and even though they had never played before, they were able to produce the most beautiful music. The nobleman was so soothed and touched by their playing that he forgave his servant and revoked the death sentence. The harp-playing servants remained wonderful musicians to the end of their days.

On another occasion, after Brigid had been caught in a rainstorm, she took off her cloak and hung it to dry on a sunbeam.

Nipper thought they were pretty good miracles. Just as good

as any other saint's. So why wasn't Brigid in *Butler's Lives of the Saints*? The only Irish saint there was St. Patrick. Why did they leave Brigid out?

The frontispiece of *Irish Saints and Martyrs* was a pencil drawing of St. Brigid covered by a tissue-like protecting page. She looked different from the statue at school. In the drawing she seemed tired and old. Even a bit fat. But in the statue in the school foyer she was tall and pretty. She held her fingers to perfect lips and gazed serenely at the floor, as if about to blow a kiss or perform yet another wonderful miracle.

14

Nipper was sprawled on his bed reading the *Big Red Enid Blyton Book*, a present from Aunt Mona. English books were strange. The weather was always calm. People had picnics by the ocean and their tablecloths didn't blow away. Everyone talked funny: German shepherds were *Alsatians*; holidays were *hols*; molasses was *treacle*—was that where the word "trickle" came from? A flashlight was a *torch*. This caused Nipper no end of confusion: Why is Philippa bringing a flaming stick down to the basement? The children went to private schools where the girls wore ties and there weren't any nuns. And the members of the Famous Five were always so polite to each other. If they got mad the worst they would ever say was something like: "Oh, Julian, you *are* horrid!" People had names like Clive and Arabella and spoke in perfect sentences, as if they were reading lines in a play. And the members of the Famous Five or the Secret Seven never swore or went to church or got into fist fights. England seemed interesting all the same. Not as interesting as Mississippi, though. The Famous Five had nothing on Huck Finn, who smoked and swam naked and caught huge catfish and had seen people tarred and feathered—even shot and killed. Huck and Tom Sawyer talked funny, too, but you always knew what they were saying. You could even understand Jim, the slave—once you got used to him.

Nipper threw down the book and went to the top of the stairs. He sat on the top step and listened. His mother and Mona were still playing 45s. He could hear the masonite kitchen table shiver and squeak each time Mona slammed down a card, and her shrill, "Put that in your pipe and smoke it!" Nipper wondered if they would play until it got too late for the Rosary. Sometimes they got carried away—especially if no one could win the last two out of three hands. Nipper was pretty sure Huck Finn didn't play 45s or say the Rosary. He wondered if the Famous Five did. He doubted it. They were too busy solving mysteries and talking funny and eating treacle. Maybe that was why English people talked funny, because they ate so much treacle.

Nipper crept down the stairs and stood in the kitchen door. Mona was raking in the cards. "Time to give this up now," she said. "Get Nipper down till we gets the Rosary over with."

"I'm here," he said.

Mona looked up. "Oh, good. Right on time. Got your beads?" Nipper pulled them out of his pocket and held them up. "All right, then. Out to the living room."

"Anyway," Sharon said, picking up the thread of an earlier conversation which had been lost in the heat of the 45s, "Brendan Flynn wasn't dropped on his head. He had some kind of disease and it made him go all funny. And sure he was premature on top of that—like Nicky was."

"What does that mean?" Nipper said. "Premature?"

"Oh, nothing," Sharon said. "Don't you be bothered about that."

Mona pinched Nipper's cheek. "It means you were born before your time."

"Mona," Sharon said.

"And you know something—I know why, too."

"*Mona.*"

"I mean, he's never liked closed-in places. I'd say that's why he was premature: he couldn't stand to stay inside you for the full nine months—had to get out."

"Mona!"

Nipper screwed up his face. "Mom, what's she talking about?"

"Never you mind. That's grown-up stuff."

Mona laughed. "Anyway, my darling, it's no odds if Brendan Flynn was premature or not. He was dropped. But what could you expect? His mother was half-drunk all the time."

Sharon looked at her sister steadily. "No, it was the measles or something when he was a baby. That's what Grandmother told me."

"What are you gettin' on with? The measles aren't going to fool up your head like that. Sure we all had the measles."

"If you gets it when you're a newborn it can turn you retarded," Sharon said. "And sure on top of that, old Mrs. Flynn used to be always leaving him out in the sun—hours on end and no bonnet or cap on him. Grandmother told me all about it. God knows we don't get much sun in Newfoundland, but we gets enough to addle the brain of a poor little infant. There's been more than one youngster turned retarded by being left out in the sun."

"Maybe he got stole by the fairies," Nipper said. "Maybe he's a changeling. That's what Pauly Mackey's mother thinks."

"Don't mind that one down there," Sharon said. "Sure she's worse than old Grandmother Flynn."

"But Brendan is not *retarded*," Mona said. "Not like Roy Driscoll—God love 'im. Sure he's always reading big old books—and them with the tiniest kind of print in 'em. He couldn't do that if he was retarded. He's just a bit . . . *off*—like Silly Willy was." She laughed. "Remember that time on Water Street when Silly Willy ran up and kissed you?"

"Don't remind me."

"That was some big smacker he gave you."

"I *said*, don't remind me."

"The colours you turned—my dear, you could've put a rainbow to shame."

"Mona, give it up."

"But, I mean now, you take it: a grown man goin' around on an old bike, wearing double-breasted suits—*wool* for God's sake—in the middle of the summer."

"Where in the name of God does he get that stuff? That's what I'd like to know," Sharon said, kneeling down. "It looks as old as the hills. I suppose it was his father's."

Mona nodded. "Long underwear, too. It's no harm to say Brendan Flynn loves his long underwear. He must find the world some awful cold place is all I can say."

"But he's pleasant."

"Oh, he's pleasant enough," Mona said. "Always tips his hat to you: 'Good morning, ladies.'" Mona put a hand to her mouth and giggled. "Sure he was calling us ladies when we were still in knee socks at St. Brigid's—younger than Nipper there. God, I used to be some embarrassed."

"What's wrong with being polite?" Nipper said. "That's what you're always after me to be, isn't it?"

"There's nothing wrong with being polite," Mona said. "But there's no need to go to hell with it. I don't expect Herb Blake to talk to me like I'm the Queen of Sheba every time I'm down to his shop buyin' a couple of pounds of bologna."

"Well, Brendan's a gentle soul for all that," Sharon said. "Even if he is a bit touched."

"And always, then, with those *books* in his face," Mona said. "He's going to walk right out in a pond someday and drown himself."

"He likes reading *Irish Saints and Martyrs*," Nipper said, kneeling before the wingback chair. "Like we got. He showed it to me one day up on the Old Road. St. Brigid is his favourite."

"Make no wonder," Mona said. "He's like a saint himself.

But sure half the saints were a bit touched." Mona lowered her voice conspiratorially. "Do you suppose that's true? You know, that the saints and holy martyrs would be singing and praying while the lions and tigers were tearing them limb from limb?" Mona shivered. "My dear, I can tell you that if I was being thrown to the lions, the last thing I'd be doing is breaking into song. I'd be just like Saint Peter in the Bible: I'd say anything I was asked to and right quick, too. Tell them I believed in the Golden Calf? My dear, I'd tell them I believed in a whole bloody herd—calves, heifers, bulls—the lot. Hartery's dog bit me once when I was a youngster and that hurt like anything. I can imagine now what it must be like having your whole leg down the mouth of some tiger."

"Well, none of our crowd are saints," Sharon said. "Never were. I don't suppose either one of us'll be thrown to the lions any time soon. No need to worry about that."

Mona fingered her emerald Rosary beads. "Now, if Brendan was a saint he'd be like St. Francis."

Sharon nodded. "Yes, he's awfully quiet for a man. And he's very gentle with the animals—which is more than you can say for most of 'em around here. Sure when the youngsters are bringing the cows up to the meadow they got 'em half-crucified throwing rocks at 'em and beatin' 'em with sticks. Brendan would never be at that."

Mona nodded and dropped to her knees. "That's true. You almost expect the little sparrows and robins to pitch on his shoulders." She laughed. "And sure they probably do. He's got enough hair sproutin' out of his nose and ears to hide a flock of geese—nests and all. What's wrong with old men? He's never heard of a pair of scissors?"

Sharon laughed. "My dear, he's too much in his own little world now to worry about stuff like that. Too busy readin' books. Anyway, at least he's clean."

"Oh yes, he's always clean," Mona said. "You have to give him that."

"Brendan doesn't like it when Paddy Dunne catches trout," Nipper said, his voice muffled by the back of the chair.

"Is that right, now?" Mona said.

"Yes. Brendan says that even trout like their little lives."

"Well, I suppose they do," Mona said.

"Nice, though, all the same," Sharon said.

"What's that?" Mona said.

"A feed of trout."

"Oh yes. I love a feed of trout. Muds now, mind you. Not browns."

"No, my dear. Sure the browns are just all bones."

"And there's no flavour to 'em."

"Not like a mud," Sharon said. "See, that's orange meat, like a salmon—I mean, in a mud."

"But they have a soul," Nipper said, getting up and flopping into his chair.

"Yes, something like salmon," Mona said. "But sweeter."

Nipper pulled his knees up to his chest and watched the light from the kitchen play on his plastic Rosary beads. "But the soul ceases to exist when the trout dies," he said.

"You know, I haven't had a feed of trout in ages," Sharon said.

"Mick had a soul, but when he died in the harness plowing up Flynn's potato field, his soul fled. Brendan told me."

Mona and Sharon turned and looked at him.

"What is that child getting on with?" Mona said.

"Something about trout having souls," his mother said.

Mona glared at Nipper. "Don't be so foolish. Trout don't have souls."

"They do so," Nipper said. "It says in the catechism. It says:

An animal has a soul, but it is not a spiritual soul like that of man, and it ceases to exist with the death of the animal. I looked it up."

"But a trout is not an *animal*," Mona said. "It's a fish."

"I *know* it's a fish. But God—"

"Now, a dog," Sharon said, "a dog could have a soul."

"Yes, a dog could have a soul," Mona said. "A dog—that's a different thing altogether."

Nipper sat up and twirled his Rosary beads. "What's different about it? Why should a dog—"

"Remember Topper, Sharon," Mona said, "when we were youngsters? He was some sweet. I always liked collies: pure gorgeous. I wouldn't be surprised if Topper had a soul." Mona shook her Rosary beads at Nipper. "But sure a fish . . . a fish is just the same as an old frog or lizard or something."

"Don't make no difference," Nipper said. "God made 'em, didn't He? They're alive, aren't they? Then they must have a soul. That's what Brendan said. That's what it says in the catechism."

Mona snorted. "So you mean to tell me that all them fish out in the ocean—all them millions, *billions* of fish out swimming around the ocean—each and every one of them has got a soul?"

"Yes."

"And that bit of salt cod we had for supper last night—that had a soul?"

"Uh-huh."

"And all the flies and mosquitos buzzin' around, tormentin' the life out of you all summer long—they got souls, too?"

"Sure."

"Go way with you! Sacred Heart, if that was the case you'd need a hundred Gods just to keep track of it all."

"Well, He is *God*," Nipper said. "He can do anything. That's His job."

"Anyway," Mona said, "what's the point in a trout or a turtle or whatever having a soul if it's just going to disappear the minute it dies? The whole reason for having a soul in the first place is that it *don't* die."

"Brendan says—"

"You can't believe everything St. Brendan tells you," Sharon said. "Sure he believes in the fairies and God knows what old foolishness."

"But I read it. It's in the catechism."

"That child reads too much for his own good," Mona said. "And why is he reading catechisms and encyclopedias at his age, anyway?"

"Well, whose fault is that?" Sharon said. "You're the one always giving him books."

"There's nothing wrong with books, God knows. But I'd watch it just the same. He's going to have his eyes ruined."

Sharon sighed. "Yes," she said. "At the very least."

"And why can't he hang around with youngsters his own age instead of that old vagabond, Brendan?"

"I don't hang around with Brendan," Nipper said. "I don't even talk to him that much. I only says hello. I just sees him up on the Old Road sometimes. Besides—"

"All *right*," Sharon said. "Can we shut up about Brendan and souls and trout and dogs and dead horses and get on with the Rosary?"

Nipper fell to his knees and propped his elbows on the sagging chair bottom. They bowed their heads.

"In the Name of the Father, the Son and the Holy Ghost. I believe in God, the Father Almighty, Creator of heaven and earth . . . "

That night, beneath a dimpled, yellow moon, Nipper Mooney lay in bed and watched the lace curtains trembling in the window box. If you caught a trout, and then when it was still alive you ate it, would the trout's soul go into your soul? No, it would flee as soon as the trout died in your stomach. And then the soul would fly out into the air. Right through your guts. A stomach wouldn't be able to stop a soul. Not even Francis Hartery's stomach. Francis could drink a whole bottle of Old Niagara and then sit down to three helpings of Jiggs dinner all smothered in pickles and mustard. Cast iron. That's how his mother had described Francis's stomach. But Nipper knew that not even iron could contain a soul. Brendan was right. That's why Mick had looked so small crumpled in the harness, so light with his glassy eye and the blue-arse flies crawling up his nose. That's why Mick had looked so empty, so . . . alone.

Because his soul had fled.

15

*W*hen Patrick Mooney came home from the mines, it was always late, long after Nipper had gone to bed. But no matter how late, he insisted on going into his son's room to see him. "I'll just take a little peek," his father would say outside the bedroom door.

"Wait till morning," his mother would insist. "He'll be too excited to get back to sleep. He won't be fit for school tomorrow." His mother would say this even as she followed her husband into Nipper's room.

In his suit and tie Nipper's father looked more like a salesman or even a Jehovah's Witness than a returning miner. Nipper sometimes wondered if his father really was a miner. Maybe he was a secret agent like in the *Famous Five* or the *Hardy Boys*. Maybe he was only pretending to be a miner, and he'd really been off on the mainland or over in Europe somewhere fighting the Russians. That's why he came home late at night—so no one would find out where he lived. Nipper would look for the shadow of coal dust on his father's face and hands, rimes of black under his short fingernails. He never saw any.

Nipper was a deep sleeper, but he usually woke up when his father came home. He would hear a car pulling up in front of the house or the thump of a dropped suitcase. And even though his mother didn't like it when Patrick went into his room so late at night, Nipper knew his father would have his way. So he would fold his arms behind his head and wait.

But one night Nipper did not wake up: not until the bed

dipped and the creaking springs stirred him from his sleep. He was surprised to see his father; he wasn't due home for weeks.

"How come you're back so early?" Nipper asked, rubbing his eyes.

"Oh, I'm just taking a little time off."

"Can we go fishing tomorrow after school?"

"Sure we can. Why not?"

And then his mother was leaning down, tucking Nipper in. "For God's sake, Pat, let the child get his rest, will you? He's got to be up for school in a few hours."

His father leaned forward and kissed Nipper on the hairline. Nipper smelled the familiar scents of cigarettes and Old Spice.

After his unexpected return, his father spent a lot of time around the house. He didn't go out much to help the farmers with their tractors and trucks; he didn't drive over to Deep Harbour. Sometimes he went into St. John's, but usually he was just "underfoot." That's what Mrs. Sheehan said about Ronnie's father when he spent too much time indoors: "For God's sake, get out from underfoot, will you?" Nipper's father didn't seem to have much to do. He took Nipper for walks up on the Old Road. One evening he showed him the cove in the Damsel's Eye where he'd caught the big mud trout when he was a boy. "Six or seven pounds, easy," he said. "Had to be. Just about ripped the pole out of my hand." Another day he made a fire with blasty boughs and the branches of a stunted starrigan. He fried pork chops and potatoes in a black, greasy pan and dipped icy water from a spring. No matter where Nipper sat, the woodsmoke blew into his eyes. He jumped up and down, circling the blaze, fanning the smoke from his face while his father chewed on a pork chop and laughed.

Nipper wondered when his father would go back to the mines, but when he asked, Patrick just shrugged. Nipper waited for the going-away ritual to begin, waited for the morning when he'd feel the bed dip, hear the creaking of the springs and look up to see his father's freshly shaven face. Nothing happened. When Nipper came home from school, Patrick was always sitting in the kitchen or watching TV.

As the weeks passed, a hush grew in the house. It was there when Annie was over playing 45s with his mother; it was there when Mona drove in from town for supper or to help in the vegetable garden.

Late one night Nipper stumbled downstairs to go to the bathroom. There was a light on in the kitchen. His father was sitting at the table in his singlet with a cup of untouched tea before him. He flicked the top of his lighter open and closed. His pack of Player's lay at his fingertips, but the ashtray hadn't been used. His father looked thin—thinner than Nipper had ever seen him. His eyes were sunken and red, his face rough with black stubble. He winked at Nipper. "What are you doin' up?"

"I got to pee."

"Oh, you're on an important mission, are you?"

"Yeah."

"Well, you better go do it. It's pretty late."

The next morning at breakfast, Nipper said, "Mom, is Dad ever going back to Nova Scotia?"

"We'll see," she said. "He's still feeling a bit poorly."

"What's wrong with him?"

She turned away. "He got a nervous stomach."

Nipper knew all about nervous stomachs. That's what he got when Sister Annunciata gave him a test or when Sister Mary Ignatius knocked on the door for a surprise arithmetic bee.

Then, one day, when Nipper came home from school, his father wasn't there. For a moment he thought he must have gone back to Nova Scotia without saying good-bye.

"He's at the hospital," his mother said. "Tests. They're going to keep him in for a while."

Days later his father, looking thinner than ever, climbed slowly out of Uncle Phonse's pick-up. He spent a lot of time lying on the daybed in the kitchen. He stared at the ceiling. He lit Player after Player and let them burn away in the ashtray. He grew quiet, didn't joke much anymore. Didn't push his clean plate away after a meal and say, "That's history." Didn't say things like, "I think I'll have some more of that cherry cake. That cake's right morish, that is." He shook his head when Nipper suggested a hike up to the Darning Needles. "Maybe tomorrow." His mother told Nipper not to have the television too loud, not to be tearing around the house with his Dinkys.

One day during recess Brigid Flynn said, "I heard your father's sick."

"Yeah."

"What's wrong with him?"

"He got a nervous stomach."

"What does that mean?"

"Don't know."

"When's he going to get better?"

"Don't know."

The hush grew, seeped into every corner of the house.

Nipper got used to the crowded medicine bottles in the cabinet; got used to soup bubbling away on the stove all the time because his father couldn't eat much else. But he could not get used to the hush. It crept up like a storm. It trickled into his small bedroom. It was in the pages of his books. In his mother's tired eyes. In Annie's pursed lips. In the way Mr. Sheehan looked at him and then turned away.

Patrick slept a lot now, but when Nipper brought him his pills or a glass of water he still smiled. He didn't shave much anymore, didn't smell of Old Spice. There was a different smell about him: a smell of medicine and mint and freshly laundered bedclothes.

His father looked bored lying on the daybed. Even Nipper would want to go back to school if he had to stay off for this long. One evening he brought him a Tarzan book to read, but his father shook his head. "I was never much of a hand for books."

"You sure?" Nipper said. "It helped me when I had the chicken pox and was bored right to death. I could read you a bit."

His father shook his head and closed his eyes.

One day after school Nipper went in to see him but he was asleep. When he was about to leave his father stirred and said, "How's my little Nicky today?"

Nipper turned around and squinted. "What did you say?"

"I said . . . how's my little Nicky today?"

"Why'd you call me that?"

His father raised his eyebrows in mock surprise. "Sure that's your name, isn't it? Nicholas?"

Nipper shrugged. "I s'pose. But you never calls me that."

His father smiled and closed his eyes.

One evening when Nipper pedalled down the road on his bike with Ronnie Sheehan perched on the crossbar, he saw Uncle Phonse turning his Chevy pick-up into their lane. Nipper went indoors. Aunt Mona was in the kitchen. They were packing up his father's things. His mother stared out the window. His father's pills, razor and toothbrush, his Old Spice—everything had been taken from the bathroom. New pajamas, still wrapped in plastic, lay on the kitchen table.

"Your dad's going into St. Clare's for a while," his mother said. "It won't be for long."

But it was long. And his mother was there a lot, too. When

Nipper came home from school, it was often Annie or Mona in the kitchen—even Uncle Phonse.

Sometimes there was no one.

The hush deepened. Now they said the Rosary nearly every night. And even the Rosary had changed. They said it slower than usual. The prayers weren't run together into a droning sing-song. You could pick out every word. The hush had fallen over the Rosary.

Nipper began to wake in the middle of the night. He tossed and turned and stared up at the black ceiling. When he finally slept, he dreamed the same dream over and over. His father was trapped in a collapsed mine. He was lying on his stomach and could barely move. Everything was black except for his eyes, which were red-veined and glowing like strange, flickering insects. But there was no fear in them, just sadness. And then his eyes began to fade into the blackness of the coal, the glowing points growing smaller and smaller. His father was slipping into the black. Always, just before his eyes disappeared completely, Nipper would wake and sit straight up in bed. For a moment he would think that he was trapped in a mine, too, but then his room would slowly materialize, and he'd make out the dresser and chair, his books jumbled on the floor.

He would lie back down and try to sleep.

When school closed in June, Nipper's father was still in the hospital. Nipper asked if he could go in to see him.

"I don't think so, Nicky," his mother said.

"But I want to tell him that I passed."

"You can put it in one of your letters. Sure I can tell him that for you."

"It's not the same."

"I know, duckie. But it's better this way."

Finally, Nipper grew used to the hush. Brigid and Ronnie

and the rest of his friends stopped asking about his father. They all played around the farms, organized games of tips, cut spruce boughs and built sweet-smelling teepees.

August came. It seemed that each day was hotter, more flooded with sunlight, than the day before. On the evening of August 14, the western sky flamed a brilliant orange and red. Nipper's mother looked at it and smiled as she washed up the supper dishes. "It'll be a nice day again tomorrow," she said.

16

Nipper Mooney did not attend his father's wake, nor was he asked if he wanted to. The funeral had a dreamlike quality. Days later, all he could remember of it was a shadowy series of images and events.

Donning a bow tie, flannel trousers and his First Holy Communion blazer.

Squeezing into new, creaky leather shoes.

His mother repeatedly running a wet comb through his cowlick until Mona had finally taken it from her. "He looks fine." Pinching Nipper's cheek. "Very handsome."

At the church, women cluck-clucked and whispered to each other when they saw him. The men looked at him with concern.

And then came a running film of images:

His mother's face hidden behind a black lace veil.

The way she splayed her arms on the top of the pew and rested her forehead on the back of her hands.

Mona's pale, contorted face.

Annie's ceaseless sniffling.

Brendan Flynn standing stiffly at the back of the church.

Monsignor Murphy's chainsaw voice breaking on the high notes of the Kyrie Eléison.

His father's draped casket floating in clouds of incense.

Nipper did not go to the graveyard, nor was he asked if he wanted to. As the coffin was loaded into the hearse, his mother ushered him over him to Annie, who immediately took him by the hand. "You go home with Annie, now," his mother said, "and be a good boy." And that's where he'd spent the afternoon,

Annie fussing over him, plying him with cookies and Freshie, asking a hundred times if there was anything he wanted.

Over the next couple of days fewer cars turned into the dusty driveway; the phone rang less often. Soon food and the remains of food were the only signs that anything out of the ordinary had happened: half-eaten casseroles and picked-over turkey carcasses crowded the small refrigerator; pies covered in tinfoil bumped on the kitchen counter. And then, two days after the funeral, Mona lugged a suitcase into the house and announced with an air of finality that she was staying—at least for a while.

"But what about Derm?" Sharon asked.

"He can get along without me," Mona said, heaving the suitcase onto the chesterfield. "At least until school starts. He's not that helpless—even if he is a man."

The next day Nipper slept late; it was almost noon when he woke to a blustery, cloudy day. But despite the long hours in bed he was exhausted, having had, as Mona called it, a night in the ashes—a night full of vague, troubling dreams, dreams that seemed to have no centre, energy-sapping dreams that left him hollow and pinched, as if he'd absorbed an electric shock. When he brushed his teeth, he saw that his face had a swollen, beaten-up look, as if he'd been crying. But if he had been, no memory of it remained.

As soon as he opened the front door, he smelled the bittersweet tang of fall in the air. He sat on the step and looked across the pocked road to the hayfield, the faint, winding shadow of the pole line. He got up and crossed the road, retracing the route he had taken a week before. The spruce and fir whispered, bending easily in the cool wind. When he reached the pole line, he wandered slowly, watching everything intently. His vision seemed especially acute: even ladybugs crawling up clover stalks seemed to leap out at him. But he could not find the exact spot where he had lain down.

Nipper gave up his search and wandered back down the road. Near the gate to Sheehan's hayfield a cluster of children sprawled. Ronnie Sheehan, as if reminding everyone that this was his territory, sat high on the iron gate tossing a softball into the air and catching it in an oversized mitt. Below him, leaning up against the fence, were Pauly, Gerard and Brigid Flynn. As Nipper approached they fell silent.

Ronnie tossed the ball high into the air and caught it. "Hey, Nipper, did you see your father when he was . . . "

Brigid grimaced. "*Ronnie.*"

"You know, when he was like . . . dead and in the coffin?"

Brigid turned and glared at Ronnie. "That's a mortal sin for you, Ronnie Sheehan. Nipper don't want to be talking about that. Anyway, it's none of your business."

"I was just wondering."

"Yeah, well, wonder about something else."

Nipper shook his head. "No," he said. "I didn't go to the wake, just the funeral. The coffin's closed up at the funeral."

"How come he died?" Pauly asked. "He wasn't old, was he?"

"Not as old as my dad," Ronnie said. "My dad's fifty."

"Go way," Pauly said. "Your dad's not that old."

"He is so," Ronnie said. "And my mom's forty-seven and my grandfather's seventy-two. I asked."

"So how old was your father?" Gerard said.

Nipper had no idea. Somehow he had never thought about it. His father was, well, parent-age, grown-up age—not an age he could think of in terms of a number. He shrugged and stared at the ground.

"Well, how old's your mother?" Ronnie asked. "They're probably the same."

"They don't have to be the same," Pauly said.

"I never said *had to be*," Ronnie said. "I said *probably*."

"I don't know," Nipper said, sitting on the lower rung of the gate. "But your father wasn't *old, old*," Pauly said. "Like my Grandfather Sean. Now he's old—eighty or ninety at least."

"No, I don't think he was old," Nipper said.

"So how come he died if he wasn't old?" Pauly asked.

"You don't have to be old to die," Brigid said. "Everybody knows that. Frankie Bussey died and he was only eight. And Denise Henehan's sister died and she was only . . . well, I don't know how old she was, but she was only a girl—not even like a teenager or anything."

"He was sick," Nipper said quietly, almost apologetically. "He had cancer."

"Our Uncle Leo had cancer," Gerard said, with a touch of pride, "but he didn't die."

"He nearly died," Ronnie said.

"Yeah, he *nearly* died. But he didn't."

"He got better and then he got killed in a car crash," Ronnie said.

"Truck," Gerard said. "It was a truck."

"That's right—truck. Rolled it in on Dangerous Turn."

Nipper craned his neck and looked out over the hayfield. "My dad was sick," he said again, as if speaking to himself. "I can hardly remember when he wasn't sick or away up in Nova Scotia. He wasn't home much at all. And when he got real sick I had to be quiet and sometimes I wasn't allowed in his room."

"Is that why your mom works in Blake's store?" Brigid asked.

Nipper paused, struggling to see the connection. "I guess. My dad was in the hospital a lot." Suddenly he felt very tired. He slumped to the ground and leaned against the fence.

"I wouldn't want to be dead," Pauly said, "because then all you'd ever get to see are your eyelids."

Brigid jumped to her feet and slapped her hands on her hips. "Pauly, you are such a little baby. How do you expect to be a priest when you grows up if you thinks stupid stuff like that? Nipper's father can see. He's just in heaven, that's all. Isn't he, Nipper?"

Nipper rubbed his eyes and looked at her. "I don't know. That's what everyone says."

"And it's true," Brigid said. "He is in heaven. He's probably looking down at us right this very minute."

Ronnie looked at her scornfully. "He is not. You don't get to go to heaven until the end of the world. You got to go to Purgatory first, unless you're a baby or a heathen and then you goes to Limbo."

Brigid smirked. "Don't you mind him, Nipper," she said in motherly tones. "Your father's in heaven."

"*Don't* believe me," Ronnie said. "I don't care. But that's what Sister Bernadette said—and she should know. Nuns know all about dead people."

Once more the children fell silent. Water gurgled in the drain.

"So are you an orphan now?" Pauly asked.

"*No,*" Brigid said. "He is not an orphan. He's still got a mother. An orphan is only when *both* your parents are dead. Paddy Dunne's mother is dead and he's not an orphan."

"Well, maybe Nipper's a half-orphan," Gerard said.

"There's no such of a thing," Brigid said.

"Why not?" Gerard said. "My dad's got a friend who's half-French. And you can be half-dead, or half-drunk."

"Or half-*cracked,*" Ronnie said. "Like old Brendan is."

"Brendan is not half-cracked," Brigid said, stepping toward him.

"That's right," Ronnie said. "He's *all*-cracked."

"He is not," Brigid said, an icy edge creeping into her voice. "He knows all kinds of stuff—even more than the nuns. And he's a very nice man."

Ronnie jumped off the fence and faced her. "Then how come he doesn't have his own house like other people? And why is he always up on the Old Road wandering around all by himself?"

"Yeah," Pauly said. "And how come he rides a beat-up old bike like we do instead of having a car or a truck? And how come he goes around dressed up like it's forty below in the middle of the summer?"

"And how come he's not married?" Ronnie said. "And he *never* goes to church."

"What are you gettin' on with?" Brigid said. "Sure your father don't go to church, either."

"He do, too."

"Well, he *goes*, but he never puts a foot inside. He just stands out on the steps with Francis Hartery and smokes."

Ronnie glared at her. "Yeah . . . well, how come Brendan's always reading big old books instead of working?"

"Brendan works."

Ronnie rolled his eyes and snickered. "All he does is some milking or drive the cows up to the meadow. That's not working—not *real* work. Sure we all does that."

"Brendan works," Brigid said. "He lives with us. I should know. Anyway, he's not that young anymore, you know. What do you expect him to do?"

"You're just saying that because he's your uncle."

"I am not," Brigid said. "It's true. And for your information he's my *great*-uncle."

"He's a changeling," Pauly said. "A fairy. That's what my mom always says."

"There's no such of a thing," Brigid said, wheeling around and pointing a finger at him. She turned again to Ronnie. "And Brendan is *not* half-cracked. *You're* half-cracked, Ronnie Sheehan. And Nipper's father *is* in heaven."

"Okay, okay," Ronnie said, tossing the ball high into the air. "Sure he is." He caught the softball and worked it into the middle of the mitt. "Who wants to play tips?"

That evening Nipper Mooney sat on his front step and watched as the cows, udders swelling, made their way down the road from Tim's Meadow. Brendan walked behind, pushing his black Raleigh and humming to himself. As he passed Nipper's house, he looked over, tipped his hat and rang the bell. Nipper waved, and when Brendan had passed he continued to look after him until he disappeared from sight, and all that could be heard was the receding tinkle of bells.

The next morning Nipper was waiting on the doorstep. As soon as he heard the cows, he ran down the lane and pushed open the gate. Once there, he hesitated and then called, "Brendan, can ... can I come?"

Brendan slipped the paperback he was reading into an inside pocket. "Sure," he said. "It's all the same to me."

Nipper closed the gate and ran up to him. "Thanks."

Brendan clucked softly at the cows. "No problem. Why do you want to go up to the meadow? You must be tired of looking at cows."

"Yeah, well . . . something to do."

Brendan flicked at a cow's haunch with his alder. "I was sorry to hear about your father."

Nipper nodded and stared at the ground.

"I dropped by your house the other evening but . . . well, I'm not much of a hand for crowds."

"That's okay," Nipper said. "There were too many people there anyway."

"I said some prayers to St. Brigid for the repose of your father's soul," Brendan said.

"What does that mean—repose?"

"It just means resting: prayers to help his soul rest easier." He glanced at Nipper out of the corner of his eye. "Not that your father's soul will need any help. He was a good man, Patrick. A queer hand. Always carrying on." Brendan shook his head bitterly. "He must have been pretty young. How old was he?"

"I don't know," Nipper said. "I'm gonna ask."

"We don't know what's in store for us, do we? Course, your dad had been sick a long time."

"Yes," Nipper said. "He was always sick." Nipper stared at the hypnotic, swaying tails and hip bones of the cows. "Hey, Brendan?"

"Yeah?"

"Something kind of *strange* happened the day Dad . . . passed away."

"What was that, now?"

"Promise you won't tell anyone? I mean, it's kind of a secret."

Brendan laughed. "Sure who would I tell—the cows? What happened?"

As Nipper talked, Brendan stared straight ahead, his face expressionless, his alder switch trailing on the ground.

When Nipper finished, Brendan looked at him sideways.

"You're sure you just didn't fall asleep?"

Nipper shook his head. "For a whole day? No way. Sure why would I fall asleep? It was morning. I wasn't tired. I just laid down for a while, then I got up and went back home. But when I got there it was suppertime."

"Is that right, now?" Brendan said softly.

"Yeah. Mona was mad at me—wanted to know where I was."

"How did you feel?" Brendan asked. "Any different?"

Nipper considered. "No. I felt fine."

"It was probably the fairies," Brendan said matter-of-factly.

A thrill rushed through Nipper. He slowed his step.

"That's what I'd say," Brendan went on. "You wandered into a fairy circle and they stole you—held you for a while. Do you remember where it was you laid down?"

"Kind of . . . but not really. When I went back, everything looked different."

Brendan nodded. "It was the fairies."

"Really?"

"Sure."

"But why? What did the fairies want with me? What did they . . . *do* with me all day?"

Brendan shook his head. "There's no point in trying to figure out stuff like that. It just happens sometimes. Besides, it could have been worse. You could have woke up twenty miles from here—away in over the barrens somewhere."

"But—"

"You say you feel all right?"

Nipper nodded. "Yeah."

"Then I wouldn't worry about it."

Nipper stopped and looked at Brendan doubtfully. "There's really fairies?"

"Sure," Brendan said, walking on. "I mean, you can call 'em what you like, but there's *something* out there. I've always thought so, anyway." He looked back over his shoulder. "And sure why wouldn't there be? It's a funny old world."

Nipper ran up to Brendan. "Do you think they'll take me—*hold* me again?"

Brendan clucked at the cows. "Now don't you go worrying about that. Sure you said you're fine, didn't you?"

"Yeah, but—"

"Well, then. They must like you." Brendan smiled. "Don't be worrying."

They walked on listening to the shuffle of the cows' hooves on the road, and Nipper Mooney marvelled at a world where a child could be stolen by the fairies and his father taken up to heaven all on the very same day.

TWO

17

*E*ach Sunday morning as Nipper and his mother drove down the Upper Road to early mass at St. Christopher's, they met Brendan walking up, heading for the Old Road. Ronnie Sheehan was right: Brendan did spend a lot of time up in the woods—particularly on Sundays. Neither the season nor the weather deterred him. In summer, he wore a faded tweed jacket and workboots; in winter, a lumpy red overcoat and gaiters. Always, he carried something rare in Kildura: a knapsack. It was usually late when he returned, sometimes after dark, his sweat-soaked hair sticking out from under his wool cap.

"You're like the Holy Trinity of the Old Road," his mother said to Nipper as they passed Brendan one morning. "You and old Brendan and Paddy Dunne. You're right in love with the Old Road. Your father was the same way. Sure it's all only woods and bog. What in the name of God do you *do* up there?"

Nipper shrugged. "Nothing," he said. "Explore. Play. Go troutin'."

That was true enough for him, but he really didn't know what Brendan did up on the Old Road. Just that he knew the lay of the land better than anyone else; tramped farther than anyone else—even farther than Paddy Dunne. And, unlike the other men, he never carried a fishing pole or rifle; Nipper would have been surprised if he had. Maybe Brendan *was* a fairy; maybe he was just going home to Sunday dinner with his fairy family. Or maybe he really was like St. Francis of Assisi: maybe he hiked the hills and barrens of the Old Road with a knapsack full of food for the animals, the jays and chickadees settling sweetly on his shoulders as he tossed them bread crumbs and nuts.

About the other member of the trinity, Paddy Dunne, there was no mystery. Paddy, with his bamboo and fishing basket, or with a shouldered axe ready to chop holes in the ice, was the Old Road fisherman—in any season, in any weather. Nipper watched him with envy; he knew he wasn't in the same league as Paddy Dunne. Even when Paddy fished the near ponds, the ones that Nipper and Ronnie frequented, he seemed to be always successful. Paddy had the gift: knew how to read the sky and wind, knew the best times of day, knew when the whole business was useless and it was just as well to haul in your line and go on home.

Nipper always felt awkward when he met Paddy on the Old Road; this didn't change even when Paddy had joined his class. Nipper always kept his head down until the last moment, then slid him a glance and muttered a quick, "Hi." Paddy would say nothing, just wave his bamboo.

And then one misty evening in late August as Nipper rounded the turn by Bitter Cherry Orchard, he nearly walked straight into Paddy Dunne.

"Sorry," Nipper said, embarrassed.

Paddy grunted and stepped around him.

"Get any?" Nipper asked.

"A few. It's gettin' a bit late in the year."

"Yeah," Nipper said, although he had never much thought about the connection between the time of year and the availability of trout.

"See ya," Paddy said, continuing down the road.

Nipper nodded and moved on, but he had only gone a few yards when Paddy called, "Hey, Mooney."

Nipper stopped and turned.

Paddy glanced at the ground, then looked at Nipper furtively. "I was . . . I was sorry to hear about your old man—I mean, about your father."

Nipper nodded. "Yeah."

Paddy took a couple of steps toward him and hesitated. "My mom died of cancer, too."

"I didn't know," Nipper said. "I mean, I knew she died ... "

Paddy switched his bamboo from one hand to the other. "I was pretty young when the cancer came against her. I don't remember too much about her. But that's what the old man said: the cancer came against her."

Nipper stared at Paddy. He had rarely heard him speak like this—give, what amounted for him, almost a speech. Nipper shifted awkwardly, struggling to find something to say. "I'm . . . I'm sorry."

Paddy narrowed his eyes.

"I mean, I'm sorry your mother died."

Paddy stared at the ground. "Yeah. Me, too." He looked up at Nipper. "Anyway," he said, turning in the road, "sorry for your trouble."

Nipper cleared his throat. "Thanks," he said. Paddy set off down the road.

But all the while Paddy Dunne had been speaking, something stirred in Nipper's memory. And as he watched him round the turn by Bitter Cherry Orchard, he suddenly remembered the boy in the rain outside the Parish Hall at the Garden Party all those years ago, and he knew with certainty that Paddy Dunne had been that boy.

On the Sunday afternoon before the start of the new school year, Nipper Mooney walked up the Old Road and took the steep path to the South Darning Needle. He climbed up on a boulder and stared into the black water. It was here where the photo of his father and him had been taken. The last dragonflies skittered across the surface, dazed, almost slow enough to be caught by hand.

Nipper looked across the pond to the barrens. Even under the brilliant sun the land seemed bleak: dead trees; grey, heavy boulders; yellow marsh that, if you tried to cross, would suck you to your knees. He squinted and studied the stands of drowned birch, the skeletal fir starrigans.

Nipper closed his eyes. He dreamed of trees hundreds of feet high with vines for swinging. But it was hard to think of yourself as Bomba the Jungle Boy in a land where the barrens wind could lash you to pieces, where you could sink without a trace into a ten-foot snowdrift. This land was too ordinary: no chance that around the next bend you might meet a lion, see a leopard dozing over its kill. No chance you would hear distant drumming from a village of headhunters or cannibals. No elephants or gazelles. The Beothucks were long gone. Even when you were stolen by the fairies, they wouldn't let you see them.

Nipper dropped a stone into the water and watched the expanding ripples. He jumped down from the boulder and set off along the path. Just as he was about to break out onto the Old Road, he heard footsteps. He stopped. The steps came on quickly, and as they drew closer he could tell by their rhythm that it was Brendan. He wondered if the old man would turn down the path but, no, he went on. Nipper stepped into the road and looked toward Kildura. Then he turned and followed after Brendan.

For the first half-mile he kept well back. But the turn-off to the Roundabout was coming up, and he wanted to see if Brendan would take it. Nipper picked up his pace until he saw the green of Brendan's knapsack, the tail of his red workshirt fluttering beneath his tweed jacket.

Brendan kept to the road.

He continued on at a steady pace. Nipper was getting tired; soon he was struggling to keep up. The next turn-off was the Damsel's Eye, and here Brendan veered off and plunged down the rocky, overgrown trail. Nipper followed, knowing that Brendan would not see him unless he stopped. If he did stop, the brush was so thick Nipper would probably walk right into him. Soon he saw water sparkling through the trees, and he checked his pace. Finally, at the edge of the clearing that rimmed the Damsel's Eye, he stopped.

Brendan had continued down to the shore. Nipper watched as he slipped off his knapsack and sat on a boulder. Brendan shielded his eyes with his right hand and stared out over the pond. Nipper remained in the trees for a few moments, then he stepped into the clearing. He walked toward Brendan, meaning to call out, but for some reason he stayed silent. Soon he had come so close to him that he was afraid to speak, afraid of startling him. Nipper felt embarrassed and silly. He turned to go back up the path, but Brendan tilted his head.

"Hello, Nicky."

Nipper started. "How did you know it was me?"

Brendan spit into the water. "Oh, that wasn't too hard. I've been coming up here so many years now it's no trouble to know if someone's following me. I didn't think it was Paddy Dunne; he's got a heavier step."

"I wasn't *following* . . ."

Brendan laughed. "That's all right. I know you don't mean any harm." He turned back to the water. "What are you doing? Not troutin' today?"

"No. Just looking around. Exploring."

"Giving the fish a break, are you?"

Nipper nodded and directed a skimmer across the still water.

Brendan sighed. "I was thinking on poor old Gerald and Max."

"Who?"

"Gerald Breen and Max Tobin." Brendan swivelled around. "You don't know about them?"

"I heard two fellas got drowned up here somewhere. I didn't know their names."

Brendan gazed out over the water. "Well, that's who they were and this is the spot." He turned and looked at Nipper. "You haven't seen the marker?"

"The what?"

Brendan motioned for Nipper to follow and set off along the path. Near a tall, spreading spruce he dropped to his knees and pushed aside the branches. "Look."

The marker, about two-feet square, was of dark-grey concrete and had been set against a slanting rock. The letters were cut deeply, the indentations filled with spruce needles and moss. They were like the Egyptian hieroglyphics Nipper had seen in his geography book; he had to brush away the needles and branches and look carefully before the letters focused and arranged themselves coherently.

IN MEMORY OF
MAX TOBIN
GERALD BREEN
WHO DROWN HERE
8 JULY 1910
RIP

"I didn't know about that," Nipper said. "Who put it there?"
Brendan shrugged.

"Why is it hidden? Why didn't they put it more out in the open—somewhere people could see it?"

Brendan laughed. "Back in 1910 it *was* out in the open. That spruce was just a little baby. It's all grown up since then."

Nipper examined the marker again. Max Tobin and Gerald Breen. The Breens and Tobins lived down on the Lower Road. Derek Breen went to St. Brigid's—two grades up from him. Nipper glanced at Brendan. "Did you know them?"

"Oh yes. Knew them well—Gerald in particular. Max was one of those who never had much to say—not to me anyway. Although he was nice enough in his way. But Gerald . . . he was a lovely fellow." Brendan smiled. "They were certainly energetic. Always skylarkin'. Always taking a dare or giving a dare. 'Boggers,' they called 'em." Brendan shook his head. "And this is where they drowned. That was an awful day. Well, *three* days really. We found Max the next evening—went looking for 'em when they didn't turn up. But Gerald . . . we didn't find poor Gerald until the following afternoon. He'd floated quite a ways down the pond, was hung up on rocks in the rapid water. I was in the boat: me, Phil Hartery, a couple of more men. I helped to pull him in." Brendan faltered. "I never thought a man's skin could be that white—frog-belly white. I can still see Gerald's hair tangled in the river weed. He had pretty long hair for them times, Gerald did." Brendan bit his lip. "God save us all. It must be an awful thing to drown."

Nipper pictured the scene. One of the swimmers getting a cramp—just about every drowning story he'd ever heard involved a cramp—and panicking; wild eyes and twisted mouth; the other fellow splashing through the water to help. And then a frantic tangle of arms and legs, the men scraping, tearing at each other, pushing each other under. From a distance it might have looked like more of their skylarking. Then, finally, exhaustion, their lungs filled with black water, hair full of weeds, and no more jokes or dares or three-day fishing trips to Shalloway Pond.

That was so long ago; Brendan had been a young man. Nipper glanced sideways at Brendan's face: his skin was wind-burned, his nose and cheeks sprinkled with fine veins, but his complexion was still smooth, not the face of someone in his seventies.

Nipper ran his fingers along the crumbling concrete marker. Concrete? Who had brought concrete all the way in here? Spent the time to carve the names and dates? A mystery. Just someone for whom a peeling wooden cross or basket of plastic flowers wouldn't do. And now the marker itself was drowned, hidden by alders and chokeberries, in the winter buried beneath mounds of ice and snow, the concrete crumbling and seeping into the ground. Only in the spring and fall were the faded names offered up, unobstructed, to the sun, the high, brilliant stars.

Gerald and Max had also been stolen. But not just for a day. They weren't ever coming back. Or maybe they had never left the Damsel's Eye. Nipper looked again at the inscription: WHO DROWN HERE 8 JULY ... Why drown instead of drowned? There was plenty of room for the extra two letters. Did poor Gerald and Max have to drown *every* July 8?

Brendan stood up and adjusted his knapsack. "I'm heading farther in the road," he said. He paused and looked at Nipper. "You want to come?"

"Sure—well, how far?"

"A good ways. You tired?"

"No. I don't mind walking. Where you going?"

Brendan turned and headed along the path. "To the ocean." He stopped and looked over his shoulder. "You ever been to the ocean?"

"No. Not that far."

"Well, come on if you're coming."

Nipper scrambled to his feet. "I'm coming," he said, starting after him. "I'm coming."

They tramped along the Old Road, Brendan's watery eyes flickering over the trees and marshes. Occasionally, he brushed his hand along the drooping alders, bent to caress a cluster of pearly everlasting. "Everything'll be fading soon," he said. "Well, I suppose that's the way God intended it."

Nipper kicked a stone and watched it careen along the road. "I didn't think you believed in God."

Brendan pulled up. "Of course, I believe in God. What are you gettin' on with?"

"You never go to church. How come you never go to church if you believe in God?"

"I go to church." Brendan extended his arms and gestured broadly. "*This* is my church."

"What?"

"I said, this—"

"You know what I mean."

Brendan slipped his thumbs under the straps of his knapsack and walked on. "I suppose I do," he said. "Well, I used to go one time—every Sunday."

"Why'd you quit?"

Brendan stared straight ahead. "You don't want to know, Nicky. Anyway, that's ancient history now."

"Come on. I won't tell anyone."

Brendan wrinkled his nose and sniffed. "Well, the long and short of it is that I had a falling out with Monsignor Murphy. A hard man, that Monsignor Murphy. That was years and years ago—when he first pitched down here. Anyway, I gave it up. I still go to midnight mass on Christmas Eve to hear the carols. It's always a full house on Christmas Eve—easy to lose yourself in the crowd. If that old frigger Murphy—God forgive me—ever saw me, he'd probably stop the service and throw me out."

"Why did you fall out with him?"

Brendan raised his hands and let them slap against his thighs. "Back then I had the fashion of saying what was on my mind. We used to discuss things—religious things." He paused. "Personal things, too. I used to ask questions. I had a lot of questions, and some of them he didn't like." Brendan glanced at Nipper with wide eyes. "And, well, to tell the truth, some of the answers he gave me *I* didn't like—that is when I even *got* any kind of an answer. We had some pretty hot arguments. We even had a couple in the confessional, if you can believe that. Anyway, I was talking to him after mass one day, and he just blew his top. Called me a heretic and a heathen—a few other things, too. Told me to get the hell out of his church. I said, all right, I'm going. And when I was on my way, *I* said a few things—things I probably shouldn't have. I had a pretty wild temper in them days."

"You?"

"Oh yes. It didn't take much to rile me up. Anyway, I never went back. I had a horse, then, Princey. Sometimes I'd ride over to Deep Harbour and go to mass there. But that's quite a distance just to go to church. And Princey was pretty old. One day I said to myself, 'Why should that poor creature have to suffer for my sins?' So I've stayed clear—except, as I say, on Christmas Eve."

"But you're supposed to go every Sunday. It's a sin not to go. I got to go. And sometimes Mom makes me put on a tie."

"Do you like church?"

Nipper considered. He liked the stained glass windows and the statues and flowers; he liked the prayer books, which were thick, and had soft, crinkly paper with colourful ribbons to mark your place; he liked the marble holy water cisterns (even though he was disappointed that the water looked and tasted exactly the same as the tap water at home); he liked the golden candle rack, where you could light a candle for someone and were trusted to leave your five cents; he liked the priest's vestments, which reminded him of superhero costumes; he liked the purple velvet pouches that held the money collected by the men of the Holy Name Society, and which led him to believe that Monsignor Murphy must be the richest person in all of Kildura.

Other things he didn't like. Confession. The worst time for church was Good Friday. Kneeling for what seemed like hours, footsteps echoing off the walls, the heavy scent of incense and smoky candles hanging on the still air. And you couldn't even rest your tailbone against the pew without having someone glare at you or give you a smack. Nipper remembered some Good Fridays when there were terrible storms—the stripped birches snapping in the wind, the cold rain falling in sheets. On those days he was sure the end of the world was finally at hand.

"I likes some of it," Nipper said. "But Monsignor Murphy is scary. Aunt Mona thinks so, too. She can't stand him. She says he's too old and stiff and mean, and they should get someone younger. And she hates his singing. She says he reminds her of the meanest of the Three Billy Goats Gruff."

Brendan chuckled. "Yes," he said, "a good description." He paused, then scowled. "A lot of so-called religious people can't see any further than the church. They think God lives there—never steps outside those big oak doors. But I see Him more clearly out here—out in the woods and barrens, in the juniper, in the eyes of the fox—the things *He* made." Brendan bent down and picked up a dry branch. "People have lived around here for years and years, but most of 'em don't know what anything *is*. It's all just bushes or woods or flowers. Well, I think that lessens what God has done—the miracle of it all."

Brendan shook his head. "There's too many who just look at something long enough to shoot at it or cut it down."

Brendan pulled up again and looked at Nipper. "One time I read about this crowd of Indians over in Australia—aboriginals, they calls 'em over there. They believe the world was created by their ancestors, who called things into existence by walking through the land and singing their names." Brendan nodded. "Now, I'm no more of a hand to sing than old Monsignor Murphy, but I think there might be something to that. That's why I decided to learn the names of all the trees and flowers and birds and things. I mean, just look at all the *variety* in the world: the lilies and fireweed and twenty kinds of goldenrod. It's such a miracle. It's like Mr. Blake says—"

"Mr. Blake who Mom works for?"

"No, no. Mr. Blake the poet. Dead and gone now these many long years. Mr. Blake said he saw eternity in a grain of sand and heaven in a wildflower. I like that. I know what he meant. I *think* I do." Brendan pointed the branch at Nipper. "Nicky, my son, you'll learn more about God in those lines or by taking a good hike in over the barrens than you will in a million churches—God forgive me."

"Brendan, how come all the poets are dead?"

Brendan laughed. "They're not *all* dead. There's still lots of poets. But if they're great poets—like Blake and Shake-speare—then people remember them long after they pass on—some of us do anyway.

"So I don't go to church anymore. I make my peace with God in my own way. I don't think He holds it against me." Brendan chuckled. "Although I admit it's a bit touchy, second-guessing God. Just think of the hard time He gave those Philistines. They probably got the surprise of their life when the thunderbolts started falling on them. The same thing might happen to me. I might be handed a one-way ticket to hell the minute I passes on. Who knows? I bet that's what Monsignor Murphy thinks—*hopes*. But *I* don't think so." Brendan took off his hat and ran his hand through his wispy hair. "No, I don't think so."

"Do you ever say any prayers?"

"Oh yes. I pray to St. Brigid. I mean, we are named for her and she is the patron saint of farmers, so I figure she must be watching over us. Anyway, she's probably not as busy as God or Jesus or the Holy Ghost. I never could understand that business about the Holy Trinity, anyway. At least with St. Brigid you know who you're talking to." Brendan paused and looked at Nipper. "Want to see something special?"

"Sure."

Brendan reached inside his shirt and drew out a silver cross and chain. "Know what this is?"

"Course I do. It's a St. Brigid's Cross."

"Yes, but they're usually made out of grass or palms, right? Like you see on Palm Sunday. This one is made out of silver."

"Where'd you get it?"

"My grandfather brought it back from Ireland, years and years ago. He worked on the boats. He was a bit like your father—didn't have much time for farming. It was a gift for my mother, and when she died it came to me." Brendan cupped the cross in his palm and looked at it thoughtfully. "And when my time comes, I'll pass it on to Brigid. You know, so it'll stay in the family. Anyway, it's only right that someone named Brigid should have a special St. Brigid's Cross."

"How come St. Brigid has her own cross in the first place?"

Brendan threw up his hands. "For the love o' God, Nicky! Is there no end to your questions?"

Nipper shrugged. "I was just wondering."

"Well," Brendan said, "the story goes that she came upon this pagan chieftain lying by a river. He'd been in a battle and he was wounded—dying. Now, he was a pagan because in those times in Ireland there were pagans *and* Christians. Christianity was just gettin' on the go. Brigid herself was brought up by a pagan—a Druid. Dubthach Donn, his name was."

"What's a Druid?"

"Sort of like a pagan priest. Anyway, this poor old pagan chieftain was stretched out by the river, and Brigid sat down next to him and comforted him. As she was talking—all about Jesus, I suppose—she took some reeds from the riverbank and plaited them into a cross. The chieftain was so impressed with her that he converted to Christianity before he died. That's how it all got started. Then people got into the fashion of making St. Brigid's Crosses out of palm fronds or reeds or straw. They'd take them to the church on her feast day, February 1, and the priest would bless them. Then the people would put them in their barns for good luck and to guard against fire. There was lots who used to put them in their houses, too. When I was a youngster, you'd see them all the time. But now it's only the scattered person does that."

"There's one hanging above her statue in school," Nipper said. "And we got an old one above the door in our barn. It's nearly black now. My grandfather must have put it up."

Brendan nodded. "Kevin used to do it. It was common one time."

Nipper took Brendan's cross and looked at it. "Is it real silver?"

"Oh yes. As real as you can get. Grandfather got it in Galway, and he asked an Irish priest to bless it. He brought Mother back silver Rosary beads, too, but those were buried with her—God rest her soul."

Nipper looked at Brendan. "Do you say the Rosary?"

"No," Brendan said, slipping the cross back inside his shirt. "Not for years and years—not since I was a child." He laughed.

"I've always thought of the Rosary as more of a social project: you need a lot of people for a good Rosary. Besides, I don't mind walking, but my knees couldn't take all that kneeling anymore."

"We said the Rosary a lot when Dad was sick."

"Did you, now?"

Nipper nodded. "We only used to say it once a week. Then, when Dad went up to Nova Scotia to work in the mines, we said it twice a week—sometimes three. And then, when he got real sick, we said it nearly every night. But he still didn't get better."

"Ah, well," Brendan said, "there's only so much you can ask out of the Rosary."

"What prayers do you say?"

"Oh, the regular ones. But I have some special prayers, too. Prayers to St. Brigid—prayers more than a thousand years old. I got them out of an old book."

"Tell me one."

Brendan stepped back. "Go on. You're not interested in that."

"I am. Tell me one."

"No . . ."

"Come on."

Brendan looked at Nipper, then clasped his hands behind his back like a child at a school concert. He closed his eyes. "May the protection of the angels and the saints encompass your going and coming; and about you be the milkmaid of the smooth white palms, Brigid of the clustering brown hair."

Nipper grinned. " 'Milkmaid of the smooth white palms?' That doesn't sound much like a prayer. It's more like a poem. Say another one."

Brendan cleared his throat. "Brigid, ever excellent woman, golden sparkling flame, lead us to the eternal kingdom, the dazzling resplendent sun." He winked at Nipper. "That's my favourite one—especially on foggy days. I bet you can't picture Monsignor Murphy saying that, can you?"

Nipper shook his head.

"Well, there's nothing wrong with a bit of variety in the world."

"Is that why you're different—because of all the variety in the world?"

"I expect so." Brendan grinned mischievously. "Of course, a lot of people thinks it was because I was dropped on my head when I was a baby."

"Were you?"

Brendan laughed and started up the road. "Now, Nicky, how can you expect me to remember something like that—all those years ago and me only a little infant?"

They walked on silently. Nipper's legs were beginning to burn. His right sock had slipped down inside his sneaker. Brendan didn't seem at all tired. "We're almost there," he kept saying. "Just around the next bend." But Nipper didn't need to be told. He had occasionally glimpsed patches of blue through the trees and hills, and the air had taken on a keen, musky scent.

Nipper lagged a hundred yards back. Brendan stopped and waited for him to catch up. They left the road and took a steep, muddy path. Soon they broke through the woods onto a boulder-strewn shelf of moss and juniper and Labrador tea. The ocean unfolded before them. To the west, Deep Harbour nestled along a finger-like bay. They walked out to the cliff edge, the crashing surf and the cries of gulls growing louder with each step.

"This is my special place," Brendan said. "I named it the Lookout."

"What do you do here?"

"Do?" Brendan shrugged. "Look at the ocean. Read. Say my prayers. Think about things."

Nipper leaned forward.

"Careful, now," Brendan said. "Not too close. That's about a five-hundred-foot drop. You goes over that edge, you're never coming up again."

Nipper held tightly to a stunted spruce and looked down the jagged cliff face. Hundreds of feet below, gulls floated buoyantly like handfuls of tossed confetti.

Brendan took a deep breath. "Smell it, Nicky? There's nothing smells like the ocean. That goes all the way back to the old country. People crossed over hundreds of years ago in them tiny, creaky little boats. Hard to believe, hey?" He stared out over the water. "Hard to believe. Course, a lot didn't make it. They say my namesake, St. Brendan did—in an oxhide boat. I could never picture what a boat like that would look like. And why oxhide? There was lots of wood over in Ireland in them times. Anyway, they say he was the first white person to ever come to this country."

Nipper felt dizzy; he clutched the spruce tighter. "In a little boat like that? That's impossible."

"Not if God is with you. And sure Brendan was a saint."

"Was he a saint then, or was he made a saint after? I mean, did he get made a saint because he was the first person to cross the ocean?"

Brendan pinched his brow then rubbed it vigorously. "You know, that's a good question. I don't know the answer to that. I'll have to look that up. Well, even if he wasn't a saint yet, I'm sure he felt that God was with him, guiding him. Saints can always feel that—all the ones I ever read about, anyway. Maybe St. Brigid was looking out for him. One of her prayers has to do with sailors." Brendan looked out over the ocean and recited:

Brigid, daughter of Dubthach Donn,
Who guides the ship from shore to shore,
We put ourselves under your protection,
For this night belongs to you:
From tonight till tonight next year,
And this night itself through God's will.

Brendan grinned. "So I guess she doesn't just look after farmers."

Nipper watched the swelling, bluish green waves, listened to the distant suck and pull of the strengthening tide. "I believe you'd have to be a saint to cross the ocean in a little boat," he said. "Look at them waves. You'd sink in about two seconds. I wouldn't try it—would you?"

Brendan looked wistful. "Well, now—who knows? I always did want to do some travelling before I dies." He grinned self-consciously. "You know where I'd really like to go?"

"Where?"

"Africa—and see all the beautiful zebras and giraffes. But that's an awful distance, Africa. If I couldn't go there, I wouldn't mind going over to Ireland. Back to the old country. I'd like to go to Galway, where Grandfather got the St. Brigid's Cross." Brendan laughed. "And an oxhide boat is probably all I could ever afford. But if one Brendan did it, then why not another?"

"Well, the first one *was* a saint. Or he became one, anyway."

Brendan laughed. "Yes, that's true. And I'm certainly no saint—although people calls me one. Oh, don't give me that look! I knows all about it and so do you. Your own mother said it to me when I met her on the road one day—let it slip out: 'Hello, St. Brendan,' she said. The look on her face!" Brendan snorted. "Anyway, what odds. There's worse things they could be calling me."

They left the cliff and sat down against a moss-covered

boulder. Brendan pointed to a spreading shrub with deep pink flowers pushing out of the rocks. "Look at that. Beautiful, isn't it?"

"Pure gorgeous," Nipper said. "That's what Aunt Mona says when she likes something: pure gorgeous."

"Lambkill, that's called. Do you suppose it would really kill a lamb? I often wondered about that. I don't know much about lambs. We've never gone in for lambs in Kildura. You have to go farther down the shore for lambs."

Brendan opened his knapsack and rummaged through it. "Want something to eat?"

"Sure. What have you got?"

Brendan pulled out sandwiches, a water bottle and a bruised apple. "Here," he said, handing the food to Nipper. "I don't want anything. You have a little snack while I go for a walk."

Nipper watched as Brendan set off along the cliff edge and disappeared down a slanting bluff. He ate the apple and one of the sandwiches. He closed his eyes, listening to the gulls, smelling the sharp scent of the sea.

And then Brendan was shaking him gently by the shoulder. "Nicky, wake up." Nipper opened his eyes and saw that the sun was sinking, the darkening sky spreading cherry-black on the horizon. "Come on," Brendan said. "We should have left earlier. It'll be dark now before we gets home."

"Ah, what odds," Nipper said, getting to his feet and stretching. "I'm not afraid of the dark."

Brendan grinned. "Let's hope your mother knows that."

Nipper paused and looked at Brendan. "How come you never calls me Nipper?"

Brendan adjusted his knapsack. "I guess you just never struck me as a Nipper. Don't feel right to me. Besides, Nicholas is a fine name. Who named you Nipper anyway?"

"Dad. It was because I was so small when I was born."

Brendan laughed. "I might have guessed. That was just like Patrick."

They headed back up the path and broke out onto the Old Road.

"Do you think we'll see any fairies?" Nipper asked.

"Probably not. It's a rare thing to see a fairy. I've only seen them a few times myself, and I've been coming up here for years and years. They likes to keep to themselves. And when you think about it, who can blame 'em? But who knows? Maybe this will be your lucky day."

"What do the fairies do? Do they have funny hats and dance around in circles? That's what Mom told me."

Brendan grimaced. "That's what they don't. A fairy wouldn't waste his time with that foolishness. In my opinion, they don't *do* anything—at least not anything we can understand. They just . . . *are.* It's like God: He didn't come from anywhere, He just *is.*"

"Well, who'd win a fight between, say, my guardian angel and a fairy?"

Brendan pushed his hands into his pockets and sighed. "Youngsters. All you minds is fighting." He shook his head. "Well, if there ever *was* such a fight—which I doubt—I imagine your guardian angel would win. You see, the fairies are angels, too—or they were one time. They got thrown out of heaven when Lucifer led his rebellion. They weren't really evil—not bad enough to go to hell. But they couldn't get back into heaven either, so they ended up here on earth: halfway between heaven and hell. This is their purgatory. Anyway, that's what Mother told me. So I wouldn't say a fairy could be as powerful as a real angel. But they can get up to all kinds of devilment just the same—some of 'em can, anyway. I don't know why. They're probably just bored to death waiting for the Judgement Day. Probably just trying to keep themselves amused. It depends on the kind of fairy you strikes. You see, they got different person-alities the same as people do." Brendan lowered his voice. "They say the fairies can appear in all kinds of different forms—even as animals. One foggy day I saw an old woman walking in over the barrens near the Damsel's Eye—right out in the middle of nowhere. An old woman with a black cloak on her and an old-time kerchief. What a feeling came over me when I saw her! And when she looked up and saw me, I went right weak—dizzy-like. It was like my legs give out. I had to sit down on a rock. And when I looked up, she was gone.

"But that was rare. You don't see fairies as much as you *feel* 'em. Like sometimes when the woods gets *too* quiet—"

"Yes! That's what it was like when I got held!"

"Well, then, you know. And you can only see them if the light is right—like that foggy day near the Damsel's Eye. And it helps if there's a stream or a brook nearby. Maybe the sound of the running water covers the sound of your walking and breath-ing until it's too late for them to disappear. It's hard to see them, but I *feel* them all the time.

"Maybe, maybe, maybe—that's all you can say about the fairies. Nobody really knows. And that's the way they like it."

"Brendan, why do you think the fairies took me—*held* me that day? Was it because Dad died?"

Brendan shrugged. "I don't know, Nicky. That was such a sad day. Perhaps they wanted to save you from it. Or perhaps Patrick wanted to see you one last time, and they brought you to him. Maybe that's where you were all that day—in the hospital room with him."

"But why can't I remember?"

"Who knows? Like I say, there's no accounting for what the fairies get up to. And maybe you will remember—some day."

"But it's so weird . . . strange."

Brendan spread his hand and gestured down the valley. "Look around," he said. "Sure it's all strange."

It was almost completely dark. Nipper kept close to Brendan. They walked in silence. A pale moon rose over the far ponds. Near the path to the Darning Needles, Nipper caught a trembling in the shadows. He stopped and watched as a figure emerged from the woods—smoothly, quietly, like a dancer. The figure hesitated in the road.

"Hello, Paddy."

Nipper started, his heart in his throat, then realized Brendan had spoken. The shadows fell away, and Paddy Dunne stood in the middle of the road, his bamboo over one shoulder, a fishing basket slung over the other. Paddy paused. Even in the half-light Nipper could see he was debating whether to walk on or stay and have to talk.

He stayed.

Nipper and Brendan went up to him. "Troutin', were you?" Brendan asked. "Get any?"

"Six," Paddy said. "Six keepers. Muds."

"Can I see 'em?" Nipper asked, surprised at his boldness.

Paddy made no answer, but laid the bamboo gently in the road. Swinging the basket around to the front, he slipped out the twig that held down the cover. He pulled out his Zippo and thumbed it into a four-inch flame. The fire lit the three faces eerily. Paddy pushed aside a layer of peat moss and revealed an eight-inch trout, its mouth open, peat grains clinging to its gluey eyes and gills.

"All pretty much like that," Paddy said.

"Nice. I wish I could catch a big trout," Nipper said.

Brendan peered into the basket. "Poor things. Swimming around all day enjoying themselves. They never thought they'd end up in a fishing basket tonight, in the frying pan tomorrow."

"Ah, come on," Nipper said. "Trout don't think."

"Not like us," Brendan said. "But they like their little lives, too."

"You always say that," Nipper said. "Sure they're only trout."

"Maybe so," Brendan said. "But they don't come willingly when they gets hooked."

Paddy pressed the moss down over the fish. "Well, all them flies the trout were jumpin' at probably didn't know they'd end up in a fish's gut tonight, either."

Brendan nodded. "I suppose you're right. It's a cruel old world."

Paddy shut the basket and replaced the twig. He picked up his bamboo and nodded almost formally. "Well, see ya," he said. And as quickly as he had appeared, he was gone.

18

*I*n Nipper Mooney's last year at St. Brigid's, the snow came early and stayed. The first storm blew out of the north on Halloween night, and from then until Christmas Eve it seemed it was always snowing. Kildura slept under a blanket of white. There were days when St. Brigid's was closed, Sundays when Sharon would not attempt the drive to church. The weather meant nothing to Monsignor Murphy. He kept St. Christopher's oak doors open for anyone who might stumble through the drifts, and would hear confessions or celebrate mass for one hundred or one or even just himself.

Nipper did not bother with fishing along the Old Road. There was too much wet, heavy snow to clear away before you struck ice, and the ice was diamond-hard and thick. He stayed at home and read one of his Tarzan books or went down to Sheehan's barn and played in the loft with Brigid and Ronnie and Gerard. Sometimes, when he was bored, he wandered up the Old Road, but under the deep snow it seemed like a different country—all the familiar landmarks buried or blurred. The ponds, covered with plateaus of moulded white, were almost indistinguishable from the barrens. Nipper tramped as far as he could, then stopped, breathing hard, looking out over the white hills, gazing up at the grey, frozen sky.

One afternoon in November, Sister Mary Ignatius knocked on the classroom door. Nipper braced himself for an arithmetic bee or a lecture from Monsignor Murphy, but the principal did not come in. Sister Bernadette got up from her desk and went to the door. "Yes, Sister?" she said. Nipper heard whispers in the hall, and then Sister Bernadette stepped outside and closed the door. The children frowned and looked at one another. When Sister Bernadette came back, she pulled the door behind her and leaned against it, still gripping the knob. Her face was as white as the snow on the windowsills. Nipper heard the door to the next classroom creak open and the children filing quietly into the hall. "You may pack up your books," Sister Bernadette said. "You'll be going home early today." Something in her tone stilled the class; there were no cries of delight, just anxious glances and puzzled looks. No one moved. Nipper was glad to be going home: the next period was arithmetic with Sister Annunciata. But he knew that something was wrong. He looked out the window to see if a storm had blown up when he wasn't looking. But there was only a thin, slanting drift of soft flakes.

Nipper wondered if there was going to be a war, if the Russians were going to drop the atomic bomb. A war was the only thing he could think of that would make Sister Mary Ignatius give a half-holiday when there wasn't a snowstorm.

"How come we're goin' home, Sister?" Ronnie Sheehan asked.

Sister Bernadette raised her fingers to her lips and closed her eyes; for a moment she reminded Nipper of the statue of St. Brigid. "Because . . . because there's been a tragedy. President Kennedy has been shot." She moved slowly to her desk and sat down. "The first row may go to the cloakroom," she said quietly.

Nipper stood up and looked at Brigid. How could someone as important as a president be shot? Did that mean there'd be a war?

As Nipper pulled on his gaiters, there was an unusual silence in the cloakroom. No jostling or laughter. Ronnie Sheehan didn't say a word. And even though the next row was waiting to come in, the children took their time clasping buckles and buttoning up coats. There's definitely going to be a war, Nipper thought. The Russians killed President Kennedy. The minute we step outside a bomb is going to fall.

Nipper watched as Paddy Dunne pulled on his mitts. He went over and stood next to him.

"Paddy, what do you think is gonna happen?" Nipper asked.

"What do you mean?"

"You don't think . . . you don't think there's gonna be a war or something, do you?"

"Why should there be a war?"

"Well, they killed President Kennedy."

Paddy looked at Nipper carefully. "Yeah, but that's not *our* country. Our country is Newfoundland. Canada. That's the United States."

"Oh," Nipper said. "So . . . there's not going to be a war?"

"No," Paddy said. "There's not going to be a war."

And he was right. When they went out into the schoolyard, the only thing falling was snow.

On the Monday morning of the last week of classes before Christmas holidays, Nipper pulled open the west door and saw Sister Bernadette lighting candles at the feet of St. Brigid. Every time someone came in, the wind roared down the hall and ruffled the flames. She looked at Nipper and smiled. "The candles won't go out. Did you know that after St. Brigid died her sisters kept a flame burning in her honour for over six hundred years?"

Nipper nodded.

"Well, then, we should be able to keep a few candles going for a single day, shouldn't we?"

"Sure," Nipper said. He watched as Sister Bernadette arranged the baskets of flowers—fresh now, as well as plastic. "Is it true that when she took her vows a flame shot out of her head?"

Sister Bernadette laughed. "How did you know about that?"

"Brendan told me. Brendan Flynn."

"Brigid's uncle?"

"Yeah. He knows all about St. Brigid. He likes all the saints, but St. Brigid is his favourite."

"Is she, now?"

"Yes. He even knows some of St. Brigid's special prayers."

"Well, you tell Mr. Flynn I said it's very commendable he's taken such an interest in our patron saint."

"What?"

Sister Bernadette laid a hand on Nipper's shoulder. "Tell him I said, good for him."

In the afternoon all the classes were marched over to St. Christopher's for a Christmas service. The church, decorated with spruce boughs and holly, smelled like Bitter Cherry Orchard. Sister Annunciata played carols on the organ and Nipper joined in the singing: "O Come All Ye Faithful," "Joy to the World." Everyone sang except Monsignor Murphy. Nipper thought Aunt Mona would have been happy about that. At the end of the service Colleen Burke stood in the balcony and sang "O Holy Night," her voice piercing and pure. Everyone twisted in their pews to look up at her.

That night, after the Rosary, Nipper pulled out volume 3-4 of the encyclopedia: BERG -CLER. For some reason he had never looked to see if St. Brigid was there. He thumbed through the B's. She was there all right. She didn't get much space, just a paragraph. But the entry said something Nipper didn't know, that Brendan had never mentioned. *She was exceedingly beautiful and to avoid offers of marriage and other temptations, implored God to render her ugly, which prayer was granted.* Could that be true? If it was in the encyclopedia, it must be true, mustn't it? Nipper wondered if that was why she looked so pudgy and plain in the frontispiece of *Irish Saints and Martyrs*. Not that she was *ugly* in the picture, but she didn't look much like the statue in school. That St. Brigid was young and pretty, with fish-shaped eyes and perfect lips. Which was the real St. Brigid? When Nipper thought about it, all the holy statues looked pretty much alike. The one in the school foyer could even be St. Theresa or St. Anne (the patron saint of miners)—or even Mary Magdalene. How would you know?

19

Nipper trudged home along the Old Road. He had tried to hike out to the Damsel's Eye, but the snow was too heavy and deep. His pants and boots were soaked. He should have stayed and played hockey on Shalloway Pond with Ronnie and Gerard.

As he rounded the turn by Bitter Cherry Orchard, Nipper smelled smoke: a strange, burning smoke that hung on the air like incense. Perhaps Gerard and Ronnie had lit a fire. But the smell wasn't right. This wasn't the sweet, woodsy smell of spruce or fir; not the thin, sharp scent of burning leaves or garbage. This was something else.

Nipper tramped on through the waist-high snow. With every step the smell grew stronger—so strong that around each turn he expected to see a blaze. He could almost imagine what the smoke would look like: thick and purple, hanging like a shroud. It was a smoke he could taste on his tongue, could imagine freezing and falling to the ground, crackling like ice.

Shalloway Pond was deserted, but Nipper saw the powdered, criss-crossing patterns of skate blades. The smell grew stronger. He lowered his head and tightened his lips against it, then pushed on through the snow.

When he reached the Upper Road, he began to run. He saw no one. As he sprinted past his house, he looked down the road and, suddenly, there it was—a cloud rising and spreading in the air—not purple, but greasy and black, coiling upward. Nipper pushed his legs harder, the infected air painfully flooding his lungs. By Sheehan's meadow he pulled up and doubled over, catching his breath, squeezing the stitch in his side. Then he continued on down the road, half-walking, half-running, past the Flynns' and Harterys', past the meadows and snow-patched barns.

At the bottom of the Dunnes' lane he saw a crowd of people and, finally, he knew. His mother was there, standing with Annie. He ran up to them, breathing hard. "Don't go up the lane, Nicky," Sharon said. But she spoke without conviction, as if she somehow understood that he had to go up.

And so he did.

The Dunnes' was totally engulfed, the roof gone. A wall of intense heat pushed out and down the lane. It had grown darker, and the bursting flames and jutting beams were the purest orange and black Nipper had ever seen. The flames licked out and upward, shooting sparks high into the sky. Intermittently, over the steady roar, the seared, crumbling wood cracked and popped like gunfire. Nipper's eyes adjusted to the light. There were many people gathered, children as well as adults, but no one was attempting to fight the blaze, or perhaps an earlier attempt had been abandoned. Nipper could see there was no point. The volunteer firemen circled the house, shaking their heads and staring into the flames. Everyone else stood well back, some peeping from behind trees, as if afraid the fire might reach out and grab them. People were strangely quiet. Nipper himself had not said a word.

He saw Brendan standing at the top of the lane, and he went and stood beside him. Brendan's face was crimson and perspiring, his eyes reflecting the flickering, orange glow. The oily smoke billowed through the black branches of the trees. Suddenly, the front wall shivered and collapsed inward, throwing up clouds of sparks and smoking ash. Nipper looked into the Dunnes'. It was the first time he'd ever seen the inside.

Brendan laid a hand on his shoulder. "You go on back to the road now," he said. "It's too dangerous." Nipper turned and saw the other children being ushered down the lane. Ronnie Sheehan tottered backwards, slipping and sliding in the slush, his eyes never leaving the smoking shell.

As Nipper stepped onto the road, Paddy Dunne and his father bolted past him. Halfway up the lane Mr. Dunne stopped and bent over, panting and wheezing. "Come on!" Paddy shouted. He grabbed his father's arm and yanked him forward. Nipper heard more shouting, and then the voices died away.

On the road, away from the flames, he stood next to his mother and Annie. They stamped to keep warm. The first stars had appeared. Nipper saw Brigid with a scarf pulled up over her nose, and he went and stood by her. "My God," she said. She raised a hand to her mouth. "Oh, my God."

And then Nipper felt a murmur float through the crowd.

He pulled his stocking cap up off his ears so it balanced awkwardly on his head, and listened. He looked from face to face, the tassel shaking with his every movement. Again he heard the murmur, rising like an echo from a well and growing stronger. He looked at his mother and Annie; they'd heard it, too.

Rosary.

Rosary? Did someone want to say the Rosary in the middle of the road? He heard it again, closer this time. But it wasn't *Rosary* they were saying. It was *Rosarie*. They were saying that Rosarie was still inside the Dunnes'.

Nipper looked up the lane. Wisps of cloud blew past a dim quarter moon. The flames had died down, but showers of sparks still floated over the tops of the black spruce, glimmering brightly, then disappearing.

Nipper was suddenly aware of the biting cold. He pulled his stocking cap back down over his ears.

Brendan came down the lane.

"You go on home now," he said. "You, too," he added, turning to Brigid.

Nipper felt sick to his stomach. Dizzy—like when he was in the confessional. "Is it true, Brendan?" he asked. "Is Rosarie in the house?"

Brendan nodded. "Yes," he said. "That's what we think. Now go on home. There's nothing you can do here. Say a prayer to St. Brigid for her."

Sharon and Annie joined them. His mother reached down and took Nipper's hand. "Come on," she said, "let's go." Brigid turned away.

They walked up the road, Annie sniffling and muttering to herself. By the gate to Nipper's house she stopped and said, "I'm coming in. I'm that upset . . . I can't go home yet. I'm coming in."

Nipper and Annie sat at the kitchen table while Sharon made tea. "God save us all," Annie said. "The poor little creature."

In the days following the fire, a haze of silence fell over Kildura; a tincture of sorrow coloured the snow and frozen air.

On a sun-drenched Tuesday morning the doors to St. Brigid's swung open. Everyone marched out and headed down the road in neat lines to St. Christopher's. Nipper sat with his class and glanced at his family pew, filled now with kneeling grade sixes. He wondered where his mother and Annie were.

Brigid stared straight ahead. Ronnie Sheehan's cowlick glistened. There was a rustle at the back of the church, and the pallbearers from the Holy Name Society began the processional. Rosarie's white casket was so small there was barely room for the three men on each side; they shuffled and stumbled, trying not to step on each other's feet. Everyone turned to look—everyone except Brigid, who continued to stare straight ahead.

What had she said? *You don't need to be old to die. Everybody knows that.* The processional passed his pew and Nipper pictured the Dunnes'—the collapsing walls, the rumbling flames, the showers of shooting sparks. He watched the casket advancing awkwardly up the aisle. What was in there? What could possibly be in there?

Resting on top of the casket, in the middle, was a bouquet of fresh, white flowers. The damp scent of the flowers drifted over to him, and Nipper was suddenly flooded with a memory.

He is in grade two. It's May: Mary's month. May 1: May Day. The students at St. Brigid's always go through the same ritual.

"May 1 is an important day," Sister Bernadette had said. "It is the beginning of the month when we pay special reverence to our dear Saviour's mother, the Blessed Virgin Mary."

A small statue of Mary is brought into each classroom. In the statue in Nipper's class, Mary clasps her hands just like she does on the front cover of the catechism; she tilts her head downward ever so slightly. Blue is Mary's colour, like the colour of her dress in the painting above the blackboard, like the ribbons the children are given to pin to their shirts and dresses—rosettes with a medal inside with Mary's picture on it and a long, blue streamer. Ribbons that make you look as if you've won something.

The children in Nipper's class help Sister Bernadette with their altar. An unused desk is brought to the front and put in the corner. Sister Bernadette covers it with a clean, powder-blue cloth and positions the statue exactly in the middle. Candles are placed on each side, and every morning during May the children take turns lighting them. When the altar is done, Sister Bernadette leaves the class and comes back a little later with two small vases of flowers—not plastic flowers like the ones at the feet of St. Brigid in the school foyer, but real flowers. Nipper doesn't know their names, but they're blue and white, fragrant and damp smelling, with touches of dew on their soft petals.

When the altar is completed, the children kneel and say the Hail Mary and the Hail, Holy Queen.

Hail, Holy Queen, Mother of Mercy; hail, our life, our sweetness and our hope! To thee do we cry, poor banished children of Eve; to thee do we send up our sighs, mourning and weeping in this vale of tears. Turn, then, most gracious advocate, thine eyes of mercy toward us; and after this our exile, show unto us the blessed fruit of thy loving womb, Jesus. O clement, O loving, O sweet Virgin Mary!

There's a statue of Mary in the hallway, too, bigger than those in the classrooms, but not as big as the one of St. Brigid. It's raised up on a table covered with a spotless linen cloth like the one covering the altar at St. Christopher's. Candles and baskets of fresh flowers crowd Mary's feet. This bigger Mary extends her arms, palms out, holding up the folds of her dress; her head also tilts downward.

She wears the tiniest trace of a smile.

Nipper stops and looks at the statue during recess. There are so many flowers. The corridor smells like a garden.

Rosarie Dunne comes down the hall. Her round, green eyes light up at the sight of Mary's altar. She stops next to Nipper and smiles. Then Rosarie leans forward. She closes her eyes and inhales the damp fragrance. At that moment, Nipper feels a shadow at his side. He looks up to see Sister Annunciata looking down, her gaze fixed on Rosarie, the flower fragrance rising around them all. Sister Annunciata's face twists into a fist, and she points a long finger at Rosarie Dunne.

"You. *You*, robbing the scent of Our Lady's flowers! Get back to your classroom."

Rosarie's thin mouth opens wide. She stares at Sister Annunciata. She starts to bawl. Turns and runs down the hall.

Nipper looks after her.

He turns back to Sister Annunciata to ask why. But she is
already gone, walking rapidly down the corridor away from him.

In St. Christopher's, Nipper looked at Sister Annunciata. She
stared at the floor with her Rosary beads held to her lips. He
wondered if she remembered Rosarie stealing the scent of Our
Lady's flowers.

The processional halted before the altar. Monsignor Murphy bowed stiffly and anointed the casket with a cloud of
incense. Paddy and his father stood in the first pew to the right
of the priest. Nipper could only see their backs, occasionally a
flash of profile. Paddy wore a black suit jacket with shiny elbows.
It had never struck Nipper how small Mr. Dunne was—not
much bigger than Paddy—how he hunched forward just like his
son. Stephen Dunne never looked at the casket, but sometimes
Paddy did, staring at it hard, then dropping his gaze to his feet.

Nipper had heard Sister Bernadette talking to Sister Annunciata in the hallway that morning. "There's nothing sadder than
a child's funeral," she'd whispered, shaking her head. "The little
white coffin like a teardrop."

Nipper looked around. The church had felt different for his
father's funeral. As the service proceeded, he noticed there was
more crying than there'd been for his father, but he didn't mind.
That was how it should be. He looked at Sister Bernadette sitting
near the aisle, fingering the missal in her lap. Her pale complexion had whitened so much that her full lips seemed almost as red
as his Aunt Mona's, who put on her lipstick so thick it caked the
filters of her Rothman's. During the Creed, Sister Mary Ignatius
clasped her hands tightly around her winding Rosary beads;
even from twenty feet Nipper could see her blue veins bulging.

Halfway through the service Nipper noticed people stirring and glancing over their shoulders. He turned and saw Brendan standing at the back of the church holding his stocking cap in his hands. He crossed himself, brushed his fingertips against his lips, and slid into the last pew.

Monsignor Murphy's sermon was short. For once, even he seemed lost for words. He talked about the child returning to the arms of the Father, ashes to ashes, dust to dust, how we are all here for just a little while, and Nipper thought, But not you. You've been here forever. Always will. You'll never die.

The organ droned, and everyone clattered to their feet for the dismissal. Nipper stood and watched the casket move back down the aisle.

Brendan had disappeared.

Outside, Nipper stood on the steps with Brigid and Ronnie. He watched Rosarie Dunne being loaded into the hearse, noticed again the hunched shoulders of Paddy and Stephen. Annie and his mother came and stood beside him, the hem of his mother's blue-black dress falling beneath her woollen coat. "Poor little thing," Annie murmured. Nipper had heard that a lot over the last few days. Poor little thing.

That afternoon St. Brigid's was closed. Once again Sister Mary Ignatius granted a half-holiday even though there wasn't a snowstorm.

Later, when Nipper wandered up the Old Road, he saw Brendan staring across Shalloway Pond, his mittened hands clasped behind his back.

"I saw you in church this morning," Nipper said.

Brendan nodded.

"Did you say some prayers for the repose of Rosarie's soul?" Nipper asked.

Brendan turned to him. "I did. I reminded St. Brigid that Rosarie was a sweet child." Brendan kicked absently at the hard snow. "But she doesn't need prayers. The poor thing didn't live long enough to cause any trouble." He smiled. "Not like some of us." Brendan exhaled deeply, blowing a cloud of white breath into the air. "Did you know Paddy and his father are moving away—out to St. John's?"

"Yeah. Mom told me."

"They're going to stay with Paddy's uncle."

"I heard."

"Stephen said he's never coming back to Kildura. Couldn't face it." Brendan sighed. "Can't say that I blame him." He turned and looked at Nipper. "You'll have the Old Road all to yourself now."

"We will."

Brendan nodded. "Yes," he said, looking out over the pond. "We will."

That night, when Nipper had put on his pyjamas and gotten into bed, the door opened. "Say an Act of Contrition before you close your eyes," his mother said.

"I already did."

"Good." She turned to leave.

Nipper sat up in bed. "Mom, do you think she did?"

Sharon stopped and looked back at him. "What?"

"Rosarie. Do you think she said an Act of Contrition before she closed her eyes?"

In the light from the hallway Nipper saw his mother's thin shoulders rise and fall. "Yes, Nicky," she said, "I'm sure she did."

Nipper sank back in the bed and pulled the quilt up to his chin. "I hope so," he said.

Sharon nodded. She switched off the hall light and closed the door quietly behind her.

THREE

20

Nipper opened the screen door and smelled cigarette smoke: Aunt Mona. She didn't come to Kildura very much these days. She was working part-time in a jewellery store in St. John's, and her old Buick was always on the blink—the pistons were just about shot. Nipper dumped his bookbag in the vestibule and went into the kitchen. It was Mona, all right. Uncle Derm must have dropped her. She'd been there for a while because the ashtray was full, and there was a crumpled Rothman's pack next to it. His mother was washing up the tea mugs.

"We'll ask Nipper," Mona said, as soon as she saw him. "Who's the best singer in the whole world?"

Nipper groaned. Mona was forever dying to know who was the best at something. But she always had her mind made up before she asked you. Nipper thought the Montreal Canadiens were the best hockey team. After all, they won five Stanley Cups in a row, right? Not according to Mona.

The best hockey team? The Toronto Maple Leafs.
The best colour? Orange.
The best flower? Devil's paint brush.
The best dancer? Fred Astaire.
The best politician? Winston Churchill.
The best painting? The Mona Lisa.

Mona had been asking people, "Who's the best?" since she was a child, and Nipper knew his mother wasn't too crazy about it. Even now she stared out the window with a dazed expression on her face, like she'd rather be doing something else, *anything* else except trying to figure out who was the best. Sharon's idea of a good game was 120s or 45s or Patience. Something where too many opinions weren't involved.

Nipper opened the fridge door and rooted around for an apple. He didn't know who the best singer in the whole world was, but he liked Connie Francis: "Who's Sorry Now?" and "V-A-C-A-T-I-O-N" and "Where the Boys Are." But he knew that if he said Connie Francis, Mona would roll her eyes and say, "Connie Francis!" Then she'd look at Sharon and say, "Did you hear that? Your son thinks the best singer in the whole world is Connie *Francis*." So Nipper just shrugged. And even though he wasn't a little African boy or a little Chinese boy, he bit into his apple and said, "I don't know. Who do you think?"

Mona plucked a Rothman's from a fresh pack and lit it. "Bing Crosby," she said, blowing smoke the colour of the Buick's exhaust toward the ceiling. "Beautiful voice: pure gorgeous. Voice like velvet. Nobody can touch Bing Crosby."

Nipper didn't know what to make of Bing Crosby. Once he saw him in a movie where he played a priest. But he wasn't much like a priest—not a *real* priest. Not like Monsignor Murphy. Bing Crosby didn't say mass or hear confessions. He played the piano and sang a lot of songs and spoke really softly, like a saint, and his eyes glowed like the eyes of Jesus in the painting in the Daily Missal, where Jesus is on his knees in Gethsemane looking up to heaven and praying because he knows he's going to get crucified. Bing Crosby led a boys' choir. The boys were supposed to be tough—real hard cases—but they were always polite to Bing Crosby. They called him "Fawdah," and in no time at all they had stopped being juvenile delinquents and were singing better than the Mormon Tabernacle Choir, which Mona said was the best choir in the whole world—even if they were Protestant. Nipper couldn't imagine Monsignor Murphy leading a choir. He was always hacking and coughing like he was going to pass out any minute. He "finds his chest"—that's what Nipper's mother had said. Mona was right about Monsignor Murphy's voice. When he sang, it sounded like someone emptying out a barrel of four-inch nails onto a concrete floor.

Sharon dried her hands on the dishtowel. "Well, I kind of like . . . Elvis."

"Elvis!" Mona said. She looked at Nipper and widened her eyes. "Elvis! Sure he's got a face on him like a baby's arse."

"Mona!"

Nipper laughed. A baby's arse. That was a good one.

"Well, what odds if he do?" Sharon said. "What's his face got to do with his singing?"

Mona shook her head. "No," she said, "Elvis is all right, but Bing . . . Bing is definitely the best."

"Who's the best woman singer?" Nipper asked. "I kind of like Con—"

"Patti Page," Mona said. She dragged on her cigarette and sang into a cloud of smoke:

How much . . . is that dog-gie in the window?

Nipper sat at the table and took off his shoes. "How do you know they're the best singers in the *whole entire world?* Maybe there's some singers over in Africa or China or England or somewhere who are even better."

"Then how come we haven't heard about them?" Mona said, rapping on the table. "If they were the best in the world, they'd be famous, wouldn't they?"

Nipper sighed. Just for once he'd like to hear Mona say, "Yes, I suppose there *could* be someone over in China who can sing better than Bing Crosby. After all, China does have the largest population of any country on earth. And Connie Francis

... yes, I believe you're right. I was going to say Patti Page was the best female singer, but now that you mention it, Connie Francis *is* better."

Some hope.

And then, the very next Saturday morning while Nipper was eating his breakfast, he heard a song on the radio that sounded ... different. He kept looking up from his corn flakes to listen. *Close your eyes and I'll kiss you* ... When that song was over another one came on: *She loves you, yeah, yeah, yeah* ... Nipper was sure it was the same group. And then there was *another* song. He didn't exactly know what he liked about the music, but he couldn't stop listening. He said to his mother, "Who's that singing on the radio?"

Sharon looked up from her sewing. "That's that new crowd—the Beatles. The station got a contest on the go. If you know all the song titles and phone in, you can win one of their records."

Nipper jumped up on the counter and squeezed in next to the radio. He turned up the volume and listened to all the songs. And when the contest was over, he thought, This Beatles crowd is definitely better than Bing Crosby—even better than Connie Francis.

Over the next few weeks Nipper couldn't turn on the radio without hearing the Beatles. When he went into St. John's with his mother to buy a winter coat, he passed a magazine rack in Woolworth's, and just about every magazine had a picture of the Beatles on the cover. He pulled one out and looked at it. The whole top part of the cover was a photograph of the Beatles, and underneath was another group who looked a bit like the Beatles: the Dave Clark Five. The headline read:

GEORGE SAYS FIVE AGAINST FOUR IS NOT FAIR!

Sharon came over to see what he was looking at.

"Mom, can I have this?"

"I suppose," she said. "I don't guess a magazine will break the bank." She paid for it, and they went for lunch in the store restaurant. As Nipper ate his chocolate sundae with walnuts and a cherry on top, he flipped through the magazine and looked at the pictures of the Beatles. They had funny hair—a bit like Paddy Dunne's—and they wore suits without collars. One of their guitars pointed in the wrong direction, and the drummer's nose was even bigger than Francis Hartery's—which Nipper hadn't thought possible.

Brigid liked the Beatles, too. "George is the best," she told Nipper during recess one day. "George and Ringo." Nipper heard on the radio that the Beatles were going to be on "The Ed Sullivan Show," and Sharon let him stay up to watch. He couldn't wait, but, finally, there they were. They looked just like their pictures. They didn't seem to be doing anything very much, just standing there smiling and strumming, but their songs were very catchy. And everyone in the audience was going crazy—screaming and bawling like it was the end of the world.

"Why are the people carrying on like that?" Nipper asked.

Sharon just tapped her foot and chuckled, but Mona pointed at the screen. "Those girls were paid to do that, you know. Paid. That's a scam."

"Oh, give it up," Sharon said. "Ed Sullivan wouldn't allow that."

Mona got up and went out to the kitchen to make tea. "Paid," she said over her shoulder. "Definitely paid."

But Nipper didn't think so.

He liked the Beatles.

The Beatles were the best singers in the whole world.

21

Nipper sat at the top of the stairs twirling his Rosary beads. Mona and his mother were playing 45s. The game sounded different tonight. Usually, there were periods of silence followed by groans or shrill bursts of laughter. But tonight there was continuous talking—lower talking than usual. And there was hardly any card-slamming from Mona. When she was really into the game, his aunt slammed down her winning tricks so hard the walls shook. Once the plaque of Pope John XXIII above the sink ended up in the dishpan. Mona had pulled it out of the sudsy water and laughed. "Probably needed a wash, anyway."

Nipper watched the blur of his twirling Rosary beads. Who's the best card-slammer in the whole world? My Aunt Mona.

He pricked up his ears. They were talking about him. Intermittently, his name floated up the stairs, and occasionally he picked out *St. Brigid's* and then *St. John's*. Finally, he heard the scraping of chairs, and his mother pushed open the kitchen door.

"Nicky, come down for the Rosary."

Nipper pocketed his beads and plodded down the stairs. As he headed into the living room, Sharon said, "Wait. Come in and sit down for a minute. I've got some news for you."

Whatever it was, it couldn't be that bad. As Mona put away the Hilroy exercise that acted as score book, she winked at him and grinned.

"You're coming into town with me tomorrow so we can get you some new school clothes," Sharon said.

School clothes. Was that all? Nipper didn't think he needed

any, but mothers had their own ideas about those things. He wasn't thrilled about trying on clothes, but it would be fun to go into St. John's. Maybe he'd get to eat in a restaurant that had chocolate sundaes.

The worst part would be the drive.

Nipper had never seen anyone drive like his mother. It was embarrassing. She had never wanted to drive and only learned after Patrick had taken the mining job in Nova Scotia. She wasn't a nervous driver, but for some reason she never shifted above second gear. Ronnie Sheehan made fun of Sharon's driving. He'd say, "Hey, Mrs. Mooney, want to hear how you drives?" Ronnie would make the sound of her shifting from first to second, and then stay on the same growling bass note until he turned beet-red in the face and ran out of breath.

Sharon would cross her arms and shake her head. "There's no need to drive like a maniac if you're just runnin' down to the shop or going to Sunday mass," she'd say.

Nipper didn't think putting a car in third gear necessarily meant you were a maniac. After all, there *were* four gears. And sure it was better for the car. That's what Mr. Sheehan had told them after church one morning: "Leavin' her in second all the time is awful hard on the engine, you know." But as far as Nipper's mother was concerned, third gear was optional equipment. Sometimes when they were driving and the engine was roaring like it was going to explode, Nipper could not keep quiet. "For God's sake, Mom, put her in third, will you?"

But Sharon would just grip the wheel harder. "Leave me alone. There's no rush. I'll get around to third someday."

Nipper didn't have much hope. And fourth gear? Reverse? Best not to think about it.

Once they got to St. John's it would be okay. Maybe she'd buy him a new Hardy Boys book. If he was lucky, he might get the book *and* a chocolate sundae.

Nipper stood up. "Okay," he said. "School clothes. Sure. Are we sayin' the Rosary tonight?"

"In a minute," Sharon said. She looked at him carefully. "We're actually going to have to get you a school . . . uniform."

Uniform.

Nipper frowned. "What do you mean—a uniform?"

Sharon leaned forward in her chair. "Well, you're ten years old now. So, starting in September, you'll be going to school in St. John's. All Angels. I've got it all arranged."

Mona grinned. "With the *Christian Brothers.*"

Nipper stared at his mother.

"It'll be good for you, Nicky," she said. "You're always surrounded by women: me and Mona—Annie. The Brothers will make a man out of you."

Nipper sat down heavily. They'll make a man out of you. What had Uncle Phonse said when his father died? *You have to be the man of the house now.* Why was everyone so concerned about him being a man when he was only ten years old?

"But you better watch out," Mona said, wagging a finger at him. "Those Brothers are a tough lot. I heard they wear black leather straps down the sides of their robes. They'd just as soon eat you alive as look at you."

Nipper pictured grim Sister Mary Ignatius, remembered the sting of her pointer and strap; the time in kindergarten when Sister Annunciata made Pauly Mackey wear a girls' tunic because he wanted to go home and cried for his mother. Could the Brothers be worse than that?

Nipper looked from Mona to Sharon. "If they're that mean, why do I have to go? What did I do?"

"You didn't *do* anything," Sharon said. She leaned back in her chair. "I've just had enough of that St. Brigid's. It's nothing but a hole. There hasn't been one ounce of work done on that building since me and Mona went there. Freezing cold in the winter, mice eatin' the school books—"

"Big old jeezly rats creepin' up from the river," Mona said, shivering.

"I don't care about that," Nipper said. "All my friends are there: Ronnie and Gerard—everybody. Anyway, what's a few old mice compared to being *eaten alive?*"

"Don't mind Mona," Sharon said. "She's just coddin' you. The Brothers aren't mean—just a bit strict, that's all. Sure, my God, they're almost the same thing as a priest. How bad can they be? And All Angels is a lovely school. I used to go there to bingo. They got a gorgeous big gym."

"And choirs and a band," Mona said. "You likes music. Maybe you'll get to learn an instrument."

"And there's a library," Sharon said. "Hundreds, *thousands* of books. You'd like that, wouldn't you?" She reached forward and took Nipper's hand. "And everything's right clean." His mother adopted the tone that told him there was no point in arguing. "You'll get used to it."

22

Gardiner Street's motley-coloured row houses leaned, shoulder to shoulder, up a steep hill to Harrison Avenue. There was a bakery, a convenience store, a dry-cleaning business, and two barbershops run by the Bowen brothers, Rick and Bill. Another brother, Jerome, operated a third shop only minutes away on Water Street. Chip bags and other trash blew in the street and on the sidewalks—especially at the intersection of Saintsbury Place, whose residents appeared to produce more litter than their Gardiner Street neighbours. In winter, Coke bottles and Jersey Milk chocolate bar wrappers stuck up from clumps of dirty snow or lay crumpled and frozen in the gutters.

But most of the trash was not the work of the Gardiner Street/Saintsbury Place residents at all. Most came from the boys who attended All Angels. The back entrance to the schoolyard opened halfway up Gardiner Street, and many of the West End boys used it as a shortcut. When the wind was especially strong, it peppered the rusting chain-link fence with scraps of trash, glued fast, like flies to flypaper. The Brothers continually pleaded with their students to "refrain from littering." It never did any good. So, in the early fall and spring, they pressed the entire student body into a clean-up regiment. Each boy was given a plastic bag and ordered out to pick the surrounding streets clean. The students scavenged up and down sidewalks and back alleys. But by the next day the garbage had sprouted again, and by week's end it flourished.

.   .   .

Sharon arranged for Nipper to drive into St. John's with Bobby Sheehan, Ronnie's older brother, who worked at the dockyard. Nipper had ridden in Bobby's rusty Volkswagen before. He had a heavy foot: he knew all about third and fourth gears.

"Bobby'll drop you at the foot of Gardiner Street," Sharon said, "and you just walk up to All Angels from there." She paused. "It might be a little . . . early."

Nipper looked at her warily. "How early?"

"Well, Bobby's shift starts at eight o'clock, so he'll drop you at about seven-thirty, quarter to. He likes to get to work in plenty of time." Nipper knew that classes didn't start until nine o'clock and the school didn't even open until eight-thirty.

"What am I going to do for a whole hour?"

"Oh, you'll think of something," Sharon said. "Holy Rosary is just across the street. That's always open. You can go in there if it rains."

Nipper groaned. "A *church*?"

When Nipper Mooney first stepped onto the grounds of All Angels, he saw an H-shaped wooden box painted a dull yellowish beige. To the right of the concrete steps was a small grotto where the Virgin Mary, hands clasped, was attended by three kneeling angels. In the centre of the courtyard stood a larger statue of the Archangel Gabriel, his wide, ruffled wings billowing behind him, his mournful gaze turned heavenward.

The schoolyard rang with the din of hundreds of screaming boys, their roughhousing a striking contrast to the air of respectability suggested by their slicked-down hair and fresh uniforms. In his grey flannels, tie, and crest-adorned black blazer, Nipper felt uncomfortably stiff and starched. His tie was suffocating him, but he didn't dare loosen it. The worst thing was that he seemed to be the only person there who didn't know anyone.

When the doors finally opened, the students were herded

into lines and marched through the school to the gym, where they would be assigned to their homerooms. Nipper gazed about in wonder. Everything overwhelmed him: the gleaming waxed floors, the larger-than-life statues of saints and angels standing solemnly at the ends of the corridors, the stairs leading to the second, *third* stories. The Brothers, arms crossed, leaning stiffly against the gym walls, also seemed larger than life, and strangely priest-like in their black soutanes. Nipper looked for leather straps and was relieved when he didn't see any.

As he stood waiting for his name to be called, he noticed the boy next to him gazing about and clutching at his tie.

"Hi ya," Nipper said.

The boy grinned nervously. "Hi ya."

"This your first time here, too?"

"Yeah."

"Where you from?"

"Portugal Cove—well, it *used* to be Portugal Cove. We just moved into town."

Nipper looked around the gym. "What do you think of the school?"

"Some friggin' big. You could put about ten of my old school into this."

"Yeah," Nipper said. "Mine, too."

"Why? Where you from?"

"Kildura."

"Whatcha doin' out here?"

Nipper shrugged. "My mother."

The boy rolled his eyes and nodded.

Nipper watched as one of the older students approached a short, squat Brother sitting on the lip of the stage. "When you havin' tryouts for the soccer team, Burr?"

Burr?

The Brother swung his legs. "I'll let you know, Mr. Walsh. Probably be in a couple of weeks or so."

"You're not gonna cut me this year, are you, Burr? I was practising all summer. Honest to God. Ask Sweeney and Stamp—they'll tell you. I scored twenty goals."

"We'll see, Mr. Walsh."

"Ah, come on, Burr. Don't be so friggin' mean—I mean, don't be so mean."

The Portugal Cove boy noticed Nipper's puzzled expression and tugged on his elbow. "That's what they calls the Brothers," he said. "Burr. Took me awhile to figure out what they were gettin' on with, too."

Class numbers and students' names began to be called. "That's me," Nipper whispered when he heard his name. "But hardly anyone calls me Nicholas. Not even Nick. It's Nipper."

"Then we're in the same class," the boy said. "They called my name, too: Joe Barnes."

"Brother Devine's our teacher," Nipper said. "I wonder what he's like."

"Guess we'll find out soon enough."

As Barnes and Nipper headed down to their classroom, Nipper wondered what else—besides the Brothers and the sheer size of the place—was making him uneasy. There was something odd, something missing that he couldn't quite put his finger on. And then, when he took his seat and looked around, it struck him: no girls. Not that girls interested him very much. But there was something unsettling about a school without girls—especially when the male teachers wore dresses.

Brother Devine was a soft-spoken sixty-year-old with a shock of white hair, a leathery complexion and thick bifocals that persisted in sliding down over his nose. Contrary to what Nipper was expecting, he wasn't at all threatening; compared to Sister Mary

Ignatius and Sister Annunciata, he was positively mild. He spent the first morning entertaining the boys with stories about Jason, Aeneas and Odysseus. Nipper was surprised when it came out that they weren't Catholic—weren't even *Christian* for that matter. Except for fairy tales, the nuns had only departed from their textbooks to tell stories about the saints and holy martyrs. Brother Devine seemed quite taken with Jason and his friends all the same, and he energetically recounted their adventures, at one point jumping up on his desk and flailing his arms about in an effort to describe how Odysseus had escaped from the Cyclops.

During lunch hour Barnes and Nipper explored the streets around the school. Nipper had never been in St. John's on his own; now he was free to roam wherever he liked. Everything interested him: the traffic, smells, stores; even the housewives in curlers and bandannas, shaking out mops on their front steps, seemed strangely exotic.

Near Madden's Bakery, Nipper and Barnes came upon a group of small boys sharing out some food. Barnes worked up the courage to ask what they had.

"Bag o' scraps," a boy said, stuffing his mouth with cake. Crumbs stuck to his chin and lips and tumbled down the front of his blazer. He clutched a bread bag full of cake and cookies.

"Where'd you get that?" Barnes asked.

"In there," the boy said, pointing to a side door into the bakery. "Twenty-five cents a bag."

"What's in it?"

"All bits o' cake and buns and stuff that they don't use. You know, the stuff off the ends when they're cuttin' up the cakes."

Barnes reached into his pocket and pulled out two dimes. "Got a nickel?" he asked Nipper.

"I think so," Nipper said.

Barnes passed him the dimes. "Then go get us a bag."

"How come me?"

"Jeez, b'y, I'm the one paying twenty cents. You're only puttin' in a nickel. You could at least go get it."

"All right," Nipper said. He went over and knocked softly on the door.

"You don't have to *knock*," one of the boys said. "Just go on in and ask for it."

"For . . . ?"

"A bag o' scraps, b'y."

A moment later Nipper was out again with the feast: sticky slices of raisin and cherry cake and jelly rolls; pieces of raisin and shortbread cookies, date turnovers and apple flips.

As they walked around nibbling on the scraps and sizing things up, a group of Portuguese sailors, aswirl in a cloud of cigarette smoke, passed them on Water Street. Nipper and Barnes stared so hard that one of the sailors must have assumed they wanted something. He stopped and, muttering softly in Portuguese, he reached into his breast pocket, pulled out a crumpled package and handed each of them a cigarette.

Barnes and Nipper looked at each other and grinned. It was only the first day of grade five, and already they had fallen into sin.

"So how you findin' All Angels?" Bobby Sheehan asked the next morning on the drive into St. John's. "Must be different than little old St. Brigid's."

"Yeah," Nipper said. "There's some size to it."

"You be careful with them Townies," Bobby said. "Don't go gettin' on the wrong side of 'em."

"What do you mean?"

"There's all kinds of gangs out there, you know: Bond Street, the Brow, Buckmaster's Circle. They comes into our dances sometimes. Half of them fellas would just as soon shoot you as look at you. And there's a lot more of them than there is of you. So don't go fallin' out with anyone, cause if you do, well, there's no one to pick up for you. It's not like at St. Brigid's."

"I don't want to go fallin' out with anyone."

"Well, make sure you don't." Bobby shifted into fourth. "How you findin' the teachers?"

"Okay, I s'pose."

"Well, I'd watch them, too—especially the Brothers. A couple of the fellas I works with on the dockyard went to school with the Brothers. They told me all about 'em. Some of the friggers sounds like real nut cases." He glanced at Nipper. "Want my advice?"

"Sure."

"Blend in," Bobby said. "Don't go doin' nothin' to draw attention to yourself. Then the Townies will leave you alone. And the Brothers, well, as long as you don't piss 'em off, they probably won't even look at you twice—unless you comes from some rich, la-di-da family. Or unless you're right smart—you know, winning scholarships and stuff like that. That's what the fellas I works with said, anyway."

"No need to worry about that," Nipper said.

"Well, just keep your eyes open is all I'm saying," Bobby said. "You'll be all right."

Brigid and Ronnie were curious about All Angels, too. "What are the Brothers like?" Brigid asked in Sheehan's loft one evening. "Are they worse than the nuns?"

"Nothing could be worse than the nuns," Ronnie said.

"I don't know about that," Brigid said, shaking her head. "I saw some of them Brothers once in church. They look an awful lot like priests to me. Just imagine having to spend all day in school with a bunch of Monsignor Murphys."

"Some of 'em are okay," Nipper said. "Brother Devine is nice."

"Who's he?" Brigid asked.

"My homeroom teacher."

"What about the rest of 'em?" Ronnie asked. "Are they all Brothers?"

"No. Some of 'em are just normal."

"Are they strict like Sister Mary Ignatius?" Brigid asked. She leaned forward. "Know what she did the other day? Made Kathy Heffernan kneel in the corner for a whole hour—on *chalk*: sticks of chalk. She could hardly stand up at the end of it."

"They're . . . " Nipper shrugged. His teachers were certainly an odd bunch. And except for Brother Devine, none of them could really teach. His French teacher, Mr. Gibson, always wore the same rumpled old suit that looked like he'd slept in it. Most days he seemed to be suffering from a hangover. Joe Barnes said he reminded him of an ugly Dean Martin. Gibson moved in super slow motion, and was so absentminded that it was easy for a student to talk his way out of a sticky situation. "Oh yes, sir, Mr. Gibson. I passed that assignment in yesterday. You were talking to Randy Dooley there by the door, and I came up and gave it to you. Remember? I saw you put it in your briefcase." Gibson would narrow his rheumy eyes and stare at the boy as if he'd never seen *him* before, let alone his assignment.

Nipper sighed. "I don't know what to make of All Angels," he said. "Not yet, anyway. But I'd just as soon be back at St. Brigid's."

"Why don't you ask your mom if she'll let you come back?" Ronnie asked.

"I did. She keeps telling me that All Angels is 'gorgeous,' and I'll get used to it."

"Well," Brigid said. "Maybe you will."

"Yeah," Nipper said. "Maybe."

23

*E*very morning, after a harrowing drive into St. John's, Bobby Sheehan dropped Nipper at the foot of Gardiner Street. In the fall and spring he would go up to the monastery next to the school and ring the bell. The housekeeper, Mrs. Critch, a sour woman with a limp and a mustache, would point silently to a corner of the vestibule and watch as Nipper bent and took up the basketball that was waiting there. This was the communal basketball that the boys could use before and after school and during recess and lunch. Nipper was too small to stand much chance of laying a hand on it when the bigger boys were around, but now, at that hour of the morning, he had the ball and the schoolyard—even the whole city—to himself.

On days when it was too rainy or cold to play basketball, or if he'd grown tired of it, he would cross Prince Street and go up the stone steps that led to Holy Rosary church. The church opened at seven o'clock in preparation for eight-thirty mass. There was rarely anyone there besides him—certainly not for the first half hour or so. Then, gradually, the old people would arrive: the men with their watery eyes and grey stubble, clutching salt and pepper caps in knobby hands; the women with their wool coats, bandannas and bulky leather purses. They wandered in slowly, their coughing and nose-blowing echoing off the stone walls. Nipper wondered if they really believed in God or if they were just coming to church because they were old and knew they were going to die soon. He watched as they genuflected stiffly and bowed their grey heads. It was always the old who came to church in the morning, the old and some of the nuns who taught at St. Anne's, the girls' school just across the street from All Angels.

But for the first little while Nipper would have the church to himself, and he carried out his own private ritual. He blessed himself with holy water from a stained marble cistern, and stared up at the enormous crucifix that hung below the choir loft. Christ's muscular, chipped body drooped forward: He looked as if He might swan dive onto the floor at any moment. His head hung wearily to one side; His crown of thorns, pointy and needle sharp, thrust into His bleeding skull. He hung there quietly, a look of pain and sadness on His bruised, bearded face.

In front of the crucifix was the candle rack. At that hour there would never be a lit candle, and Nipper would take one from the tarnished brass box and light it. The scents of candle wax and incense mingled. Nipper dropped a penny into the wooden contribution box—even though you were supposed to pay at least five cents. He had heard that people sometimes stole from the box, and once Joe Barnes said that paying only a penny amounted to the same thing. Sometimes Nipper expected Jesus to raise His head and shout down a warning from the cross. But He remained content to hang in silence.

The altar was always decorated with fresh flowers, especially on holy days. The damp scent of roses and chrysanthemums hung heavily over the polished woodwork and marble statues, the velvet-lined pulpit and oak pews. Nipper found the scent overpowering, so he would go and sit in the last pew on the east side of the church, where the sunlight slanted through the stained glass windows. Nipper had examined all the windows, but there was none for St. Brigid. The window just above him showed the Archangel Michael holding a flaming sword high above his head. Emerald eyes burned in his young face; his jaw jutted forward, and his hovering, graceful wings made him look like an eagle about to take flight. At his feet there was an inscription in Latin, and one morning Nipper copied it down:

Sancte Míchael Archangele, defénde nos in proelio; contra nequítias et insídias diáboli esto praesídium. Imperet illi Deus; súpplices deprecámur: tuque, Princeps milítiae caeléstis, Sátanam aliósque spíritus malígnos, qui ad perditiónem animárum pervagántur in mundo, divína virtúte in inférnum detrúde.

He wondered what it meant. Maybe Brendan would know.

As the sunlight spilled through Michael's lean body, or the rain drummed rhythmically on the copper roof, Nipper Mooney listened. The church creaked and echoed, the old people whispered and coughed. He glanced through the musty hymnals and prayer books, the outdated Sunday bulletins and, finally, when he became bored, he prayed.

Nipper had wondered one morning if he could turn simple prayers into Indulgences. Perhaps if he said enough prayers, they could be built up into a kind of holy bank account. One hundred Acts of Contrition might make up for those times when he would forget to say his nightly prayer.

He wondered how many prayers it would take to atone for looking at Mickey Welch's dirty picture.

Mickey had shown up at All Angels one morning with a photo of two naked women: a real photo—not something cut from a magazine. It looked and felt exactly the same as the photos parents took of birthday parties or First Holy Communions. The women were not beautiful, or even very attractive. Only one could be seen clearly. She lay on a rumpled bed staring at the camera, one hand dangling over the edge, the other clutching a lock of the second woman's curly hair. The second woman's face was buried deep between the other woman's legs, and her backside, white and overexposed by the flash, took up most of the lower part of the photo. The wallpaper in the upper right-hand corner of the room was torn and peeling, and although the photo was black and white, Nipper was sure the wallpaper was blue: he had seen the same pattern in Brigid's front room.

All of this was shocking enough, but then Mickey announced in a dramatic whisper that the photo had been taken in a whorehouse somewhere on Gardiner Street. This led to an argument about which house it might be. Barnes and Nipper spent many a lunch hour climbing up and down the street, sizing up the houses. What they were going to do if they figured out which one was the whorehouse, they hadn't really thought about. But every time they met a woman walking along Gardiner Street, they glanced up to see if they would recognize the face from the photo.

With so much occasion for sin, Nipper thought it a good idea to make his soul as clean and white as possible and store up this whiteness like a squirrel storing nuts. That way he would have some protection against those times when he would be bad. So he would kneel, bow his head, and begin to recite his prayers one after another in a long litany: Hail Mary, Our Father, Glory Be, the Act of Contrition. Nipper was very fast—he had had plenty of practice saying the Rosary at home. The prayers spilled off his tongue as rapidly as the cupcakes and cookies sailed along the conveyor belts at Madden's Bakery.

After some practice Nipper found that he could say the prayers and think about other things at the same time. But eventually the prayers got mixed up:

Hail Mary Mother of God who art in heaven hallowed
be the Holy Ghost and I am heartily sorry for having
offended thy kingdom come Amen.

The last words spun and echoed in his head. When he looked up, dazed and prayer-drunk, all the colours and smells of Holy Rosary were sharpened. The world glowed like a technicolour movie: Christ's thorns bit deeper, Michael's eyes and sword burned brighter. Nipper felt so holy he trembled and could hardly breathe. Sometimes he stayed in the trance until the ringing of the bells for the eight-thirty service finally snapped him out of it.

With the sun blazing in Michael's hair and sword above him, and most of the world still asleep, Nipper Mooney sat alone with the chipped, bleeding Jesus, and the dying old people and his penny candle. He looked out from the last pew of Holy Rosary and watched the world rub the dust from its eyes.

24

*W*hen the weather was fine, Barnes and Nipper continued to use their lunch hours to explore the city. One day when Barnes was home sick, Nipper decided to go off by himself. In a little alley at the top of Prince Street, he came across a fruit store with a window display of bananas, grapes, plums and other strange, brightly coloured fruits. Nipper thought he recognized some purple mangoes from a picture in his geography textbook. As he stepped inside, a bell jangled, and he was greeted by the scent of Christmas: oranges. On Christmas morning he would always find an orange or a banana stuffed into the toe of his stocking. Outside of that, the only fruit that made a regular appearance in the Mooney house was the apple.

A thick drift of sawdust blanketed the shop's hardwood floor, and sawdust crept into Nipper's socks as he wandered among the bins, drinking in the tropical scents of pineapple and coconut, and studying some wooden crates stamped with Chinese characters.

The shopkeeper eyed him suspiciously. "Can I help you?" he asked.

"No, that's all right," Nipper said. "I'm just lookin'." But the smells were so wonderful that he worked up the courage to point and ask, "What's them things?"

"Kiwis."

"What wees?"

"*Ki*wis," the shopkeeper said. "From New Zealand."

"Oh." Nipper watched as the man bent and opened a box of bananas. "Umm, how much are the bananas?"

"Twenty-five cents a pound."

"Can I get one?"

"One pound?"

"No, one banana."

The shopkeeper reached into the box, plucked a plump banana from a bunch and laid it on the weigh scales.

"Five cents."

"That's all?" Nipper had thought that such an exotic Christmas fruit coming all the way from Africa or wherever would be much more expensive.

"You want it?"

Nipper searched his blazer pocket and handed over the five cents. The banana felt smooth and cool in his hands. It was only a five-cent purchase, but he felt grown up, like he had done something romantic. He took one last look around, one last deep breath, and went out through the jangling door.

Two boys sat on the shop's front step, their legs jutting awkwardly into the sidewalk. Their school ties were loose and slewed around their necks. One of the boys was blond; he picked at his fingernails. The other one French-inhaled a cigarette. As Nipper stepped around their outstretched legs, they glanced up at him.

"Whatcha got there, buddy?" Blondie said.

They were older boys, and Nipper hadn't expected them to speak to him. "Nothin'," he said, startled. He kept walking, but he could hear the boys murmuring to one another. Then they got up and followed him.

"Nothin'?" Blondie said to his back. "Looks like a banana to me."

"Yeah," Nipper said. "A banana."

"Monkey food," Smoker said.

"That's right," Blondie said, laughing. "Hey, buddy, you don't want that. That's only for apes and gorillas." He sprinted ahead and stopped in front of Nipper. "Why don't you give that to me." Nipper looked up at him with wide eyes. The hardness of the boy's expression sent a trail of goose bumps running up and down his legs. He opened his mouth to speak, but his voice had gone. Nipper stared into Blondie's narrowed eyes. Just when he was about to hand over the banana, Blondie pushed him hard in the chest. Nipper backed up on the foot of Smoker, who cursed and shoved him violently into Blondie.

Blondie stepped back and swung.

Nipper struck out blindly with one hand and tried to protect his face with the other. The banana fell to the sidewalk. Blondie punched Nipper hard in the nose; blood spurted over his white shirt. Nipper had never been punched in the face before, and the touch of the fist on his skin sickened him more than the blood or the pain. The banana lay crushed on the sidewalk.

The boys ran off down the street.

Nipper felt himself starting to cry, but he swallowed hard and leaned up against a parked car until he got his breath back. A group of girls from St. Anne's passed by. They whispered and giggled, glancing back over their shoulders at him. Nipper reddened and turned away.

After the girls had gone, he straightened his blazer and tie, wiped some of the blood from his face with a piece of Kleenex, and went back to All Angels. As soon as he entered the classroom, the boys whistled and crowded around him.

"Someone jumped Mooney!" More boys came running. "What happened? Who jumped you?"

"Nobody." Nipper didn't want to talk about it, but when Brother Devine came in, he insisted on the details.

"I bought a banana," Nipper said. "A couple of guys tried to take it off me."

"A banana?" Brother Devine rolled his eyes. "Why didn't you just give it to them?"

"I was going to—"

"I mean, it's not worth getting beat up over. I would have expected more from you," he said. "Fighting out on the street like a hooligan. Who were they anyway? From this school?"

"Yeah. In grade seven or eight."

"What did they look like?"

"A blond fella and another guy."

"I knows them, Burr," Mickey Welch called out from the back of the class. "I betcha that was Frankie Forristall and Gene Crocker up in grade seven. They're always pickin' on fellas." There was a murmur of agreement all around.

Brother Devine shook his head. "Toughs," he said under his breath. He banged out the door, then quickly stuck his head back inside. "Quiet until I get back."

About ten minutes later Nipper was summoned over the PA to the office. When he got there, Blondie and Smoker were leaning up against the counter with their heads down. Brother Devine stood over them with his hands on his hips and a rigid expression on his face that Nipper had never seen before. He looked at Nipper.

"That them?"

Nipper nodded.

"Right," he said. "All of you into the office and we'll wait for Brother Bannister." They trooped into an untidy, dusty room and sat down. On the wall, just behind the principal's chair, hung a black strap.

Brother Devine shook his head at Blondie and Smoker. "You're some big men now, aren't you? Beatin' up on a young fella half your size. And over a *banana*. Sacred Heart, don't they feed you at home? If you're that poor off go up to the monastery, and Mrs. Critch'll give you a bowl of soup and a few crackers."

Bannister finally arrived. Brother Devine quickly told him

what had happened, glaring the whole time at Blondie and Smoker. Bannister clasped his hands behind his back and listened silently. When he had finished, Brother Devine winked at Nipper and went back to class.

The principal of All Angels was like no other grown-up Nipper had ever seen. He was a big man with a ruddy complexion. His black glasses held thick Coke-bottle lenses, making his eyes shift in and out of focus and roll like marbles. Nipper thought that if he had to look at him for very long he'd get carsick.

Bannister sat behind his desk and rapped a pencil against a coffee mug. Blondie and Smoker grinned nervously at each other. Nipper ran over his story in his mind, but it was hard to concentrate with the strap peeking out over the principal's right shoulder. Finally, Bannister stood up and took in the three boys with his odd eyes. "I refuse to tolerate fighting," he said. "Look at you," he said to Nipper, pointing across the desk. "That shirt is ruined, you know. Ruined. What's your mother going to say? Out in the street carrying on like a bunch of . . . Indians."

"But Burr—"

He silenced Nipper with a wave of his hand. Then he turned and took down the strap. "And you, Mr. Forristall," he said to Blondie, "I've had it with you. Stand up and hold out your hand." Blondie got up and ran his hand up and down the side of his blazer. Bannister had seemed like an old man to Nipper, but when he raised the strap over his head and brought it down, he looked like a twenty-year-old. The first blow shattered the air in the small office; the coffee mug jumped on the desk. Forristall sucked in his breath with a whistle and promptly shook out his hand. "Again," Bannister said. He dealt out six blows on each hand. After the fourth, Nipper could see tears coming into Forristall's eyes. "Back to your class," Bannister said when he'd finished. Forristall jammed his hands into his blazer pockets and rushed out of the room. Bannister turned to Crocker. Nipper felt no pity for either of them. As far as he was concerned he could have given them a dozen more.

When Crocker had left, Bannister looked at Nipper. "Stand up."

Nipper's mouth went dry.

"What?"

"Stand up and hold out your hand."

"What for, Burr? I didn't do nothin'. They jumped me. I didn't want to go fightin'."

"Hold out your hand." Bannister's eyes pitched and rolled in his head; a gold tooth gleamed through his parted lips. Nipper closed his eyes and slowly brought up his hand. When Bannister struck, Nipper nearly lost his breath. It was like picking up a live wire. Bannister gave him three hard blows.

"The other hand."

Nipper could hardly see through his tears, but he managed to obey.

"Now back to your class," Bannister said, as he hung up the strap. "And no more fighting."

Nipper stepped into the outer office with his hands jammed under his armpits and tears streaming down his face. The secretary, Miss Jackson, stared at him; Nipper turned away. When he got to his classroom door, he lingered outside until he had gathered himself together. He hoped no one would know he'd been crying. He opened the door and went in. Everyone stopped what they were doing and looked. Brother Devine stared at him curiously.

"What happened, Nipper?" he said.

"He strapped me. Brudder Bannister. I didn't even do nothin', and he strapped me."

Brother Devine frowned and ran his hand through his white hair. "Sit down," he said softly.

Nipper slumped into his seat.

"Page 62," Brother Devine said to the class. "The first three sums, please."

Nipper opened the book, but the numbers were jumbled and out of focus. He stared up at the blackboard. Brother Devine crouched down by his desk.

"I'm sorry you got strapped, Nipper. Brother Bannister, he . . . he shouldn't have done that." Brother Devine squeezed Nipper's shoulder and went back to his desk.

After school, when Nipper climbed into Bobby Sheehan's Volkswagen, Bobby flicked at Nipper's shirt and whistled. "Shit, did someone take a swing at you?"

"No," Nipper said, "I'm all right."

"What happened?"

"It was in the gym, during recess. I got hit in the face with the basketball."

"Oh, you got your bell rung, did you?" Bobby said. "Well, just remember: it's like fallin' off a horse. You got to dust yourself off and get back on again."

"Yeah."

Nipper gave his mother and Brigid the same story. Part of him wanted to tell them what had really happened, wanted to insist on going back to St. Brigid's even if it was dirty and cold and full of mice. But he didn't say anything.

"For God's sake, Nicky," Sharon said. "Be more careful in the gym from now on, will you? Keep your eyes open."

"You don't need to worry about that," Nipper said. "I will."

25

"Mom, I don't think I can sing."

"Of course, you can sing," Sharon said. "I hears you singing along with the Beatles on the radio."

It was the beginning of Nipper Mooney's third year at All Angels, and his mother wanted him to try out for the choir. She had heard that, unlike the athletic teams, the choir practised during school hours, so there was no reason why he couldn't participate.

Nipper still found it hard to believe that All Angels even *had* a choir.

"But they don't sing Beatle songs in school choirs. Not at All Angels, anyway. Besides, just because I likes the Beatles it don't mean I can sing like 'em."

"Go on. Sure you got a grand voice. You sounds just like Paul McCarthy."

"Mc*Cartney*, Mom. McCartney."

"You know who I mean—the cute one." She ran her hand through his hair. "That's why I sent you out there in the first place: so you could get into things like that. I'll drive you out to the concerts if that's what you're worried about."

Nipper sighed. "Oh, all right. At least I'll be able to get out of class for the practices."

At the first rehearsal it quickly became clear that Brother McDonald, the choirmaster, was not a Beatles fan. He looked more like a boot camp sergeant than a musician, which seemed fitting, because Nipper soon found out that most of the songs they sang were of the military variety. When it was discovered that he actually could sing and was assigned a solo in the Christmas concert, it wasn't "O Holy Night" or "Joy to the World." It was the "The Ballad of the Green Berets":

> *Fighting soldiers from the sky,*
> *Men who jump and men who die,*
> *Men who mean just what they say,*
> *Those brave men of the Green Berets.*

It struck Nipper as odd to sing an American war anthem in a concert celebrating the peace and joy of Christmas.

"Hey, Burr, how come I got to sing 'The Green Berets'? It's not very Christmasy."

" 'The Ballad of the Green Berets,' " McDonald said, "is a fine, uplifting song for any season."

"But—"

"And remember: it's about soldiers—so don't make it too pretty."

It wasn't just the choice of songs that Nipper found odd. Brother McDonald also read to the choir just before every performance. "It'll calm you down," he said. "Settle your nerves." The boys could certainly have used the calming down. Nipper wasn't an expert on singing, but he was pretty sure the Mormon Tabernacle Choir didn't have anything to worry about. He thought the reading might well have worked—except that McDonald's favourite author was Edgar Allan Poe. Before concerts, the choir would huddle in a corner of the dressing room, and while the other performers raced around in pursuit of lost props or made last-minute adjustments to their costumes, McDonald stood before them and launched into "The Raven" or "The Tell-Tale Heart":

I held the lantern motionless. I tried how steadily I could maintain the ray upon the eye. Meantime the hellish tattoo of the heart increased. It grew quicker, and louder and louder every instant. The old man's terror *must* have been extreme! It grew louder, I say, louder every moment—do you mark me well?

They marked him well. Some of the younger boys marked him so well they could barely talk, let alone sing. Nipper sometimes thought they'd have to be carried to the stage. It was little wonder that when he asked Mona what she thought of their first performance, she said they'd improve once they got over their stage fright.

One evening Ronnie Sheehan phoned Nipper and told him to meet him at Pauly Mackey's house.

"What for?"

"It's a surprise," Ronnie said.

"What?"

"Just meet me there."

When Nipper went into Pauly's yard, he saw Ronnie, Gerard and Pauly gathered near the basement door.

"What's goin' on?"

Ronnie stood up and pointed at Pauly. "Show 'im."

Pauly sighed and opened the door. They went inside and headed down to the basement.

"I never should have told you," Pauly said. "I should've kept it to myself."

"Kept what to yourself?" Nipper asked.

Ronnie stopped on the stairwell. "I suppose you heard that Stan's Takeout burned down last week?"

"Yeah."

Ronnie jerked his thumb at Pauly. "You know his old man is the guy who keeps the cigarette machine topped up?"

"Yeah."

"Well, the machine wasn't burned right through. He managed to save some smokes. They're down there."

"And that's where they're staying," Pauly said. "My dad'll kill me if he finds out we took any."

They trooped into the basement. The cigarettes were heaped in two oversized cardboard boxes. Some of the packages were blackened at the edges, the cellophane missing or twisted and curled by heat, but most seemed as good as new.

"Jesus," Gerard said. He jammed his arms to the elbows into one of the boxes and let the packages run through his hands as if they were Spanish coins in a pirate chest. "How many are there?"

"A hundred and forty-two," Pauly said. "Assorted."

"Assorted?" Gerard said. "That's even better."

Ronnie grinned. "Ours for the taking."

"I don't know," Pauly said. "What if Dad finds out?"

"No one's gonna *find out*," Ronnie said. "We'll just take . . . oh, fifty. They won't be missed."

Pauly's eyes widened. "Fifty? Are you sure? Maybe Dad counted them."

"That's what he never," Ronnie said. "Why would he count them? He's just gonna throw 'em out. He said so himself, didn't he?"

Pauly didn't answer.

"Well, didn't he? That's what you told me."

"Yeah, but what if he changes his mind?"

"He won't change his mind. Sure he can't sell 'em like that. They're damaged goods."

"Well . . ."

"Pauly, there are 142 packs of smokes there," Ronnie said. "Doesn't that strike you as a bit of an opportunity?"

"What do you mean?"

"Pauly, it's like that thing Sister Mary Ignatius is always gettin' on with in religion. A . . . a what do you call it? Nipper, what's that word—you know, when someone knows that something is going to happen? When they gets a sign?"

Nipper pondered. "Oh, you mean a portent?"

"Yeah, that's right—a portent."

"Like that old piece of rag we camped out in last 24th of May," Gerard said, "that leaked like a bastard and just about drowned us all. That was a poor-friggin'-tent, too."

"Very funny," Ronnie said. He turned to Pauly. "Pauly, God has dropped into our laps 142 packs of cigarettes—"

"Assorted, don't forget," Gerard said.

"*Assorted* cigarettes," Ronnie said. "You can't let your old man throw 'em away. That's a waste."

"Yeah," Gerard said. "Just think of all the poor people over in Africa and China with *no* cigarettes."

"But my old man—"

"Won't miss them," Ronnie said. "He's only gonna throw 'em out. That's waste. And you know what waste is, Pauly? That's a sin is what that is—a mortal sin."

"Oh," Pauly said. "If that's the way you feels about it, maybe we should just donate 'em all to the Missions. The missionaries could give 'em out to the Indians down in Peru. Anyway, how do you know this is not a temptation? Maybe the devil is tempting us."

Ronnie sighed. "Pauly, a pack or two of smokes left on a counter or poking out of your grandmother's purse is a temptation. This is *142* packs. In open boxes in your basement." Ronnie reached into a box and plucked out a pack of Rothman's. "Pauly, God does not believe in overkill. One hundred and forty-two packs of cigarettes—"

"Assorted," Gerard piped up.

Ronnie glared at him. "*Assorted* cigarettes, in cardboard boxes is not a temptation. It's a friggin' gift for God's sake."

Pauly went to the stairwell and looked up. "Well, I don't know . . ."

Ronnie paced around the basement. "Pauly, did you burn down Stan's Takeout?"

"Of course not."

"Did Gerard?"

"No."

"Did Nipper?"

"No."

"Did I?"

"Well . . ."

"Jesus Christ, Pauly, I did not burn down the friggin' takeout!"

"There's no need to curse," Pauly said.

Ronnie took a deep breath. He raised his clasped hands to his lips and stared at the ceiling just like Monsignor Murphy did before he elevated the chalice. He spoke very quietly. "Pauly, the way I see it is that God, in the form of an electrical short-circuit, burned down Stan's Takeout. And by so doing, delivered unto us 142 packs of—" he glanced at Gerard—"*assorted* cigarettes." Ronnie laid his hand on Pauly's shoulder. "So, what are we gonna do?"

They decided on twenty-five packs. Ronnie didn't want to take any Cameos or Matinees, but Pauly insisted they take a complete selection. "You just can't take all the Export "A"s and Rothman's," he said. "The old man'll know we were at 'em for sure. You got to take an assortment."

"All right, all *right*," Ronnie said. "We'll take the friggin'

Cameos and Matinees. Maybe we can give 'em away or sell 'em to the girls."

The next evening they smuggled the cigarettes out of the house and brought them down to Sheehan's loft, where they hid them in the rafters. Twenty-five packages. Assorted.

26

Coming out the Old Road from fishing, Nipper saw Brigid at the head of Shalloway Pond standing by her bike.

"Nicky, when did you start smoking?"

Nipper dropped the cigarette and stepped on it. "Oh, I don't smoke," he said. "Not really. Just every now and then." He looked at her bike. "What's the problem?"

"That," Brigid said, pointing to the rear wheel. She dropped to her knees and glared at the tangled bicycle chain. Nipper leaned forward and glimpsed the swelling of her small breasts, the skin pale, yet somehow glowing, her nipples hidden, pushed into the tightly woven fabric of her top.

She stood up and shook her head in mock despair. "*I* can't fix it," she said. "Can you?"

Nipper crouched down and shrugged. "No," he said. "The wheel's gonna have to come off."

"I better get Dad to take a look at it."

"Yeah."

Brigid wrinkled her dark brow and bent again over the bike.

"Brigid, how come you don't call me Nipper anymore?"

"Because it's not your name," she said. "Not your real name. It's just a nickname."

"Yeah, I know. But it's what everyone calls me. Well, everyone except Mom and Brendan . . . and you."

Brigid brushed back her hair and frowned. "I don't like it," she said. "It makes you sound like . . . like a mosquito." Then, quickly, she sprang forward, and her mouth was on his neck, high, below the left ear. Nipper felt the parting and pursing of her soft lips, the tip of her tongue—the bite of small teeth. He inhaled sharply. A tide of goosebumps flooded his body. From what seemed like a great distance, he heard her bicycle crash to the ground.

Brigid pulled away and looked at him mischievously, smiling with her moist, black eyes. Nipper raised a hand to his neck and blushed. Brigid's eyes crinkled with laughter, but she didn't blush. Nipper had heard that people with dark complexions never blushed—couldn't.

"Why did you do that?"

Brigid raised her shoulders high and dropped them. "I don't know." She reached down and picked up her bike. "I guess I just felt like it."

Nipper rubbed his neck and grinned. "You're crazy."

Brigid leaned against the bike and crossed her arms. "You have pretty eyes," she said. "Your lashes are like spiders' legs."

Nipper's face burned again. "Is that good?"

Brigid nodded. She began to push her bike down the road. "Sure," she said, looking over her shoulder. "That's good."

That night, as Nipper brushed his teeth, he examined the marks on his neck. Brigid had broken the skin only slightly, the jagged imprint barely perceptible. He stroked the scar. His body felt strangely hollow and unfamiliar—like the face that stared back from the mirror.

FOUR

27

Nipper Mooney started grade eight in September 1967, the last month of the "Summer of Love." His homeroom teacher was Brother Crane, who had just transferred to All Angels from St. Mark's, where he had been known as the toughest teacher in the school. When Crane first walked into the classroom, the boys immediately saw that his reputation was well-deserved. According to the grapevine, he had been a champion boxer, and his build and gait bore this out. Even when he strode to the blackboard, he hunched his shoulders and bobbed his head as if making for the centre of the ring to touch gloves with an opponent. But unlike other boxers, he never took off his fighting face.

Brother Crane taught all classes except Latin and French, and it probably wouldn't have made much difference if he'd taught those as well.

The Latin instructor, Brother Simms, was also new to the school. He was a flustered, moody man who usually sported a three-days' growth of beard. In spite of this, he always reeked of aftershave. Joe Barnes said that the aftershave wasn't soothing his face as much as it was fertilizing it. The face itself needed all the help it could get. The line of his chin jutted awkwardly toward the floor; his flat, squashed nose looked like something a child might have made out of playdough; his sleepy brown eyes had a weird way of gazing off in opposite directions. Simms might have been blown up in a war and not properly put back together. He told the class later in the year that he had been in a motorcycle accident: someone had opened a van door, and he crashed through it at fifty miles an hour. The boys thought it was cool that he had a motorcycle (the first Brother they'd ever heard of who had even taken a ride on one), but it also—perhaps unfairly, Nipper thought—made them sneer at him for being stupid enough to run into a van door.

Brother Simms hated Latin and made no effort to disguise his feelings. He knew very little more than his students, and probably not as much as some of the smarter ones. It was easy to trip him up. Nipper figured this out one day when Simms was coming around checking homework. Nipper had been taking the opportunity to finish an English composition. Somehow, he lost track of where Simms was, and he suddenly looked up to see the teacher reaching for his scribbler. Nipper was about to blurt out an excuse and hand him the Latin homework, but Simms was already busy with the English composition. After a moment he grunted approvingly, laid the scribbler back on Nipper's desk, ticked a red mark on it, and moved on.

Brother Patterson, the French teacher, wasn't much better. He was a short, rough character who also coached the soccer team. It was well known that, when he chaperoned the senior dances, he often separated couples if he thought they were getting too close. He was also famous for carrying a six-inch hunting knife in case, as he put it, "things got out of hand."

As a French teacher, the best that could be said for Patterson was that he made no pretence about his shortcomings. Unlike Simms, he didn't bother with conjugations and vocabulary. The textbook was never officially opened at all that year, although Nipper occasionally glanced through it to look at the pictures. One showed a group of girls in miniskirts taking photos of the Eiffel Tower; in another, a jovial French chef held up a tantalizing tray of pastries. As that class was just before lunch, Nipper found himself turning to the pastry photo more and more.

Because Brother Patterson didn't know any French, he came up with the odd notion of having the boys sing. This was especially odd because he knew less about singing than he did about French. He would bring a reel-to-reel tape recorder to class and hand out song sheets. The first time he did this, the boys groaned, anticipating some boring folk music in the "Frère Jacques" line. But the music turned out to be Québécois pop music performed by sultry female singers who dripped sexuality with every phrase. The class sang along phonetically, never having a clue as to what they were actually saying.

> *Des mots et des gestes, voila ce qu'il reste*
> *De ce grand amour, qui a trop duré*
> *Des mots et des gestes, voila ce qu'il reste*
> *De ce grand amour, qu'il faut oublier*

The worst thing was that, while Patterson was absolutely tone-deaf and completely lacking in rhythm, he still considered it his duty to stand before the class bellowing out the words in a flat St. John's brogue and waving his hands about like a demented traffic cop.

It was a strange way to spend forty minutes, and occasionally it got even stranger. Sometimes Patterson showed films. But the boys were not introduced to the cinema vérité or films about Québécois or French culture. Instead, they were treated to Donald Brittain's *Canada at War* series. Episode thirteen, "The Clouded Dawn," was Nipper's first introduction to Hitler's death camps, and he found the images of walking skeletons, and corpses being bulldozed into mass graves both repulsive and riveting. As handcuffed Nazi war criminals were led into the Nuremberg trials, the narrator matter-of-factly announced their crimes. One was accused of beating prisoners' testicles until the men died.

It wasn't French, but Nipper was certainly learning something.

In most ways Nipper Mooney's fellow students were typical. Many of them had been together since grade five, and some since kindergarten. In deference to their boxer-teacher, they were a little quieter than in previous years. The majority fell into the drone category: neither bright nor stupid, never too saucy, never too outspoken. They did their time stoically. Barnes experimented with clock-watching. He had seen a television show about telekinesis and had become convinced that, if he stared at the classroom clock long enough, and willed hard enough, he could speed up the hands. Nipper knew that was ridiculous, but he wished him luck all the same.

Larry Harvey, the class clown, could imitate all the Bugs Bunny cartoon characters with uncanny accuracy, and had used this talent in previous years to get out of scrapes. If he was called upon in class and didn't know the answer, he would make a joke in the voice of Foghorn Leghorn or Tweety Bird. The first and only time he tried this on Brother Crane, he was greeted with stony silence. Larry was reduced to entertaining the boys in the hallways and schoolyard. Joe Barnes, with his wacky notions and impulsive desire to comment on everything and anything, was next in line to the clown throne.

The resident tough guys were Ralph Picco and Danny Hickey. Both acquired their status mainly through appearance, reputation, and the fact that Picco hailed from the Brow and Hickey from Bond Street—areas of St. John's that often erupted into violent gang wars. Nipper had never seen either of them fight, and Hickey in particular seemed a rather gentle sort in spite of his scruffy exterior. Still, they obviously weren't the kind to tangle with.

Dean Williams, who sat behind Nipper, was the "brain."

Williams knew *everything*—not just the everyday academic information, which he generously served up in a bored monotone to anyone who might ask, but also a wide range of useless information and trivia: sports, politics, music. He could rhyme off the names of all three Supremes, and probably their middle names and birthdays if you really wanted to know. Williams was clearly bored by the whole useless exercise of school, and spent most of his time daydreaming or smirking at his bungling teachers.

Bob Dinn and Phil Smith were the token athletes. Both played second string on the junior hockey team, although Smith enjoyed greater status because he was also a spare on the basketball team.

And, as in most classes, there was a geek or "bird," as they were known at All Angels. His name was Darrell Wiggins.

28

*N*ipper had seen Darrell around the school ever since he'd come to All Angels in grade five, but he had never spoken to him. On the first day of grade eight Darrell was assigned the seat in front of him, and with Dean Williams sitting behind, Nipper found himself sandwiched between the intellectual extremes of the class.

This wasn't Darrell's first attempt at grade eight. He was two or three years older than the rest of the boys, but he looked much older. The tallest boy in the school and the skinniest person Nipper had ever seen, Darrell wore enormous horn-rimmed glasses, behind which his round head bobbed on a thin, stalk-like neck. His face was a startling combination of clashing colours: skin, milky white; buck teeth, a dirty canary yellow; nose, a bruised and splotchy red. When he had an outbreak of acne and flashed his cracked incisors, his face looked like a partridgeberry pancake sizzling in a frying pan. Nipper had never seen a sorrier case. At least God Love 'im Roy Driscoll had *looked* normal.

No matter what the season, Darrell was cursed with a perpetual cold. His nose was always running, and he constantly wiped it with a finger, the back of his hand, or, more rarely, a soiled handkerchief. Most of the boys were convinced he was dying. In science class that year they studied various diseases, and every time they came across a new one someone would whisper, "Maybe that's what Darrell got." Joe Barnes held it was a toss-up between scurvy and beriberi. He asked Darrell if he ever ate any fruit. Darrell grinned and said he liked potato chips.

"But you can't just live on chips," Barnes said. "You must eat other stuff."

"Oh, I eats other stuff," Darrell replied. But what that stuff might be he refused to say.

Perhaps the strangest thing about Darrell was his voice—an odd, hooting baritone that made Nipper think of a sick owl. When he spoke, he lowered his head as if addressing the floor, making it all the more difficult to understand him. Not that he talked much. During that whole year, he hardly spoke except to borrow a pencil or a sheet of paper—items he was continually without. He usually sat quietly, staring around with a vacant grin on his face like someone who had been saved by a missionary.

Nipper was surprised that the boys in the class didn't make fun of Darrell—at least not in the traditional way. They didn't call him names like Pimple Puss; didn't take his bookbag or try to trip him up. What they did was more subtle and much worse. Early on in the school year, Ralph Picco dubbed Darrell the class mascot. The rest of the class acted accordingly. They spoke to him like he was a six-year-old or a puppy. They reminded him in the cloakroom at the end of the day to zipper up his parka so he wouldn't catch cold. They checked to make sure he had the proper books for his homework—even though he never did any homework as far as anyone could see. They told him to watch out for the cars.

Brother Crane's first order of business for the new school year was the attendance. When he called Darrell's name, he paused. "So, Mr. Wiggins, you're back for another year, are you?" Darrell grinned nervously and stood up. "You don't need to stand, Mr. Wiggins." Darrell sank back in his seat and fidgeted with his pencil. Crane poised a pen over the register. "Well?"

"What's that, Burr?" Darrell said.

"Brother Bannister tells me you're gracing grade eight with your presence for a . . . *third* time, I understand?"

"Yes, Burr."

"Going to pass this year, are you?"

"I dunno, Burr."

"You don't know? That's not a very positive attitude. Sure you're after sitting through all this stuff so many times now you should be able to sing it."

"Yes, Burr," Darrell said.

Nipper sensed that Crane didn't have much use for Darrell. He didn't have much use for any of the boys if it came to that, but Darrell was a special case. Crane seemed to be waiting for him to slip up, and Darrell seemed eager to oblige. The first time Darrell failed a test or didn't know a history date, Crane merely crossed his arms and glared. But this soon degenerated into taking his test paper, crumpling it into a ball, and flinging it at him. Then, in the third week of school, Darrell became the first in the class to meet Crane's personal strap.

While the Brothers did not, as Mona had suggested, wear straps down the sides of their soutanes, there was an official school strap—the very one Nipper had been introduced to in grade five with Blondie and Smoker. All of the boys were well acquainted with it. Traditionally known as the Black Doctor, it was twelve inches of glossy, plastic-like material that looked as if it had something to do with plumbing. It had hung on Bannister's office wall for years. Perhaps Crane had doubts about its efficiency, because after he had taken the attendance on the first day of class, he dipped into his briefcase, took out a long, white strap, and held it up for the class's inspection. He had constructed it himself out of linoleum and electrical tape and christened it with a boxer-like nickname: the White Bomber. As the year progressed, the boys found that most of the other teachers preferred it to the Black Doctor. This pleased Brother Crane no end. Regularly, there would be a tap on the door, and some sheepish boy would mumble that Brother so-and-so had "sent me for the strap, Burr." Crane would reach into the top left-hand drawer of his desk, take out the White Bomber, and bring it to the boy. Or he might make the boy come in and get it himself, and the culprit would stand before the class, embarrassed and trembling, while Crane pressed him for the details of his crime. There was a predictable uniformity to the replies: "Talking, Burr." "Didn't do me homework, Burr." "Pipped off, Burr." "Was copyin' Burr."

Darrell Wiggins was known for missing a lot of days, and, in spite of the fact that he lived close by on Saintsbury Place, for always being late. His mumbled reply when asked to explain his tardiness never varied: "I just left the house, Burr." When absent, he usually said he'd been sick, and, as far as Nipper was concerned, it was hard to argue with him: Darrell looked like someone close to death at the best of times.

In mid-October, Darrell missed three days in a row, and returned just in time to get back his latest math quiz. Crane moved up and down the aisles dispensing the test papers, nodding at this one, grunting at the next. When he reached Darrell, he stopped, studied the paper silently, and then slapped it down on his desk with such force that Nipper jumped. He risked a quick peek: 15 percent. Darrell had made only 8 percent on the previous quiz, so Nipper thought he was doing well. But Crane was not impressed. He executed an abrupt about-face, marched quickly to the front of the class, and sat on the edge of his desk. "You cannot expect to pass, Mr. Wiggins," he said slowly, "if you refuse to come to school."

"I was—"

"Yes, I know. You were sick." Crane reached across the desk and pulled the White Bomber out of the drawer. "Come here, Mr. Wiggins."

Darrell stood up, but didn't move.

"I said . . . come here." Darrell refused to budge. Crane

pursed his lips and looked at him coolly. "Don't make me come down there." Darrell peered at Crane and glanced around the room as if sizing up all possible avenues of escape. Then he wiped his nose on his sleeve and shuffled up to the front of the class.

Darrell towered over Brother Crane. He swayed slightly from side to side as if blown by a strong wind. Crane grasped the White Bomber tightly in both hands. He sighed and shook his head. Teacher and pupil looked at each other. "Hold out your hand," Crane said. Nipper glanced across the aisle at Barnes. Their eyes said the same thing: *If Crane straps Darrell with any force at all, he'll probably kill him. Doesn't he know Darrell's got scurvy or something?*

Darrell rubbed his hand on his leg and brought it, shaking and jerking, up to shoulder level. "A little lower, please," Crane said. He straightened Darrell's hand, raised the strap high over his head, and brought it down with a loud grunt.

Darrell yanked his hand away. The strap sliced through the air and slapped viciously against Crane's leg.

Nipper felt it. Barnes felt it. *Everyone* felt it. Crane certainly felt it. He buckled over and grabbed his leg. "You bastard!" he gasped.

"Jesus!" Barnes said. "Crane said 'bastard'!"

Darrell looked on in horror as Crane groaned and clutched at his leg. Then Darrell twisted around three times in tight circles, like some clownish figure skater executing camel spins. He looked around wildly, ran to the door and bolted down the hall.

He didn't come back for another three days. Nipper was surprised he came back at all. On the morning he returned, he spent a long time in the office with Crane and Bannister. Nipper didn't know what they said or did to him, but when Darrell came in and took his seat, he was trembling and even paler than usual.

But if Bannister and Crane expected Darrell to change his ways, they were mistaken. As the weather grew colder, Darrell's tardiness and absenteeism increased. After he had missed a day a couple of weeks before the Christmas holidays, Crane waited for the bell, closed the door, and sat on his desk.

"Where were you yesterday, Darrell?" he asked.

Darrell stood up awkwardly. "Home, Burr."

"Home? *Home?* Oh, you were sick again, were you?"

"No, Burr."

Crane took off his glasses, rubbed the bump between his eyebrows, and waited.

"The storm, Burr," Darrell blurted, shifting his weight from one foot to the other. "Because of the storm."

A titter ran through the class.

"Because of the . . . " and here Crane paused and looked at the boys in wonder to verify that he had heard the word correctly. "Because of the . . . *storm*, Darrell?"

"Yes, Burr."

"There was a storm yesterday?" Crane said. "I remember it snowed yesterday for a while. But I don't remember a storm." Crane suddenly wheeled around and pointed at Nipper. "Mooney, were you in school yesterday?" Was he in school? Of course, he'd been in school. Crane had given him two on each hand with the White Bomber for failing a science quiz.

"Yes, Burr, I was here."

"And where do you live?"

"Kildura, Burr."

"How far is Kildura from here?"

"I dunno. Five, six miles?"

"Five miles. Yes, I'd say that was a good estimate." Crane stepped toward Darrell, who jabbed at his dripping nose with a bony finger. His nervous shuffle stepped up a notch. "Nipper Mooney came to school yesterday, Darrell, all the way from

Kildura. The storm didn't stop him—and sure he's only a little runt." The class erupted into laughter, which immediately shrank, but then flared like a bonfire when they saw that Crane would let it run its course. "And you know something else, Darrell? I bet you any money that, if I went across the street to St. Anne's, those good Sisters would tell me that all their little girls managed to get to school yesterday, too. Girls, Darrell. *Girls.*" Crane moved closer to him. "Now, Darrell, you're not a girl, are you?"

"No, Burr."

"You're sure, now? You don't sit down to pee, do you?"

More laughter from the class.

"No, Burr."

"Well, I'm glad to hear it." Crane leaned up against his desk. He pinched his lower lip. "Darrell, where do you live?"

"Saintsbury Place, Burr."

"But you're no . . . *saint*, Darrell, are you?" The class laughed dutifully. Darrell stared at the floor. "Yes, Darrell," Crane said, "you live on Saintsbury Place. In fact, I know your house. And you know something, Darrell? I believe I could walk from here to Saintsbury Place in oh . . . five minutes. In fact, I'm sure I could." Crane stared hard at Darrell. "Couldn't I?"

For the first time Darrell stood perfectly still. He offered no response except to insert the index finger of his right hand into his ear. He withdrew the finger, wiped it on the leg of his flannel trousers, and looked at Crane.

"Prob'ly."

"No, Darrell, not probably," Crane said. "*Definitely.* I definitely could. Darrell, you know, if I went out to the schoolyard, I believe I could throw a rock from here down to your house. Think so?"

Darrell's nose-flicking and shuffling resumed; his pointy Adam's apple rose and fell.

"Prob—"

Crane stepped toward him.

Darrell paused and resumed his shuffle. "Definitely," he said.

"That's right," Crane said softly. "I definitely could." Darrell sat down and opened his exercise book. "I didn't tell you to sit." Darrell bounced back up. "First row, stand up," Crane said, looking all the while at Darrell. The boys obeyed uneasily, glancing around the room at each other. Was the bastard going to punish the whole class just because Darrell didn't have enough sense to come to school? "Out to the cloakroom—*quietly*—and get your coats and boots on," Crane said. "Move. Second row," he said, waving them on. "No talking."

"Where do you think we're goin'?" Barnes whispered to Nipper as they put on their coats. "Holy Rosary?"

"Nah. It's Friday, but it's not the first of the month."

"Is it some holy day or something?"

"I don't think so."

"Arts and Culture Centre?"

Nipper shrugged. "I dunno."

When the boys were bundled up, Crane led them down the hall, past the trophy cases jammed with tarnished, dented trophies, down the steps and out the ground-level door. They assembled, shivering already, under the basketball net.

"Now," Crane said, "we're going on a long, difficult mission. It's going to be dangerous, and some of you may not make it back."

The boys looked at each other. Barnes stuck up his hand. "Where to, Burr? Arts and Culture Centre? To look at the paintings?" Barnes loved the Arts and Culture Centre because he had once seen an exhibition of nudes there. "No," Crane said. "But Darrell knows. Where we going, Darrell?"

Darrell looked around in a daze. "I dunno, Burr."

ED KAVANAGH

"Well, you should, Darrell. It's a journey you've been known to undertake yourself—on occasion." Crane paused. "We're going to your house." Darrell swallowed and bit his lower lip. "What for, Burr? There's no one home. Mom's gone to work."

"That's all right. I don't want to talk to her." He looked around at the boys. "Now stick together and no loud talking." Then he added wryly, "Conserve your strength." Crane studied his watch. "It's twenty-five after nine." He looked steadily at Darrell. "You take the lead."

Darrell moved awkwardly to the front of the pack, and the class headed across the icy schoolyard. Darrell shuffled along on his long legs, the hood of his parka tied tightly around his chin, his red idiot mitts pulled halfway up his forearms, his buck-teeth yellow against the sparkling snow.

They proceeded past the monastery, continued beyond the courtyard statue of the Archangel Gabriel, down the lane, and out the chain-link gates to Gardiner Street. The scent of fresh bread from Madden's Bakery hung on the cold air. Nipper looked at his watch: nine twenty-seven. The line of boys curled lazily onto the sidewalk. Crane halted them in front of Bill Bowen's barbershop.

There was little traffic on Gardiner Street at that time of the morning. Crane walked into the middle of the street, looked up and down, and waved the boys across. They turned into Saintsbury Place. The street was dotted with dented garbage cans. At least half had been knocked over by dogs and cats. Libby's bean tins and twisted egg cartons spilled onto the street. They gathered at number 12, a yellow, peeling row house. The boys bunched on the sidewalk and overflowed into the street, but it didn't matter: Saintsbury Place was a dead end.

"Halt, men," Crane said loudly. "You, too, Darrell," he added. Ralph Picco laughed, but most of the other boys only managed a grin.

An old woman in the adjoining house pulled back the curtain from an upstairs window and looked down. Nipper could see her lips moving and, a moment later, a man joined her. They stared curiously. Crane pulled his sleeve back theatrically and peered at his watch. He raised his eyebrows at Darrell. "Well, Darrell, I was wrong. It didn't take five minutes after all; it took three. Three and a half, if you want to get picky."

Darrell didn't say anything. He wiped his nose on the back of his mitt and stared at the sidewalk.

29

*A*s Nipper walked along the crowded corridor one January morning, he glimpsed someone ahead of him, a stranger. Perhaps it was a teacher, a substitute. But then he saw long, red hair and decided it was a woman. It occurred to him that, with the exception of Miss Jackson—who was about eighty and didn't really count—he had never seen a woman in All Angels before. There was something peculiar about the way she moved, and he suddenly realized it wasn't a woman at all; it was definitely a male. Brother Bannister had visited Nipper's class the day before and announced that a new student would be joining them. Where the boy came from, or why he was starting school so late, he didn't say. "You will make him welcome," he'd ordered. Perhaps this was that boy.

Everyone turned and stared as he passed. Nipper lost him momentarily in a throng of jostling grade sevens, but then, sure enough, he saw that he'd stopped outside Nipper's classroom door. He looked behind the door, checked the number and disappeared into the room. Nipper found him in the cloakroom hanging up his coat. The boy felt someone behind him and turned around. He was about sixteen, with freckles, a broad nose, and a thick, muscular body.

It was Paddy Dunne.

"Jesus," Paddy said. "Look who it is."

He pulled a black plastic comb out of his back pocket and ran it through his long hair. He was wearing a short-sleeved shirt, and, as he preened, Nipper could see the muscles rippling in his forearm and its fine covering of blond hair. There was hair above his upper lip, too—not exactly a mustache, but close.

Nipper hadn't seen Paddy since Rosarie's funeral. He didn't know what to say.

"What are you starin' at?" Paddy said. His voice was softly gruff. The tone suggested that he wasn't much interested in the reasons for Nipper's staring; it was just the most appropriate thing to say at that moment. For Nipper's part, there were so many interesting things about Paddy that, if he'd attempted a truthful answer, he wouldn't have known where to begin. Well, no: he would have begun with his hair. Paddy's hair had always been long, but this was different. It looked very out of place. After all, the boys from All Angels supported three barbershops within minutes of the school. Most of them visited one of the Bowen brothers at least once a month, where many were given the All Angels special: a brush cut flat enough to land model airplanes on. Nipper wondered what Brother Crane would have to say about Paddy's hair. A few nights before, Nipper had seen an item on TV about recruits for the Vietnam war. The young men, many with shoulder-length locks, were shown lining up for the army barbers. They folded their arms and watched grimly as the clippers buzzed over the heads of their comrades already in the chairs. In a short while, all of the recruits stood around in their singlets looking very bald, very embarrassed, and very much the same. Nipper wondered how long it would take before something like that happened to Paddy.

Next would have to be his school uniform—or, more precisely, his lack of school uniform. At All Angels the boys wore grey flannel trousers, a black blazer with the school crest, a white shirt (long-sleeved), a school tie and, preferably, black shoes. The best that could be said for Paddy was that he was wearing *parts* of the uniform. Nipper had noticed his short sleeves because he was not wearing a blazer. A school tie hung loosely around his neck, but it was much too small for him. His pants were indeed grey, but made from some thick, jean-like material. And, when he slipped off his gaiters, Nipper saw a pair of faded black sneakers.

All of this Nipper noted and marvelled at. But the thing that struck him most was how much Paddy had grown. He wasn't a boy at all anymore. He was a man.

"Well, what are you starin' at?" he said again, wiping the comb on his pant leg.

"Oh, nothin'." As Nipper took off his coat and hung it up, Barnes and Bob O'Grady tumbled into the cloakroom laughing and lightly pummelling each other. They pulled up abruptly and stared at the stranger.

Paddy rolled his eyes, picked up his battered school books, and went out into the classroom. The other boys stopped what they were doing and looked him up and down. "Any extra desks?" he asked. Nipper saw that the question was directed at him. It wasn't a very complicated question, but for some reason it seemed to overwhelm him.

"What?"

"Any extra *desks*," he repeated. "Shit, have I got to be saying everything twice?"

"Desks? Oh yeah," Nipper said, pointing to the last one in Barnes's row. "No one sits there."

Paddy sauntered down the aisle, swung himself into the desk, and began to lazily unpack his books. This task accomplished, he stuck out his legs and clasped his hands behind his head.

Paddy looked at Nipper curiously. "So what's the teacher like?"

"Crane? He makes Sister Mary Ignatius look like a saint." Nipper grinned. "Remember her?"

Paddy shook back his long hair. "I remembers the old battleaxe. She still there?"

"Yeah," Nipper said. "My mom says she'll be like Monsignor Murphy—they'll never be able to shift her."

Paddy sat up. "You still go up the Old Road?"

"Sure. All the time."

"Got the place fished out, have you?"

"No. No need to worry about that."

"How's old Brendan? He still go up there?"

Nipper nodded. "Yeah. Not as much as he used to. He's slowin' down a bit. But I still see him."

Paddy settled back in his desk. "Tell him I said hello."

"Sure."

"I'll probably be gettin' a car soon," Paddy said. "I'll take a run up and see him myself. Do some fishing."

"Well, you know all the good spots."

Paddy grinned. "Yeah."

Nipper slipped into the opposite desk and shook his head in disbelief. "Jesus, Paddy, what are you *doin'* here?"

Paddy sat up and sighed. "Good friggin' question."

The bell rang, and Brother Crane strode into the classroom. He looked at Paddy silently, took out his register, and motioned him to the front of the class. As they stood talking, the boys watched and waited for a confrontation. They made an incongruous pair: Crane with his black soutane and shiny white collar, his short hair neatly parted and fastidiously greased and combed; Paddy with his bastardized school uniform and unruly red locks spilling far down over his collar.

But, for some reason, Crane chose not to notice. Paddy went back to his seat, seemingly oblivious to the thirty pairs of eyes that followed him. They had prayers, and when Crane called the roll, he gave Paddy a quick introduction. Then the class carried on just like it was an ordinary day.

.   .   .

That night Aunt Mona drove in for supper. As Sharon was pouring the tea, Nipper said, "You'll never guess who joined my class today. Paddy Dunne."

Mona widened her eyes in surprise. "I knew he was going to be at All Angels," she said. "But I didn't think he'd be in your class. Isn't he supposed to be in grade . . . what? Ten?"

"Yeah," Nipper said. "Maybe even eleven. How did you—"

"That's a sin, putting him back to grade eight. Course, they did the same thing to him at St. Brigid's. Well, you can only hope they know what they're up to."

"How did you know he was going to be at All Angels?" Nipper asked.

Sharon laughed. "My son, there's nothing going on in St. John's, now, that Mona don't know about."

"Millie Foran," Mona said, "in my card club. She knows Paddy's father—Stephen. She told us about it one night. She said Paddy was at Our Lady of Victory—at least that's where he started in September. Anyway, he got into trouble over his hair. Is it really long or something?"

Nipper nodded. "Pretty long. Probably the longest in the whole school."

"Well, they told him to cut it, and of course he wouldn't. Said he'd quit first. So they suspended him for a while."

"Yes," Sharon said. "It was a week or more, I believe."

Nipper looked at his mother in surprise. "How do *you* know?"

"Oh, I got my contacts, too. But I didn't know he was going to end up in your class."

"Why didn't you tell me he was coming to All Angels?"

"I was going to. Besides, I figured you'd run into him sooner or later. He's kind of hard to miss."

"*Any*way," Mona said, "Paddy said he wasn't going back—was gonna try for a job on the waterfront. Longshoreman. He got an uncle, I believe, who's a longshoreman. What's his uncle's name, Sharon?"

"Frank. They went to live with him after the fire."

"That's right—Frank. On his mother's side, he is. Stephen, of course, wanted Paddy to stick it out in school. Told him that if he didn't he'd end up on a garbage truck just like he did. Pleaded with him, apparently. But Paddy said there was no way he was going back to Our Lady. Said all they did there was crucify him. Anyway, Stephen knew one of the Brothers at All Angels, and he managed to get him in there."

"Which Brother?" Nipper asked.

"Oh, my God, what's his name . . . Devine. Brother Devine." Mona laughed. "Good name for a Brother when you think about it."

Nipper nodded. "He's one of the nice ones. I had him in grade five. He's a bit nuts, though."

"What do you mean?" Sharon said. "I thought you liked him."

"I do like him. But he used to do weird stuff. Like once he was teaching us about the Holy Trinity—you know, how it's three persons but still only one God? Well, a bunch of fellas couldn't understand it, so he told us to think about it like a hockey team. Like the Montreal Canadiens."

"Like a *what*?" Mona said.

"Like a hockey team. God was the owner, and Jean Beliveau was Jesus. Beliveau was a player, but he was the coach, too. I can't remember who the Holy Ghost was—the referee, I think. Brother Devine said that Jean Beliveau, Jesus, was a great player who everyone looked up to. He always did the right thing, but he was still capable of getting a penalty every now and then—you know, like a real human being. I can't remember how he put it exactly. It was kind of confusing. Joe Barnes asked if the Toronto Maple Leafs would be like, you know, the Philistines—"

"*Any*way," Mona said, "this Brother Devine pulled a few strings. Him and Stephen had a meeting with the principal. What's his name again?"

"Bannister," Nipper said.

"That's right, Bannister. They talked him into letting Paddy go to All Angels. Well, I suppose it was Brother Devine who did most of the talking. You could hardly ever get two words out of Stephen. Bannister said it was okay for him to come for the time being, but Paddy was on 'probation.' The first sign of trouble and he was out. And he was going to have to get around to sprucin' himself up, too. At least a bit."

Nipper could well imagine that part of Bannister's speech: *You must understand my position, Mr. Dunne. If I permit one student to come to school like that, then the others will claim the same privilege. And that I cannot have. But for now we'll see how he makes out.*

"So he's in your class," Mona said. "Small world. That must be some hard on him all the same. He must feel like a sore thumb stuck in there with all the grade eights. How's he making out?"

"All right," Nipper said. "So far, anyway."

Nipper had thought that, with the addition of Paddy Dunne to his class, things might liven up. But they didn't; not at first. Except for his hair, no one took much notice of him. In most ways Paddy was a model student. He sat silently at the back of the room and at least went through the motions. He seemed to have lost his outspokenness. Nipper wondered if Sister Mary Ignatius and his other teachers had succeeded in squeezing it out of him. Perhaps he just couldn't be bothered anymore.

The class carried on with their routine of mangling French songs with Brother Patterson, mixing up the dative and accusative cases with Brother Simms, and doing their best to stay on the good side of Brother Crane. One afternoon Crane was called to the office. When he came back, he pushed open the door and glared into the classroom.

"Who was talking?"

No one looked up.

"Was that you, Barnes?"

"No, Burr."

"Then who?"

Silence.

"No one? We've got ghosts in the classroom, do we? Phantoms?" Crane slumped against his desk. "Well, you're all nice and quiet now," he said. "Quiet as the dead. Apparently, it's at least *possible* for you to shut up. Too bad you can only do it when it suits you." Crane stood up. "I'm going to ask you one more time: Who was talking?"

Silence. Nipper ran a finger along the top of his science book.

"I'm running out of patience," Crane said. He reached into his desk drawer and pulled out the White Bomber.

Thirty pairs of eyes stared down at their desks.

Crane sighed. "You're all sticking together on this, are you?" He sucked his teeth. "Okay, if that's the way you want it: fine. First row, stand up. Mr. Power, you can have the honour of warming up the strap for the rest of them."

Power grimaced and glanced around the room. He got up and walked down to Crane. He offered his hand.

The boys watched. How many would it be? How hard?

Crane swung.

Shit, Nipper thought. Three on each hand: medium to heavy.

As Nipper waited, he glanced at Paddy Dunne, who seemed more bored than anything else. And then it was Darrell's turn.

He shuffled to the front, flicking at his dripping nose. As he offered up his hand, his whole body shook. Paddy frowned and looked out the window.

The boys filed, row by row, to the front of the class. Now Paddy stood before Crane. No one had ever seen him being strapped before. He put out his hand nonchalantly, as if he expected Crane to read his palm rather than strike it. Crane didn't look Paddy in the face. He dealt out the blows in a mechanical, businesslike manner. Paddy didn't flinch. When the sixth blow had fallen, he remained standing with his hand still outstretched. "That's it, Mr. Dunne," Crane said. "You can go now." Paddy stared straight at Crane for a moment, the hint of a smile flickering on his lips. He turned and went back to his seat.

"That fucker," Barnes said, when they were putting on their coats after school. "That's not one bit fair, you know."

"Yeah," Nipper said. "Anyway, at least it's not as bad as the friggin' shoulder-pinching. That's what I hates." Nipper had always wondered about shoulder-pinching. Perhaps it was a course the Brothers had to take in the seminary. It was the one thing that just about all of them did. And with Crane, it always happened the same way.

Nipper is reading quietly. Crane stops by his desk. Nipper closes his eyes and prays for him to move on. And sometimes, sometimes he does. But if not, a piercing pain shoots through his shoulder as Crane digs his fingers deeply into the muscle, pinching the nerve.

"What's that for, Burr?" Nipper moans, attempting to squirm out of his grasp. "I wasn't doin' nothin'."

"That's for doing nothing. Imagine what'll happen if you *do* something."

In Nipper's class, only Darrell and Paddy were spared.

"Why do you think he doesn't pinch Darrell?" Nipper asked.

"Too friggin' skinny," Barnes said. "Crane probably wouldn't even be able to *find* his muscle."

Nipper shook his head. "Maybe. But I'd say he just don't want to touch him. I wouldn't."

"Yeah," Barnes said, "I never thought of that."

But why he left Paddy alone they couldn't say.

Ralph Picco also left Paddy alone. From the moment Paddy had first arrived, Ralph hadn't said a word to him. Nipper could tell that Ralph didn't relish the prospect of losing his "toughest guy" status to a hippie. Not that Paddy made any attempt to usurp him. He'd never said a word to Ralph, either. Still, it must have played on Ralph's mind. Nipper often saw him glancing at Paddy, attempting to size him up.

One morning in the washroom Nipper heard Ralph talking to Barry Kerrivan, a tough guy from one of the other grade eight classes. "Dunne's like one of them mutes—never opens his gob," Ralph said. "And he should get a haircut. He looks like a fucking caveman or something." Kerrivan laughed, Ralph's eyes lit up, and soon Paddy was known all over the school as "Caveman" Dunne.

Nipper had to admit that, in some ways, it was a good nickname. With his heavy build, broad face and long hair, Paddy did look a bit like a caveman. No one, of course, not even Ralph Picco, had the nerve to call him that to his face, and for a while Nipper wondered if Paddy was even aware of it. But Picco took the communal use of the nickname as a victory for himself, a consolidation of his position.

The other tough guy in the class, Danny Hickey, didn't seem to take much interest in these matters, but Nipper heard him talking to Ralph while they were fooling around in the gym one day. Danny told Ralph he had it all wrong. If he was worried about Paddy Dunne being considered a harder case than he was, then he should never have dubbed him "Caveman."

"Why not?" Picco said.

"Think about it. Makes him sound like a boxer or a wrestler or something."

"Like a *wrestler?*"

"Sure," Danny said. "Just picture it: In this corner, Mad Dog Vachon. In this corner . . . Caveman Dunne."

Picco tilted his head and squinted his eyes. "Are you telling me," he said, "that everyone is calling him Caveman because they thinks he's tough, and not because they thinks he's just, you known, *dumb?*"

"I dunno," Hickey said. But Nipper could tell that he did know, and that was exactly what he thought.

"Fuck," Picco said, scowling.

Ralph Picco turned to Darrell in the cloakroom after school one day and gave him a playful punch on the arm. "How's it goin', Elvis?" His failure with Paddy's nickname hadn't stopped him from christening Darrell with that one.

Darrell winced but managed a grin. "Fine, Ralph," he mumbled.

"That's good, Elvis. You got a date tonight, or what?" Everyone laughed. Darrell grinned again and bent down to pull on his gaiters. "Oh, I knows you, Elvis," Ralph said. "You probably got a dozen women lined up just waiting for you." He gave Darrell another punch. "Don't you, now?"

"Not me," Darrell mumbled, his skinny neck blushing scarlet.

"What? You mean you don't even have *one* girlfriend," Ralph said. "I finds that hard to believe—good-lookin' fella like you."

"No, I got no girlfriend," Darrell said, straightening up and digging his mitts out of his coat pocket.

"G'wan, Darrell. You just wants to keep 'em all for yourself now, don't you? And here's poor old Ralph dyin' for a piece o' tail. Jesus, Darrell, I thought you were my buddy. Well, all right for you."

Darrell picked up his bookbag and started for the door. Ralph stepped in front of him. "No, Darrell, you're not goin' nowhere—not until you gives me the name and phone number of one of them hot pieces you knows."

Darrell grinned weakly and attempted to push past Ralph.

"Well, I never knew you were that greedy," Ralph said, looking around and winking. "You wants to keep all that pussy for yourself, don't ya?" Ralph caught Bob O'Grady's eye and motioned him to the door to watch for teachers.

"Leave 'im alone, Ralph, for fuck sake," Danny Hickey said. "He wouldn't know a pussy if he tripped and fell headfirst into one."

"That true, Elvis?" Ralph said. "I bet you'd love to get some nice hot pussy, wouldn't you?"

Darrell pushed forward; Ralph stepped in front of him.

Suddenly everything went dead quiet. Nipper turned and saw Paddy standing in the doorway. "Leave 'im alone, Picco."

Ralph glanced quickly at Hickey, then raised his eyebrows at Paddy. "What's buggin' you?" he said. "We're only havin' a bit o' fun."

"Go on home out of it, Darrell," Paddy said. Darrell glanced uneasily at Ralph, then pushed his way out through the crowd.

Paddy watched Darrell leave. He turned and reached for his coat. The boys waited for Ralph to say something, but he remained silent. Once again, they started talking and skylarking. And then came a cold, bald statement: "It's none of your fucking business anyway." All sound died in the cloakroom as abruptly as if the plug had been pulled from a stereo. Paddy stood before his coat hook with his back to Ralph. He zipped up his jacket and sighed, raising his shoulders high on the intake of breath, letting them fall on the exhalation. Ralph stared at him with narrowed eyes, his fists clenching and unclenching. Paddy turned around slowly and looked Ralph up and down. He stepped toward him, shook back his hair, and folded his arms.

"You know, Picco, you thinks Darrell is nothin' but a poor fuckin' retard, don't you?" He leaned forward and pushed his face close to Ralph's. "And maybe he is. But at least he's not a prize arsehole like you." Ralph swore and stepped back; a muscle twitched in his cheek. He glowered at Paddy, then glanced quickly at Hickey, who shrugged. Ralph turned back to Paddy, then looked around at the rest of the boys. Suddenly, Ralph grabbed his coat off the hook and put it on. Paddy watched him for a moment, then headed for the door.

Ralph wheeled around. "Fuck you, Caveman," he said to Paddy's back. "I'm not scared o' you."

Paddy stopped. He turned around slowly and looked at Ralph. Paddy's body flinched, then tensed. A flush started at his shirt collar and crept up his face. "What did you call me?"

Ralph paused and blinked. "You heard me. I said I'm not scared o' you."

"I don't give a fuck if you're scared of me or not. I asked you what you *called* me."

Once more Ralph looked at Hickey. "Don't be lookin' at him," Paddy said. "He got fuck all to do with it. What did you call me?"

Ralph rubbed his fingers over his lips.

"You gonna answer me?" Paddy said.

Ralph looked at him, then turned away. "I never called you nothin'," he said stiffly. He picked up his books and walked quickly to the door.

Paddy stepped into the doorway and pushed an open palm into Ralph's chest, pulling him up straight. "You listen to me good now," he said. "If you call me that again, or fuck with me—or with Darrell—I'm gonna have to give you a good knockin'. Got it?"

Ralph stared at him. Then, almost imperceptibly, he nodded. Paddy dropped his hand. Ralph pushed past him and disappeared down the corridor.

Paddy watched him go, then looked around at the rest of the boys. "And that goes for ye, too."

30

Nipper was wondering what Paddy Dunne was writing with his special pen. As soon as Brother Crane had announced the silent period, Paddy had taken the pen from his shirt pocket, screened his paper with his arm, and begun to write. He lost himself totally in the work.

The bell rang, startling him.

A sheet blew off his desk and floated across the aisle. Nipper picked it up and looked at it with surprise. Paddy had been copying something from the history book, but what amazed Nipper was that the handwriting was the most beautiful he had ever seen—rhythmic and flowing, each letter perfectly formed and connecting effortlessly with the next. And there was more. The margins were covered with tiny, graceful drawings: unicorns, centaurs and fish. Nipper became so absorbed in the paper that Paddy reached over and pulled it out of his hand. Nipper wanted to tell him how impressed he was, but Paddy's pursed lips and flushed cheeks warned him not to say anything.

Still, before class in the afternoon, Nipper went up to him. "Did you have to learn how to do that stuff, or can you, you know, just *do* it?"

"What?"

"That fancy writing and drawing."

"There's nothin' to that," Paddy said shortly. "I just fools around with it when I got nothin' better to do." He glanced around the classroom. "You don't need to be tellin' anyone about it, either."

"Why?" Nipper said. "I wouldn't mind knowin' how to do that."

"I *said* . . . keep it to yourself."

Even though Paddy showed no signs of improving his uniform or cutting his hair, there was no showdown with Crane. This was a source of mystery and debate in the class. The boys had seen their teacher strap a student for something as insignificant as a missing school tie. The poorest boy in the class, Gerry Bowering, always wore sneakers because his family couldn't afford winter boots for him. On snowy or rainy days Crane made him take off the wet sneakers. One day the water had soaked right through to Bowering's socks. When Crane came into class and saw the wet sock prints on the floor, he glared at Gerry and pulled out the White Bomber.

"Come here, Mr. Bowering."

Two on each hand: medium to hard.

Barnes suggested that maybe Crane was afraid of Paddy. Nipper found that hard to believe, but as the days wore on, he began to wonder.

He also wondered why Paddy had such a hard time with his school work. Every time a marked paper was returned, he would look at it uneasily before turning it over to see the grade. Sometimes he didn't bother to look at all.

One lunch hour, as they walked up Prince Street, Nipper said, "Hey, Joe, why do you think Paddy Dunne always gets put back?"

"Because he fails," Barnes said.

"Yeah, I know that. But why?"

Barnes shrugged. "I guess he's just a bit stunned."

"But he don't *sound* stunned. I mean he's not like Darrell. And sure when he's asked something, he knows the answer—well, some of the time, anyway. I mean, he knows as many answers as I do."

"I dunno," Barnes said. "Maybe he just don't study."

"Yeah," Nipper said. "Maybe. Hey, you know something else about him?"

"What?"

"He's really good at . . . "

"What?"

"Oh, ah . . . fishin'. He's a really good fisherman, Paddy is. When he lived up by us—you should have seen the trout he used to catch."

After Paddy's run-in with Ralph Picco, the boys were extra careful whenever Paddy was around. Darrell didn't know what to make of his new-found freedom. He seemed pleased to be rid of unwanted attention, but he couldn't figure out why he was suddenly being ignored. But, if his classmates consented to leave him alone, Brother Crane did not.

Nipper didn't know why Darrell had never picked up the basic All Angels survival skills. When Darrell was summoned to the front of the class for a strapping, the rest of the boys would roll their eyes and settle in for yet another drawn-out scene. Just about everyone was afraid of the White Bomber, but Darrell's terror embarrassed them. Nipper had taken a lesson from the confessional. He had long since learned that the best way to get through a strapping was to offer your hand, grit your teeth, and get it over with as quickly as possible. When you got back to your seat, it helped to sit on your hands. There was really no way to guard against tears, although Crane would usually have to dispense at least ten of his medium-to-heavy blows to make most of the boys cry. There was little shame in it. Nipper knew that, if Crane really wanted to, he could make anyone cry, Picco and Hickey included.

But Darrell had never mastered the short, quick, let's-get-this-over-with approach. Brother Crane had learned to be careful when using the White Bomber on Darrell. Their encounters had evolved into a painful black comedy. Crane watched in exasperation as Darrell began his ritualistic dance: he shifted his weight from one foot to the other like someone in urgent need of the bathroom; he swallowed and wiped his lips with his bony fingers; he ran his hands incessantly up and down his rumpled blazer. All this served to put Crane into an even nastier state of mind. When he finally swung, he struck like he might not get another chance.

One morning, after a strapping, Darrell made his way slowly back to his seat. His yellow teeth were locked in a rigid grimace, his eyes clenched shut, but tears still leaked down to his pimply chin. Nipper had never seen him in such a state.

There had been something different about the strapping. It had even sounded different. During lunch, Barnes and Nipper made Darrell show them his hands. His fingertips were cut and bleeding, the undersides of his forearms swollen with purple and red welts.

When Paddy came into the class that afternoon, Nipper called him over. "Get a load of Darrell's hands," he said. "Crane made minced meat out of him. Show 'im, Darrell."

Darrell sniffled and then offered his hands, palms up, for Paddy's inspection. "The bastard," Paddy said under his breath. He pushed back Darrell's sleeves, swore, and shook his head. "Listen, Darrell, we all knows what a prick that Crane is, but you brings half this on yourself, you know that?" Darrell stared at Paddy with hurt, uncomprehending eyes. "Look, for one thing, if you got to get strapped, don't go dancin' around like a friggin' yo-yo. Half your problem is that you moves around so much the fucker don't know where to hit you. So don't be pullin' your hands away. That's why he's catching you on the fingertips and arms. Hold your hand out straight, take it in the *middle* of the hand, and then let it give a little once he hits you. The middle is where it don't hurt so much. Jesus, there's nothin' worse than gettin' cracked over the *fingertips*. Hold your hand out flat and take it like a man." Paddy's eyes softened. "Fuck, b'y, I don't know what else to be tellin' you."

As Darrell walked up the aisle for his next strapping, Nipper saw him look over at Paddy. When he offered his hand without any of the usual fuss, Crane looked at him curiously. He seemed uncertain as to how to administer the blows.

In the cloakroom after school, the boys crowded around Darrell and congratulated him. Even Ralph Picco was impressed. "Way to go, Darrell," he said.

31

Nipper sat under the stained glass window of the Archangel Michael. He still continued his morning ritual at Holy Rosary, but he had long since given up his litany of prayers. One afternoon, in grade five religion class, he had bragged to Brother Devine about all the early morning praying he was doing. Brother Devine shook his head. "Mr. Mooney, you're wasting your time. One prayer, said fervently and sincerely, is infinitely better than a hundred tossed off with no thought, no *feeling* behind them. Prayers, in case you didn't know it, are not like popcorn."

So Nipper had begun to read. Now he sat under Michael with *Tom Sawyer, Huckleberry Finn* and all the *Hardy Boys* he could lay his hands on. The old people always smiled and nodded at him as they crept up and down the aisle. Nipper wondered why they were so friendly—until he realized they thought he was reading a prayer book.

Whenever he got the chance, he hunched down in the school library next to a steaming radiator, and while the other boys played basketball or skylarked in the classrooms, he lost himself in a book. His classmates couldn't quite figure it out. If he was such a bookworm, why wasn't he a brain like Dean Williams?

Nipper read all kinds of books: novels, history, the encyclopedias. Sometimes he found pictures of art nudes that he shared with Barnes. Those Manets and Raphaels were about the only thing that could get him into the library when he wasn't forced to be there. Barnes hated reading—especially poetry. Once he asked Nipper to help him with an assignment on E.J. Pratt's "Sea-Gulls."

> *For one carved instant as they flew,*
> *The language had no simile—*

"What the frig is a *carved instant*?" Barnes said. "It don't make any sense."

"It's not supposed to make *sense*. It's supposed to make you *feel* something."

Barnes screwed up his face. "Yeah," he said. "Sick." Later, in class, Barnes put up his hand.

"Yes, Mr. Barnes?"

"Hey, Burr, you know these famous authors we studies? You know, like E.J. Pratt and Shakespeare and Alfred Lord Tennyson and all them guys?"

"Well, not personally, Mr. Barnes, but I am acquainted with their work."

"Well, like, they're the best writers in the whole world, right?"

"Yes, Mr. Barnes."

"So, like, they're supposed to be great . . . communicators, right?"

"I believe an argument could be made for that position, yes."

"The best communicators in the *whole world*, right?"

Crane sighed. "Do you have a point, Mr. Barnes?"

"Well, I was wonderin', like, if they're such great communicators, how come we need someone like you to tell us what they're tryin' to say?"

It was the only time Nipper had seen Brother Crane lost for words.

· · ·

It wasn't just the books that drew Nipper to the library. Like Holy Rosary in the early morning, there was hardly ever a crowd. He was surprised, then, one afternoon to look up and see Paddy Dunne slipping into the seat opposite him.

"Whadaya at?" Paddy said. Nipper raised his book and displayed the cover: a Zane Grey western. "Any good?"

"Not bad. Not as good as Louis L'Amour."

Paddy nodded and opened a binder. He took out a sheet of paper and studied it.

"What's that?" Nipper asked.

"Friggin' English composition. Crane's making me write it over."

"Whatcha get?" Nipper asked. "Not that it's any of my business," he added. Paddy frowned and slipped the paper back into the binder. Nipper turned again to Zane Grey, but he felt Paddy looking at him across the table.

"D minus," he said suddenly. "All you got to do is blow on it, and it'll turn into an F." He leaned across the table and shook back his hair. "What did you get? An A I suppose."

"No, I didn't get no A. I got a B."

"Nothin' wrong with that."

"Tell it to my mother. When I showed it to her, it was like I failed or something."

"What's her problem? There's nothin' wrong with a B. I wouldn't mind gettin' one."

"Yeah, well, she keeps sayin', 'If you can get a B you can get an A. You just need to work a bit harder.'"

"Sounds like my old man," Paddy said.

"I guess they're all alike."

"Yeah. Guess so."

Paddy picked up the composition and glared at it. Then, on impulse, Nipper said, "You want me to have a look at it?"

Paddy looked at him quizzically. "Why?"

"I dunno. Maybe I could give you a hand or somethin'. I mean . . . if you want."

Paddy stared down at the paper. "Just between you and me, hey?"

"Sure," Nipper said. "No sweat."

Paddy looked down at the paper again, then slid it across the table. Nipper quickly read through it. Crane had assigned the cheery topic "Death," and Paddy had written about Rosarie's funeral. Once again, Nipper was struck by Paddy's calligraphy, but his spelling and sentence construction were terrible. Nipper's composition, like most of the others, had been about the death of a pet. Paddy's essay described how he felt when he saw a fly walking across Rosarie's casket. He had wanted to go over and brush it away, but couldn't move. It was a good essay, Nipper thought. Too bad it looked like it had been written by someone in grade three.

"Well?"

Nipper came around the table and sat down next to him.

"It's not too bad. But the first thing you got to do is get your spelling straight." He pointed at the paper. "What's that word supposed to be?"

Paddy took up the paper and ran his index finger along the line until he stopped at the word. His lips parted to form the syllables. "What's wrong?" Nipper said. "Can't you read your own writing?" Paddy glared at him and laid the paper down. Nipper thought he was going to leave. Then he quickly picked it up again and read the sentence aloud:

"I looked at the cofin. I was serprized that I coudnt move."

Nipper looked at Paddy. "That's not how you spell surprised." He got up and brought a dictionary over to the table. "Look it up," he said, pushing it toward him. Paddy took the dictionary and began to slowly leaf through the pages. It seemed to take him forever just to find the *s*'s. Again, he mouthed the word, but then Nipper noticed that Paddy was looking under the *se*'s instead of the *su*'s. "Here, let me have a look," Nipper said. "Just to save time." He found the word and showed it to Paddy, glancing at him sideways as Paddy's eyes flickered over the page. Nipper wrote "surprised" and some of the other misspelled words in the top margin. "Okay, why don't you read me the first bit."

Paddy sighed and took up the paper.

But he had barely struggled through his own first sentence when Nipper finally understood: Paddy Dunne couldn't read.

32

The janitor was mopping down the hallway. Nipper could hear the mop sloshing back and forth and the creaking of the step-pail. The class was struggling with a math exercise when there was a rap on the door. Brother Crane answered it and stood talking to someone. The scent of industrial soap wafted through from the hallway. The boys heard low laughter, then Crane stepped aside and held the door. Two people came into the classroom: Brother Spencer, the homeroom teacher of the grade nine class down the hall, and a boy.

The boy's head was completely swathed in bandages.

Everyone sat up and stared. Spencer noted their expressions and gave a satisfied grin. He directed the boy to the centre of the class and stood behind him, his thick hands gripping the boy's shoulders. Every now and then he worked his fingers into a double shoulder-pinch. The boy shifted in pain; Spencer pushed down on his shoulders to hold him still.

The boy wore his school uniform, but his grey flannel trousers were threadbare at the cuffs, his shoes were scuffed and dusty, and his school crest had been ripped away from his breast pocket at the top left-hand corner. He stood with his hands clasped behind his back like the pictures of Prince Philip Nipper had seen.

The ends of the bandages drooped loosely around the boy's neck and shoulders. Uneven, grotesque slits had been left for his eyes and nose. There was no slit for the mouth.

Crane turned to the class. "No, this is not a history lesson.

Brother Spencer has not brought us a mummy today—although he certainly looks like one. Wouldn't you say so, Brother?"

"Yes, I suppose he does," Spencer said. "But this is nothing so grand as an Egyptian king."

Suddenly, the pieces of the boy—the shoes, the shabby uniform—jelled with his size and height, and Nipper realized who he was: Bill Tobin, a student in Spencer's class. His father owned a farm just outside St. John's. His friends at All Angels called him Farmer Tobin. He was as strong and unflappable as one of his father's workhorses, and was known for being almost immune to strapping. His hands, torn and callused from baling hay and doing other farm chores, withstood the strongest blows of the White Bomber or Black Doctor with ease.

The gauze near his nose blew rhythmically in and out with his heavy breathing.

Nipper felt dizzy. The turkey sandwich he'd had for lunch started to come up; he put his head down and pressed the back of his hand against his mouth.

"No, this is not an Egyptian," Spencer went on. He had the kind of voice that made everything he said sound like shouting. "This is a boy who doesn't know"—he plunged his fingers deep into Tobin's shoulders—"*how-to-shut-up!*" Tobin gave a cry that was lost in the bands of gauze and twisted out of Spencer's grasp. Spencer grabbed him once again by the shoulders. "You see, Brother Crane," he said, "I figured the only way to teach this boy how to be quiet would be to make it impossible for him to speak. Nothing else seemed to work. Do you have any boys like that in your class? I wouldn't like to think so."

"Well, Brother," Crane said, "I think I can safely say that I've got a few yappers in here. In fact, if I wanted to bandage them all up, I'd have to use every first-aid kit in the school."

"Yes," Spencer said. "I wouldn't be surprised." He sized up the class, his eyes coming to rest on Barnes. "I know Mr. Barnes over there. He's got more tongue on 'im than an old rubber boot."

"That he does," Crane said, glaring at Barnes. Barnes grimaced and hunched down in his seat.

"Well, Brother," Spencer said, "I must be taking my little project off to the other classes. I believe it would benefit them all to get a peek at him." He steered Tobin abruptly toward the door, but the boy lurched blindly and barked his shin on a corner of Crane's desk. He gave a muffled cry that sounded like a curse.

"What was that, Mr. Tobin?" Spencer said.

"It's perhaps better that you didn't quite catch it," Crane said grimly.

"Yes, you're probably right. Thank you, Brother," Spencer said, pushing Tobin outside.

The door closed. Crane sat at his desk and looked down at the class. "Back to your exercises," he said. He gave a sly grin. "And no talking."

The boys looked around at each other and then turned back to their work. There was no sound except the rustling of paper and the scratch of pencils. Then Nipper heard a voice.

"That's not right, you know."

Crane looked up and scanned the room. "Someone has something to say?"

"I said . . . that's not right."

Crane got up and came around his desk. He folded his arms, inclined his head slightly to the left, and looked down the aisle. "Well, this is a special occasion. You're offering us your opinion on something, are you, Mr. Dunne?"

"Doin' that to that young fella. It's not right."

"Really?" Crane said. He gave a short laugh. "And since when have you become an expert in these matters?"

"I'm not saying I'm no expert—"

"No, that's right. You're not."

"That don't mean I don't know when something's not right. Doin' him up like that and bringin' him around like he was one of them freaks in a circus." Paddy shook his head. "It's not right."

"*Freaks* in a circus?" Crane spat. "You're a fine one to be talking about *freaks*. You traipsing in here, day in and day out, looking like a bloody streel. Hair on you like a hopped-up hippie."

"That haven't got nothin' to do with it. Besides, Jesus had long hair, too, you know. Was He a hippie?"

Crane froze. He looked at Paddy with such ice that Nipper felt the whole room grow cold. Crane walked slowly down the aisle. When he got to Paddy's desk, he stopped and turned toward the front of the class. For a moment, there was absolute silence. "Mr. Dunne, you don't pretend to compare yourself with Our Lord, the Saviour of the world—and of *your* miserable soul, do you?"

Paddy stared at Crane's back. His lips were tight. "All I'm saying is that He had long hair, too—longer than mine, according to some of the pictures I seen of 'im."

Crane turned and pounced. He grabbed Paddy by the shirt with both hands, yanked him out of his desk and slammed him against the back wall. Paddy's head cracked against the concrete. Barnes tumbled out of his seat and stumbled up the aisle. Paddy's eyes glazed over, but he brought his hands around and grabbed Crane by the forearms. They stood locked together, their faces only inches apart.

"Now, you listen," Crane said, breathing heavily. "Nobody here is interested in your opinion—least of all me. So you better shut that mouth of yours or I'll shut it for you." He adjusted his grip and pushed Paddy tight against the wall. "Do I make myself clear?" Paddy blinked. "Well, do I?"

The bell rang.

"Nobody move," Crane said. Nipper could hear the other classes spilling into the corridor. Everyone waited. It was probably only half a minute, but it seemed like an hour. Then, abruptly, Crane let Paddy go and stepped quickly away from him. Paddy reached up and felt the back of his head. "Now get out of here," Crane said. "The whole bloody crowd of you."

Silently, the boys started putting their books away. Crane looked at Paddy one last time, then turned and left the room.

Paddy moved unsteadily to his desk and picked up his books. "Are you all right?" Nipper said. The boys all looked at him. Ralph Picco and Danny Hickey came and stood next to his desk.

"Yeah," Paddy said. "I'm okay."

After school, Nipper passed Farmer Tobin waiting for his bus at the bottom of Gardiner Street. Tobin stared straight ahead, oblivious to everything going on around him. He stood as still as a real mummy. The bandages had left red marks on his face, and tiny bits of sticky residue still clung to his chin and eyebrows.

33

Barnes didn't know what to make of Nipper helping Paddy with his English composition.

"Shit, if he wants help, why don't he go to Dean Williams like everyone else?"

"Because he asked me, that's why."

"Must be because you're a bookworm."

"Must be," Nipper said.

For three days they met in the library at lunch hour. The more Nipper worked with Paddy, the more he realized that his problem was that he couldn't get down on paper what he was hearing in his head. When he told Nipper what he wanted to say, the sentences sounded fine, but when he wrote them out, they ended up as misspelled fragments. In the end, Nipper had him dictate, and he wrote out the composition for him. Paddy copied the finished product. As he was doing this during their last meeting, he looked up. "Crane's going to know I didn't write this."

"Didn't write it *by yourself*," Nipper said. "But sure they're all your ideas. I just helped you get them down and fixed up the spelling. But it's your composition." Paddy didn't look convinced, but he turned back and finished the work.

When it was done, it was impressive. Paddy had used a special, long art paper, and, with his handwriting, the essay looked like an ancient scroll.

Before the first period in the afternoon, Paddy went up to Crane while he sat writing in his register. He held out the composition.

Crane took it and looked at it sceptically. "What's this?"

"Composition, Burr. I redone it."

Crane looked at it briefly, then he held it away from his desk and let it fall to the floor. He turned back to the register as if Paddy wasn't there. The class fell silent. Paddy stood looking at Crane. Nipper could only see his back, but he could picture the tightness in his face. Paddy reached down, picked up the paper, and held it out again to Crane. "Burr, it's my composition, the one you told me to do over." Crane looked up, took the paper, and again let it fall to the floor. Once more Paddy picked it up, but this time he placed it on the desk and headed back to his seat.

Crane stood up and came around his desk. He picked up the paper. "You can take this back, Mr. Dunne. I don't want it."

Paddy turned. "Why not? I done what you asked."

"Oh, is that right?" Crane said. "You did?"

"Sure—"

"Mr. Dunne, this composition is obviously on the wrong-sized paper. Anyone can see that. I specified . . . ?" He raised his eyebrows and looked around the class.

"Eight and a half by eleven," someone muttered.

"That's right," Crane said. "Eight and a half by eleven." He held out the paper to Paddy. "I can't read this."

Paddy shoved his hands into his pockets.

"You don't want it?" Crane crumpled the paper into a ball and threw it into the corner wastepaper basket.

Nipper closed his eyes. *You fucking prick.*

"Mr. Dunne," Crane said, "if you're not going to play by the rules like the rest of the boys, I think you better write out chapter four of our religion text three times."

"I'm not doing that," Paddy said quietly.

"Oh yes, you will," Crane said. "And you can take an F on your composition."

Paddy shrugged. He walked back down the aisle and dropped heavily into his seat.

34

Nipper was having trouble with his Latin declensions. That's how Brother Simms put it. "Your Latin declensions leave a lot to be desired, Mr. Mooney." *Your* Latin declensions. Nipper wanted to say, 'They're not my friggin' Latin declensions. I don't want the goddamn things. English suits me fine, thank you very much.' And it wasn't like Simms himself was mad for Latin. Every time he opened the textbook, he got a sour puss on him. That's what Mona said when she saw Nipper staring at his liver and onions. "Get the sour puss off you, b'y. There's lots of youngsters over in India and China would love a feed of liver and onions."

Nipper hated Latin. He would eat liver and onions every night of the week if he didn't have to do Latin. And the very first verb they had to learn, on the very first page of the text, was *amo*: "to love." They should have started with the verb *to hate* or the verb *to annoy* or the verb *to torture.*

Simms made Nipper stay after school to work on Latin declensions. *His* Latin declensions.

"But I can't stay. I'll miss my ride back to Kildura. There's not a bus until five o'clock."

"That's all right, Mr. Mooney. You can use the extra time to do some translation."

Simms kept him in until four-thirty, when the school was closed and locked. Nipper stepped out into the wet, empty courtyard and looked at his watch. He walked over to Holy Rosary and sat in his pew at the back. He looked up at the

Archangel Michael and thought, I'm spending half my friggin' life in this place.

Nipper wandered down the Upper Road looking for Gerard and Ronnie. He went up Flynn's lane and saw Brigid stacking milk cans by the dairy. Nipper thought of the prayer to St. Brigid that Brendan had taught him. *Milkmaid of the smooth white palms, Brigid of the clustering brown hair.* This Brigid's hair was black.

"Where were you yesterday?" she asked.

"Friggin' Latin. I had to stay in."

"Why do you have to do Latin? We don't."

Nipper threw up his hands.

Brigid stacked the last can and wiped her fingers on her jeans. "You want to go up to the loft for a while?"

"Sure."

They climbed the rough ladder and slumped against the sweet-smelling bales. The straw pricked Brigid through her top, and she reached behind to push down the hay. She twisted to get herself comfortable, and each time she did, Nipper saw the muscles twitching in her dark neck, and the blue vein leading up to her black hair. Her hair was already flecked with fine straw. She leaned back. Nipper moved closer to her.

"Say something to me in Latin," she said.

Nipper rolled his eyes. "I don't know any. That's why that frigger Simms makes me stay after school."

"You must know *some.*"

"Sure you knows what Latin sounds like. It's the same as in church."

Brigid turned to him and clenched a fist beneath her chin. "I know. But say something, anyway."

Nipper drew a deep breath. "Mea culpa, mea culpa, mea máxima culpa. Or, as Joe Barnes says, Me a cowboy, me a cowboy, me a Mexican cowboy." He grinned. "There. Happy now?"

"Say something you learned in school."

Nipper sighed. "Amo, amas, amat—"

"What does that mean?"

"It's the verb 'to love.'"

Brigid smiled. "It sounds better in French."

"Yeah," Nipper said. "Anything sounds better than Latin."

Brigid straightened her legs and searched a lock of hair for straw. "Ronnie and Gerard made some new tunnels the other day. You want to go in?"

Nipper fidgeted and brushed at his nose. "You know I don't like the tunnels."

"Yeah, but if we go in there, no one will see us." Brigid popped a straw between her lips and stared up at the ceiling. "And we won't have to worry about Gerard or Ronnie or anyone."

"Why should we be worrying?"

"Well, just in case," Brigid said. "You know them. They'll make fun."

"They'll make more fun if they knows we're in the tunnels by ourselves."

Brigid nodded. "Maybe. But it's nice and cosy in there."

Nipper remained silent.

"I'll go first," Brigid said. "The tunnel out to the shutter is pretty big. It won't cave in."

"I'm not worried about it caving in," Nipper said. "I just don't like being in small places. It makes me sick; you know that."

"But once you go through, there's lots of room. The tunnel goes right out to the shutter. We can open it up."

Nipper looked into Brigid's black eyes: restless eyes, like those of a small animal. He wanted to ask her if she felt different being so dark. Maybe it wasn't Brendan who was the changeling at all. Maybe it was Brigid. If there were still Beothucks, he wouldn't have been surprised to learn that the fairies had stolen the real Brigid and replaced her with a Beothuck baby.

Brigid's hair was moist and shiny, like wet coal, and her fingers were long and slender and beautiful, even though she bit her nails to the quick. Her bottom lip was fuller than the top. And Nipper thought, All that stuff about bleeding and curses that Ronnie Sheehan was always getting on with, that couldn't apply to Brigid. And sure what odds if it did? All he knew was that, when he was with her, he felt excited and calm at the same time.

Nipper looked toward the tunnel entrance. "All right," he said. "You go first."

Brigid crawled inside. And even the sight of her disappearing into the blackness made beads of sweat form on his forehead. He heard her knees brush the floor, and then she called, "I'm here," her voice muffled by the wall of hay bales. He heard the creak of hinges as she pushed open the huge shutters. "There's lots of room. You can stand up and everything."

Nipper went to the tunnel entrance and dropped to his knees. He looked in.

It was like facing the confessional.

"Nicky, are you coming?"

It's not just going in, it's coming back, too. But even as the thought flickered through his mind, he entered the dark tunnel. *Brigid just went through and she's all right and if I go fast I'll be there too in a second but if I go too fast maybe I'll jar a bale loose and it will all come down on top of me and I'll be shut in like in the confessional, drowned like poor Gerald and Max in the Damsel's Eye, smothered like Rosarie in the fire, buried like Dad in his coffin . . .*

Nipper glimpsed a sliver of light. The air cooled, became fresher.

He was through.

Nipper couldn't help it: he scrambled to the shutter and gulped the fresh air. The scent of cow manure was strong, and the wind moved gently in the meadow where Mick's soul had fled.

Brigid was sitting by the shutter. Nipper slumped next to her and put his head between his knees.

"We don't have to do this anymore," Brigid said quietly. "I didn't know it was that bad."

But now Nipper was more embarrassed than sick, and he couldn't look at her, although he wanted to very badly.

Brigid laid a hand on his knee. "Don't worry," she said. "Everybody's got something wrong with them."

Nipper swallowed painfully and looked at her. The breeze from the shutter ruffled her black hair, which was even more flecked with straw. Her dark face was as smooth as the Botticellis in the encyclopedia. Nipper said, "Brigid, remember that time up on the Old Road when you bit my neck?"

Brigid chewed her lower lip and nodded.

"Well . . . do you think . . . do you think you could do that again?"

Brigid made no answer, but turned and nuzzled him as Mick used to when he was looking for treats. The touch of her lips and tongue flooded Nipper's body, and she bit deeply and gently and for a long time.

When she stopped, Nipper caught his breath. "Can I do that to you?"

Brigid pushed her crow's-wing hair from her neck and the taste of her skin was all salt and sweat and cherries as if she bathed in cherry water. And her skin was wafer-smooth and hot and he felt her beating heart and although he could not see, he knew she had closed her dark eyes.

When it was time to leave, Nipper said, "I'll go first."

He paused before the tunnel entrance, then quickly slipped inside. The fear and nausea were still there. But there was something else, too. And as he emerged on the other side, his heart thumped wildly with a different kind of panic.

35

*E*very day after school Nipper met Brigid in front of Blake's store.

"You're spending a lot of time with Brigid Flynn these days," his mother said one evening when he came in to get Cokes for them.

Nipper shrugged. "Yeah. She's nice."

"Yes," Sharon said, handing him his change. "*Very* nice."

Sometimes they went for walks up the Old Road; Nipper knew lots of places where no one would ever find them. Sometimes they even sneaked into the Mooney barn and necked beneath the cross of St. Brigid. But when it was cold or rainy, they went up into Flynn's loft. Nipper didn't find the tunnels quite so bad anymore—as long as Brigid was with him. As long as at the end of the tunnel, she would be there.

One evening when he left the barn, he saw Brigid's mother staring out the window at him and frowning. Nipper kept his eyes on the ground. At least her father hadn't noticed anything—or, if he had, he didn't seem to care. Then one day Brendan gave him a funny look.

"Aren't you gettin' a bit old to be playing in the hayloft?"

"Well, yeah, I s'pose. I mean . . . it's just somewhere to go."

Brendan's watery eyes lit up. "*Oh*," he said. "I see. Goin' to church, are you?"

"What?"

"Nothing," Brendan said, winking. "Nothing."

Nipper liked lying next to Brigid—liked slipping his cool hands under her shirt, feeling the goosebumps form on her

252

warm skin, feeling her body arch and turn into him. At night, he curled into a ball with his hands tight between his legs and savoured the lingering scent of her warm breath, the salty taste of her skin. He remembered how her closed eyes shuddered and twitched, how his face flushed and burned when it was framed by her black, tumbling hair. She was so perfect, serene—almost like a saint herself. *Milkmaid of the smooth white palms* . . . Why were some saints the kind you prayed to and others the kind you weren't allowed to touch? How could something so beautiful be a source of sin?

A mystery.

One evening after supper, Nipper went over to the cherry bookcase and took out the *Family Catechism*.

What is a mystery?
A mystery is a truth which we cannot understand.

What is a supernatural mystery?
A supernatural mystery is a truth which we cannot fully understand, but which we firmly believe because we have God's word for it.

Nipper closed the book. God's word. Cross your heart and hope to die. Lots of things he wanted to know about were mysteries. Why didn't Jesus appear to everyone in the world at the same time? Why didn't God send more Jesuses so everyone could be saved right from the very beginning? Why did the missionaries bring God's word and smallpox all on the same boat?

Why was it a sin to touch Brigid?

To let her touch him?

To ask her to take off her top in the loft when he knew—*thought*—that she would?

Nipper flipped through the pages again.

Why are sins of impurity and immodesty especially dangerous?

Sins of impurity and immodesty are especially dangerous because our nature is strongly inclined toward them, they are easily committed and soon develop into habits which are very hard to break.

Nipper grimaced. You're telling me.

What should we accustom ourselves to do when unchaste thoughts and desires enter our mind?

When unchaste thoughts and desires enter our mind we should accustom ourselves to pray immediately to Our Lord and to His Blessed Mother for strength to overcome the temptation.

What are the chief means of preserving the virtue of chastity?

The chief means of preserving the virtue of chastity are to avoid carefully all unnecessary dangers, to seek God's help through prayer, frequent confession, Holy Communion, and assistance at Holy Mass, and to have a special devotion to the Blessed Virgin.

Oh no, Nipper thought. Not frequent confession. He imagined confessing to Monsignor Murphy about being in the loft with Brigid. *Monsignor, remember that time back in grade one when I told you I didn't have any bad thoughts? Well . . .* Nipper flipped to the back of the catechism: "Problems and Exercises."

Godfrey, a lad inclined to be lazy, is bothered with many

temptations to sin. May he justly blame all of them on the devil? Explain your answer. Advise him how to overcome his temptations.

Nipper closed the catechism and slipped it back into the case. Sorry, Godfrey, he thought. I think you're on your own.

36

It was getting close to spring; the snow was melting around the basketball nets. After prayers one Monday morning, Brother Crane pointed at Nipper, Bob O'Grady, Barnes and Paddy Dunne.

"You, you, you and you," he said. "Off to the gym and wait for me." When he said "gym," Nipper knew right away what it was about: bingo. There was always a bingo on Saturday nights, and they were being detailed to take down the chairs. O'Grady, Barnes and Nipper bounded up the stairs: any excuse to get out of class was welcome.

They ran into the gym and swung themselves onto the lip of the stage. Paddy followed at his own pace. When he came in, he looked at the chairs and swore. "Gettin' us to do their friggin' work," he said. "Slave labour—that's all they thinks we're good for."

Nipper grinned. "What odds. At least we're not stuck down in the classroom. I'd rather be here any day."

"Sure," Barnes said. "Bit o' fun."

"Right," Paddy said, shaking his head.

The minute Crane turned up and began pacing in front of them, Nipper began to have second thoughts.

"All right," Crane said. "I want the chairs on the trolleys and the trolleys under the stage. *Neatly*, if you don't mind. If they're not lined up right, they won't fit. And don't take all day."

They began. The only good part was the racket of the collapsing and stacking, which they enjoyed and did nothing to soften.

Crane stood near the stage, barking at them like a warehouse foreman. "Come on, O'Grady, get the lead out." Nipper looked over at O'Grady and saw him struggling with three chairs. He staggered to one of the trolleys and dropped them with a crash. "Harder than it looks," he muttered.

Paddy was the best worker. He often picked up four or five chairs at a time. Nipper could barely handle two, so he scurried about, frantically collapsing chairs and stacking them one by one, hoping Crane would see the value of speed over brute strength. It didn't work. "Come on, Mooney!" Crane yelled. "You can take more than that." Nipper collapsed three chairs and carried them, half-walking, half-running, to a trolley, where he promptly tripped, sending himself and the chairs spilling onto the floor. Crane rushed over, grabbed him by the shoulders and shook him violently. "What do you think you're doing?" he shouted. "You're useless. You're all bloody useless. I'm no better off than if I had a crowd of girls up here. Pick 'em up," he said, shoving Nipper toward the trolley. Nipper saw Paddy with his hands on his hips, breathing heavily, having just parked a full trolley under the stage. "What are you looking at?" Crane snapped at him. "Get to work." Paddy bent and picked up four chairs, struggling to get them adjusted neatly in his arms. Crane looked at him for a moment. "Come on, Dunne," he said. "You can take more than that. Big strappin' fella like you." Crane strode briskly across the floor and stood behind him. "That's all? I thought you were supposed to be a tough guy." Crane paused. "Or do they call you Caveman for nothing?"

Nipper had moved to the stage with his trolley, and now he looked across at Paddy. His heavy breathing ceased. He stared at the chairs with cold eyes. And then everything seemed to happen in slow motion. The muscles in his arms and shoulders relaxed, and the chairs fell to the floor, their crashing ringing thin and faraway. Nipper saw Paddy's right hand curl into a fist, which he brought gently over to his left hip. Then, slowly, he began to straighten up. As he did so, his fist flew out, gathering speed and power, describing a graceful arc, so that he looked like a discus thrower entering his first spin. But Paddy did not spin into additional circles. His fist whipped blindly behind him and crashed into Crane's jaw with a wet smacking sound that echoed throughout the gym.

Crane's head snapped back.

His eyes turned into glassy doll's eyes.

His knees crumpled and sagged, and he dropped vertically to the floor, as if a puppeteer had abandoned his strings.

He pitched forward and lay still.

No one spoke.

A truck ground its gears chugging up Gardiner Street. The boys stood frozen, Barnes still clutching a chair to his chest. They stared at Crane and then moved in unison to where he lay. Paddy looked down at him indifferently.

"Holy fuck," Barnes whispered. He looked at Nipper, then back at Crane. "Holy *fuck*!" he said again. He glanced quickly at Paddy, who stood with his fist still clenched. Barnes made as if to speak to him, but then stopped and turned to Nipper. "Shit. You don't think he's . . . *dead*, do you?" Before Nipper could answer, Paddy starting walking down the centre of the gym toward the main entrance. He never looked back. He pushed open the heavy fire doors, letting in a collage of street sounds, then disappeared down the concrete steps.

The doors banged closed.

"What are we goin' to do?" Barnes said, looking back down at Crane. "What if he's dead? Shit, Nipper, there's not a joog in 'im."

Nipper struggled to get his thoughts together. "He's . . . he's not dead," he said. "You don't die from gettin' punched in the face." His throat was so dry he croaked and caught on the words.

"Go get someone," Barnes said.

"Me? I'm not going. *You* go."

"Like fuck," Barnes said. "O'Grady, you go." But O'Grady just stared at Crane as if he hadn't heard.

"There's no way I'm goin'," Barnes said. "No *way*."

Nipper looked down at Crane. "Jesus," he said. He turned and headed quickly for the door. "Shit," he said under his breath. "Shit, shit, *shit*." He took the stairs two at a time, ran down the hall, and turned into the general office. Miss Jackson sat typing furiously.

Nipper went up to the counter. "Excuse me, Miss," he said hoarsely. Miss Jackson kept pecking at her typewriter. "Miss," he said louder. "Miss!"

She turned and looked at him. "I suppose you've come for the strap, have you?"

"No, Miss, I . . . I . . . "

"What's wrong?" she said, getting up. "Are you sick or something?"

"No, Miss, I . . . I got to see Brother Bannister." As soon as Nipper had spoken, he wondered why he'd said that. He could easily have told her what the problem was.

"What do you want to see him about? He's busy, you know."

"It's . . . it's about Brother Crane."

"What about him?"

"I . . . I . . . "

"Oh, for God's sake, take a seat," she said. "I'll ask him if he can see you." Nipper felt numb. His whole body burned with pins and needles. He sank into a chair and closed his eyes. Miss Jackson turned back to her work.

Nipper twisted in the chair and looked at Bannister's office door. When was she going to tell him? A copy of the *Annals of St. Anne de Beaupré* lay on the next chair; he picked it up, began to leaf through it, threw it down and went back to the counter.

"Miss."

Miss Jackson spun around and glared. "What *is* wrong with you?"

"Miss, I think I better see Brother Bannister. *Now.*"

The secretary adjusted her glasses. She picked up the phone and pressed a button. "Brother, can you come out, please? There's someone here to see you. I think it might be important." She listened for a moment. "No, it's a student." She glanced at Nipper. "What's your name—Mulrooney, is it?"

"Mooney."

"Mooney," she repeated into the phone. "In grade . . . ?"

"Eight," he said.

"Eight." She listened again. "Uh-huh. All right, then." She hung up. "He'll be right out."

Almost immediately the door opened, and Bannister stood there with his pipe in his hands.

"What's your problem today?"

"Burr, you better come up to the gym," Nipper said. "I think there's something wrong with Brother Crane."

He didn't know why he said, "I think." Bannister's strange eyes narrowed; his long face grew grave.

"What do you mean? What's wrong with him?"

"I . . . I think you just better come up to the gym." Nipper moved to the door and stood looking back at Bannister like a puppy enticing his master for a walk.

Bannister took off his glasses and slowly cleaned them with the hem of his soutane. He placed them carefully back on his nose and gestured with his pipe toward the door. "Lead on, Macduff," he said.

Nipper rushed out into the hall. He wanted to run, but

Bannister plodded along in no special hurry. Nipper kept having to wait for the principal to catch up. "What's wrong with him?" Bannister asked again. "Is he sick?"

"Well . . . *sort* of."

When they finally got to the gym, Crane was sitting up, dazed. Barnes and O'Grady sat on the stage looking at him. The principal ran over and helped Crane to his feet. He staggered and laid his hand on Bannister's shoulder. "What's wrong with you, man?" Bannister said. "Did you faint?"

"No, Burr, he didn't faint," Barnes said.

Bannister shot him a stinging look. "Get back to your classroom."

The boys headed quickly across the gym floor and down the stairs. "No one's gonna believe this," Nipper said. "No one's *ever* gonna fuckin' believe it." Suddenly Barnes laughed. "What's so funny?"

"Well, just think about it," Barnes said. "Brother Crane, our tough, boxer-teacher. Who'd of thought he'd have a glass jaw?"

Nipper didn't know what to think. But that was the last All Angels ever saw of Paddy Dunne.

FIVE

37

*F*or high school, there were two major changes at All Angels. During the summer before Nipper entered the ninth grade, mice-infested St. Brigid's had finally been condemned.

"Thirty years too late if you want my opinion," Sharon said.

Mona nodded. "Nothin' but a hole. Always was."

Uncle Phonse worked on the demolition. "It was the easiest job I ever had," he told Nipper. "We hardly needed the heavy equipment—just went in and started swingin' away with the sledgehammers. The walls collapsed like popsicle sticks—rotten right through. And mice? My Jesus, I never saw the like. You couldn't put your foot down." Phonse shook his head. "No, there certainly wasn't much to that old school. A good wind could have done the job."

"What happened to the statue?" Nipper asked.

"The one of St. Brigid?"

"Yeah."

Phonse shrugged. "Beats me. All that stuff was long gone by the time we got in there."

With no money for a new building, it was decided to bus the students to schools in St. John's: All Angels for the boys, St. Anne's for the girls. After four years of getting up at six-thirty to ride in with Bobby Sheehan, Nipper had the luxury of sleeping in an extra hour.

It took him awhile to get used to seeing his fellow Kildurans hanging out on the school steps or roaming up and down Prince Street or Gardiner Street. They looked odd in their blazers, ties and grey flannel trousers. Sharon laughed when she saw Ronnie

Sheehan in his new uniform. "My God," she said, ruffling his hair, "you're *gorgeous*. Done up just like a stick o' chewin' gum."

Ronnie clutched miserably at his collar. "Jeez, it's one thing to wear a tie in church," he said, "but *every* day?"

"Don't worry," Nipper said. "You get used to it."

Even Brigid looked different in her chocolate-brown uniform. Still pretty good, though. He'd always liked Brigid in a dress. This one was on the short side, too—well, for a school uniform. Sister Mary Ignatius would never have allowed that at St. Brigid's.

His four years in the city had made Nipper something of a celebrity, and during lunch hour he showed the Kildurans around, pointing out Noseworthy's fish and chip shop, where it was easy to walk out without paying, Madden's Bakery, where they could buy a bag of scraps (the price had gone up to fifty cents), and Downton's Groc. and Conf., which offered the cheapest cigarettes.

As Ronnie Sheehan, Billy Fleming and Nipper trudged up Gardiner Street on their way back to school, they passed a group of grade tens sitting on Madden's steps, smoking. Nipper knew them: they were in the Buckmaster's Circle gang. He had always remembered Bobby Sheehan's advice about keeping a low profile at All Angels. He automatically dropped his gaze to the ground, but Billy looked over at them and said, "How you gettin' on?"

"Jesus," Nipper said under his breath. "Don't be talkin' to them."

One of the boys got to his feet and sized them up. He spit and flicked his cigarette butt into the street.

"Not bad."

"Glad to hear it," Billy said. The boy sat back down and watched as they walked on. Nipper was surprised he'd even answered. Things had definitely changed. With a Kildura gang at All Angels, he wouldn't have to face the Townies alone. St. Brigid's had left Billy and the other Kildurans a little rough around the edges, and over the next few weeks word spread among the other gangs that it was better not to mess with the farm boys. Even the guys from Mundy Pond and the Brow took pains to stay out of their way.

As they continued up the street, Nipper told Billy and Ronnie about the photograph and the mysterious whorehouse.

"It's number 66," Billy said. "It *was*, anyway."

"What?"

"The whorehouse. It was number 66."

"Shit, how do you know?"

"Everybody knows that, b'y. Anyway, it's been closed for years."

There was also, on that first day of high school, a noticeable absence. Darrell Wiggins, having turned sixteen and struck out at grade eight for the third time, had finally quit. And although Saintsbury Place was, as Brother Crane had demonstrated, only a three-minute walk from the school, Darrell seemed to have vanished. Nipper saw him only twice during that whole school year: once in Holy Rosary on Ash Wednesday, and once walking up Gardiner Street with his mother. Nipper had never met Darrell's mother, but he was sure it was her: she was as tall as him, and even skinnier, if that were possible. With her flat hair and lumpy wool cardigan, she looked like a fifty-year-old Olive Oyl. Mother and son ate up the sidewalk with great loping strides. Darrell seemed remarkably calm. His teeth were as yellow as ever, but his acne was clearing up, and he swung the shopping bag he carried in a light, carefree manner.

Paddy Dunne had never come back to All Angels—not even to

pick up his books. For weeks after he'd left, his faded jacket hung in the cloakroom.

Then, one morning, it was gone.

Nipper heard through Mona that Paddy had gotten his wish and was working on the waterfront with his Uncle Frank. But on all his excursions downtown, Nipper never once ran into him.

38

Nipper and Brigid sat near the south shutter in Flynn's loft. It was growing dark; soon it would be pitch-black. Nipper didn't want to leave. Leaving would make school the next day come even quicker. He looked at Brigid through the dying light. Her face was as flushed as it ever got: he could almost imagine a tinge of red under her dark skin.

"You going to the dance Saturday night?" she asked.

"Sure," Nipper said, taking her hand. "Don't we always?"

"Yeah."

Nipper peered at her sideways. "What are you thinking about?"

"Just wondering something."

"What?"

"I was wondering . . . " She turned to him. "Do you ever go to confession anymore?"

Nipper sat up. "Why do you want to know that?"

"I was just, you know, wondering."

Nipper slumped against the wall. "No. I tells Mom that I do—tells her I goes the first of the month in town—you know, with All Angels. But I don't really go. I just sits in the church."

"When was the last time you went?"

Nipper shrugged. "Don't know. A long time ago."

"Did you still get sick like you used to?"

"Sometimes."

Brigid bit her full lower lip. "If you went again, would you tell about me—about *us*?"

Nipper sighed and shook his head. "What for? It can't be a

sin to be with you—no matter what it says in the friggin' catechism. It's a *good* thing. Some days in school it's all I think about." Nipper grinned. "Know something?"

"What?"

"I think that if old Monsignor Murphy had ever done—you know—what we do, he probably wouldn't be half the mean old frigger he is. The Brothers, too."

Brigid smiled. "Probably not."

Nipper looked at her. "Do you still go?"

"Yeah. Mom makes me sometimes. But I don't tell everything."

"You have to tell everything," Nipper said. He wagged a finger at her. "It can't be just 'bad words' and 'I disobeyed my mother.' That's what Sister Mary Ignatius said: *All of your sins. Truly and heartily sorry. That is a good confession.* Remember?"

Brigid grinned. "I remember. Hey, you know she's teaching at St. Anne's now?"

"Really?"

"I saw her the other day. She's teaching grade eleven, so at least I haven't got her for anything, thank God."

"Sister Bernadette there?"

"She's at Our Lady of the Seven Sorrows. She was nice, Sister Bernadette was."

"Yeah," Nipper said. "I think I might've had a crush on her."

Brigid giggled and poked him in the ribs. "A crush on a *nun*? That's sick."

"Well, she's pretty."

"Yeah, I suppose—I mean, for a nun." Brigid took Nipper's hand and slipped it under her shirt. "Are you ever going back to confession?"

Nipper turned and brushed his fingers along her fine hair. "No," he said. "I don't have anything to confess."

39

One Saturday night at the dance in the Kildura Parish Hall, Nipper saw Dougie Whalen lounging by the men's washroom, carefully patting his greased-down hair. Whalen threaded his way through the crowded dance floor and strutted nonchalantly up to two guys from Deep Harbour who were standing by the stage. One of them had his head down, lighting a cigarette, and Whalen decked him with a right cross that sent the cigarette flying into the air. On cue, about ten Kildurans appeared from out of nowhere and piled on top of the strangers.

Nipper had been waiting for it to happen.

It was a rare dance when there wasn't at least one fight. Guys from St. John's, Deep Harbour or the Brow would turn up, and sooner or later a scuffle broke out. The reason was just about always the same: a non-Kilduran would ask one of the Kildura girls to dance, and her boyfriend, or some Kilduran who *wanted* to be her boyfriend, or someone who just couldn't stand to see a sweet, innocent Kildura girl dancing with some stranger from Deep Harbour or wherever, would have a few words with the stranger. Soon they'd be into it. The visitors, no matter how tough, hardly ever won—they were simply outnumbered. There was no letting the two main players settle the matter on their own. As the girls screamed and chairs skidded across the dance floor, the Kildurans pounced on the outsiders in a kind of feeding frenzy. None of the Kildura tough guys—Whalen, Les Penny, Max Sinnott—thought there was anything wrong with ganging up. They argued that when they went to Deep Harbour or up to the Brow, the same thing happened to them. It was

271

almost expected that if you went to a dance in enemy territory you came back cut up and bruised—often worse. But the wounds were battle scars, marks of honour. To return home in the same condition in which you'd left was almost a disgrace.

Dougie Whalen had a long-standing grudge against the guys from Deep Harbour. They were led by a tough named Benny Black and known as Benny Black and the Forty Dirtnecks—a name Benny had coined himself. Whalen and the Kildura gang referred to them scornfully as "Randy Ben and the Dirty Fortnecks."

Nipper had heard why Whalen had it in for the Dirtnecks. One night after leaving a dance at the Deep Harbour Legion Hall, he had been surprised by Benny Black and a half-dozen of his cohorts. And while Whalen showed plenty of gusto in facing down a gang of drunken Dirtnecks on their own dance floor, he was deathly afraid of water and couldn't swim a stroke. In his mind, it was a gross violation of all racket ethics, when they promptly threw him off the wharf. Whalen never forgave the Dirtnecks. "Christ," he grumbled, "it's one thing to beat the shit out of a fella. But there's no need to try and friggin' *drown* him."

Nipper looked over at the fight; more Kildurans were joining in. He was glad Brigid had gone home early: she hated the rackets, and this was a bad one. The Dirtnecks could certainly have used the help of Benny Black and their thirty-eight comrades. Nipper shook his head. He was sick of the bravado. There were times when he was drawn into the rackets, too—either to back up a friend or to save face. It was expected—even from runts like him. The fights were all different, and yet they were all the same. Sometimes guys got a black eye; sometimes they ended up in the hospital—a scenario which was looking more and more likely for the two Dirtnecks. Nipper rarely inflicted much damage on his opponents, but he did show a remarkable resistance to fists and boots; so while he wasn't known as a fighter, he'd developed an odd reputation for being difficult to scar.

Nipper caught a ride home with Andy Turpin and Max Sinnott, both of whom had been into the thick of the fight. As they drove up the Lower Road, they saw two people walking along the shoulder near Aylward's Service Station. "Look," Sinnott said. "That's them Deep Harbour guys." Nipper thought for a moment that he was going to stop the car and start round two. He hoped not. The Dirtnecks looked as if they'd taken about as much as they could for one night. Their shuffling reminded him of the pictures he'd seen of columns of First World War soldiers blinded by poison gas: the men stumbling through the mud with dirty bandages over their eyes, one outstretched hand resting on the shoulder of the man in front.

Nipper prayed that Sinnott would drive on by, but Turpin said, "Haul her in, Max." They pulled onto the shoulder, and Turpin rolled down the window. "Hey, you want a run up the road?"

The Dirtnecks stopped and sized up the car. Their faces, in the cold neon from the service station, were so bruised and swollen that Nipper couldn't make out their expressions, but he sensed they were scared to death. The Dirtnecks looked at each other.

Turpin jumped out and pushed down the front passenger seat. "Come on," he said, gesturing into the car, "hop in." The Dirtnecks looked at each other again; then, without a word, they shuffled up to the car and squeezed painfully into the back seat.

"You don't mind a little detour, do you, Nip?" Sinnott asked.

"No, not me."

"Suppose you guys are goin' back to the Harbour, are you?" Turpin said.

"Yeah."

Sinnott put the car in gear, and it screeched out onto the highway. As they shot by Kildura's meadows and barns, Nipper kept waiting for Sinnott to make an abrupt turn onto some little side road where they would take the Dirtnecks out and give them a second beating.

"How come you're walkin'?" Turpin asked.

"Friggin' car wouldn't start," the Dirtneck next to Nipper said. His friend stared silently out the window.

"Shit, not your night, is it?" Sinnott said. "But sure the same thing happened to us one time up on the Brow. Remember that, Andy? I had that blue '59 Chev. We come out after the dance, and not a bloody joog in the car."

"Yeah, but that was because them fuckers from the Brow were after rippin' off the distributor cap," Turpin said. "We had to walk all the way home. Took us about two friggin' hours."

"And then when we goes back to get the car the next day," Sinnott said, rolling down the window and spitting, "there's the Chev with no hubcaps, no radio, the antenna cracked off—"

"And not the one bit o' gas in her," Turpin said.

"Dry as a fuckin' bone," Sinnott concurred. "Siphoned off. Yes, my son. That crowd from the Brow—they're some hard bunch."

Turpin turned around and waved an Export "A" package. "Anyone want a butt?" The talking Dirtneck took one and placed it carefully between his bruised lips.

"You guys ever go up to the Brow dances?" Turpin asked, lighting the cigarettes with his Zippo.

The talking Dirtneck exhaled a cloud of smoke. "Oh yeah, the scattered time."

"Well, you're lucky you're not walkin' home out o' there tonight," Sinnott said. "Lord Jesus, it'd be sun-up by the time you got back to the Harbour."

They sat silently as the car sped through the night. Sinnott turned off the highway and headed down the winding road to Deep Harbour. "Where do you fellas live?" he asked.

"Just across from Harvey's Bridge," the talking Dirtneck said. "We'll both get out there."

They pulled up in front of a shabby bungalow criss-crossed with metal scaffolding. A gaudy sign advertised an aluminum siding contractor. Turpin held open the door as the two Dirtnecks climbed out. Nipper heard the ocean softly lapping, caught the sharp scent of salt and rotting fish. A thin slice of milky moon nestled low over the ocean.

The silent Dirtneck cleared his throat. "Thanks for the run."

"Yeah, thanks," his friend said.

"No problem," Turpin said.

"You guys coming to the dance next week?" Sinnott asked.

The talking Dirtneck grimaced. "I don't believe so."

Sinnott hit the gas and the car fishtailed in a tight circle. Turpin lit a cigarette and switched on the radio. Nipper put his legs up on the seat and grinned. The best group in the whole world was singing "All You Need Is Love."

40

In 1970, Nipper Mooney started grade eleven, his final year at All Angels. As he looked around the room that September morning, it struck him how much the face of his class had changed since grade five. A lot of students had dropped out: most recently, Bob O'Grady in grade nine and Ralph Picco in grade ten.

That afternoon in the cafeteria, a tall, lanky boy came over and slumped into the seat next to him: Ray Peddle, who lived in Waterford Heights, just across the tracks from the Lower Road in Kildura. Peddle was in one of the other grade eleven classes: the "brain" class. Nipper didn't know him too well, but he seemed like a nice guy. At least he never *acted* like a brain.

Peddle drummed his fingers on the tabletop. "I heard you're a good singer."

Nipper sat up and squinted at him. "Well, I sings. I don't know how good. Who told you that?"

"A couple of guys. You used to sing in the choir, didn't you?"

"Yeah—back in grade seven."

"Uh-huh. You know Randy Scott?"

"A bit. He's finished school, isn't he?"

"Yeah. Last year."

Nipper nodded. "What's on your mind?"

"Me and Randy got a band started. We need a singer. Interested?"

Nipper laughed. "You're brave. You haven't even heard me yet."

"You can't be any worse than us." Peddle leaned forward. "Listen, come over to the house on Saturday afternoon. We can have a little jam." He pulled a pen out of his blazer pocket and scribbled on a napkin. "That's the address."

Nipper took the napkin and looked at it. "Hey, what kind of songs do you do? Don't sing 'The Ballad of the Green Berets,' do you?"

Peddle raised an eyebrow. "Why would we do something like that?"

"Just kidding. So what do you do?"

Peddle shrugged. "The Doors, Stones, Beatles—stuff like that."

"Okay," Nipper said. "Sure. I'll be there."

Academically, there was good news and bad news. The good news was that Brother Crane had been transferred to Ontario. Nipper didn't know anyone, including the other teachers, who was sorry to see him go.

The bad news was that their new homeroom teacher would be Brother Spencer: Brother Spencer who bandaged up boys and marched them around to the classrooms; tall, wiry Brother Spencer with the sharply cut features, receding hairline and thin, humourless mouth; Brother Spencer whom the boys had dubbed "No Lips."

When they heard the news, Barnes looked at Nipper and groaned. "Shit—how are we supposed to get through a whole year with No Lips Spencer? That frigger is ten times worse than Crane ever was."

"I know," Nipper said. "Sure did I tell you what he did last year?"

Barnes grimaced. "What? Nothing would surprise me."

"It was last winter," Nipper said. "Remember when we had all that silver thaw? Well, this bunch of grade ones and twos had made a kind of skating rink next to the monastery. It was about thirty feet long, and they were sliding on it. Old Brother Thomas came to the door of the monastery and yelled at them to give it up. 'You're going to break your necks,' he said. The kids stopped for a while—you know, until he went back in—but then they started up again. The monastery door opened, and who should come down the steps but—"

"Spencer."

"Yeah. I suppose Brother Thomas must have thought that if the boys wouldn't listen to him, why not pull out the heavy artillery."

"What happened?"

"Well, one of the little fellas never saw 'im. Spencer came down the lane, and he stepped onto the ice just as buddy—about seven, he was—was finishing his run. He slid down the ice whooping and flailing his arms around. Then he saw Spencer. He tried to dig his feet into the ice, but that wasn't gonna stop 'im. He just kind of spun around like one of them rocks when they're playin' curling. And the poor frigger—"

"Jesus, he never . . . "

"He did. Banged right into Spencer—knocked him over just like a bowling pin. Spencer got up—you should've seen the eyes on 'im—but then he slipped and fell down *again*. Jesus, it was just like one of them Charlie Chaplin movies."

"What did the kid do?"

"He just lay there on the ice. I thought he was after hurting himself, but he was too scared to move."

"What did Spencer do?"

"Picked him up by the scruff of the neck and gave him this vicious kick in the arse—sent him right into a snowbank."

"Prick."

Nipper had had his own run-in with Brother Spencer when he was in grade ten. He had started to grow his hair long, and occasionally he saw Spencer staring at him unpleasantly in the corridors. Then one afternoon his biology teacher, Mr. Carter, didn't turn up for the last period. Brother Bannister instructed them over the PA to read quietly. Most of the boys went out to the cloakroom and put on their coats so they could avoid the rush when the bell rang. Nipper slipped into his brown, fringed cowboy jacket and came back to his desk.

As they sat reading, someone walked into the room. The class had been relatively quiet; now an absolute silence fell. Nipper didn't bother to look up; he knew who it was. He was sitting in the first desk by the window, and he heard Spencer's shoes click across the waxed floor until he stopped directly in front of him. Nipper kept his eyes glued to his book. The fluorescent lights buzzed. Spencer flicked disdainfully at his fringes with a yardstick. "Howdy, Buffalo Bill," he said in an awful Western accent. "Where'd yuh park yuh hoss?"

Some of the boys laughed uneasily. Nipper didn't know what to say, but Spencer clearly wanted an answer. He looked up at the Brother's poker face and tried to read his mood. Nipper supposed that even someone like Spencer made an occasional joke. Nipper jerked his thumb toward the window. "Oh, just out there in the parking lot." The words were barely out of his mouth when Spencer reached back and slapped him so hard across the face that Nipper fell out of his desk and sprawled in the aisle.

"Take off the coat," Spencer said, looking down at him. He turned and glowered at the rest of the class. "All of you." The boys jumped up, scattering books and pens, and headed back to the cloakroom. Nipper struggled to his feet and took off his jacket. Tears ran down his stinging face, blurring his vision.

He wanted to kill Spencer.

Wanted to take his goddamn fucking yardstick and jam it down his throat.

Wanted to ram his ugly no-lipped head against the blackboard until the shit he had for brains spilled all over the fucking waxed floor.

Spencer grabbed him by the arm. "This school day is not over for another twenty minutes, cowboy. *I'll* tell you when you can put on your coat."

Nipper yanked his arm away and went out to the cloakroom.

Now, for his final year at All Angels, No Lips Spencer would be his homeroom teacher. Nipper wondered if he would remember him as Buffalo Bill.

He hoped not.

41

The jam session with Peddle and Scott went well. They had microphones and fancy electric guitars. They were good players, too—particularly Peddle. They hadn't found a drummer yet, so it was just the three of them. Nipper had never sung through a microphone, but once he got used to it, he thought he sounded pretty good. A lot better than he'd thought he would. And at least they were doing real songs.

"When do I get to hear you?" Brigid asked on the bus one day.

"Whenever," Nipper said. "You want to come to the next practice?"

"Okay." She jabbed him with her elbow. "I suppose you'll forget all about me when you become a big rock star."

Nipper grinned. "Probably."

Brigid jabbed him again. "What are you going to call the band?"

"Promise you won't laugh?"

"I won't. What?"

"Well, Scott wanted to call it the Organized Confusion . . . "

"Yeah?"

"But Peddle wanted to call it the Elastic Band."

"So which one did you pick?"

"They said it was up to me. So I figured we'd compromise and call it the Organized Elastic Confusion Band."

"Bit long, isn't it?"

Nipper shrugged. "It'll do. It's not like we're trying to be the Beatles or anything."

. . .

Nipper had heard that every year Brother Spencer singled out one boy in his homeroom for a particularly hard time. From the first days of September, it became obvious that in their class Joe Barnes was to be that boy. Soon he was playing the same adversarial role with No Lips as Darrell had played four years earlier with Brother Crane. Spencer picked on him for everything, from the way he tied his tie to the kind of pen he used for his homework.

During lunch hour one day, Barnes tagged along with Nipper, who wanted to get a book from their classroom. Barnes was in a playful mood. When he stepped inside the door, he jumped up on the first desk; then he skipped down the entire row, executed a crude tap dance, whirled around, and bowed.

He looked up to see Brother Spencer sitting at his desk with his daily planner opened before him.

Nipper stood in the doorway looking from one to the other. Barnes blanched, frozen, as if a witch doctor had cast a spell on him. Spencer stood up. He raised his hands and clapped: once, twice, three times. Then he crossed his arms and went to the doorway. "Good-bye, Mr. Mooney."

"But, Burr, we were just—"

"*Good-bye*, Mr. Mooney."

The door closed in his face.

A few weeks later, the class was filling out a job-interest questionnaire. *Do you like to work with others? How many books did you read last year? Please specify fiction or non-fiction. Do you consider that you're good with your hands?* Nipper saw Wayne Rose lean forward and whisper something to Barnes. Rose must have asked about the questionnaire, because Barnes turned back to his sheet and studied it with a puzzled expression.

Nipper looked to the front of the class to check on Spencer. He was reading, resting his head on his hand. He turned a page of his book and glanced up just as Rose whispered again to Barnes.

Lying on Spencer's desk was a heavy blackboard protractor. Barnes turned to Rose to answer his question. Spencer dropped his eyes back to his book, but Nipper saw his right hand creep spider-like over the desk and come to rest on the protractor. Nipper tried to catch Barnes's eye, but he was too engrossed in the conversation. Nipper waited for Spencer to jump up or say something, but he turned back to his book and pretended to read. Every few seconds he glanced up.

And then Barnes sensed that he was being watched.

He turned around and looked to the front of the class—just as Spencer stood up and hurled the protractor at him. Barnes threw up his hands and ducked, but he was too late; the protractor hit him in the face and fell heavily to his desk, where it wobbled back and forth like a spent spinning top.

Barnes raised a hand to his face; it came back bloody. Blood dripped onto his questionnaire. He examined the blood with glassy eyes, as if unsure what it was. Then he stood up and stared at Spencer.

"You fucking prick."

Spencer looked at him expressionlessly. Barnes pressed a hand to his face and rushed down the aisle. He kicked open the door and disappeared into the corridor.

The class stared at Spencer. His naturally flushed complexion had faded to a sickening egg-white; his thin lips seemed to disappear entirely. Nipper waited for him to do something, *say* something. But he just stood there. Finally, Nipper got out of his desk and ran out into the corridor. It was empty, but, like Hansel and Gretel's bread crumbs, drops of blood pointed the way. Nipper followed the drops downstairs and pulled open the door to the washroom. Barnes was leaning over a wash basin, running the cold-water faucet full-blast. He took his hand from his face and let the blood drip into the basin. "That bastard," Barnes said, sniffling. "That fucking *bastard*."

"Let me see." Nipper bent down and looked at Barnes sideways. A jagged, two-inch cut ran over his left eyebrow; already a purplish bump swelled underneath. Nipper tore a roll of paper towels from the dispenser and submerged a thick handful into the water. "Here," he said. Barnes took the towels with a shaking hand and put them to his face. Blood and water flecked his shirt and tie.

"That's going to need stitches," Nipper said. "Jesus, he could've fucking blinded you." The heavy wooden door creaked open, and through the mirror they saw Spencer standing in the doorway. Nipper turned around. "He's bleeding."

"Get back to class. I'll take care of it."

"We've got to get the first aid kit."

"Back to class, Mr. Mooney," Spencer said quietly. "Now."

"He should go to the hospital. He needs stitches."

"I *said* . . . I'll take care of it." Spencer held open the door. "Go."

Nipper stepped out into the corridor, then glanced back. Through the closing door, he saw Barnes standing hunched and shaking by the wash basin. He seemed very small. He stared into the mirror holding a fistful of bloody paper towels to his face.

Brother Bannister took Barnes to St. Clare's in the All Angels van. The cut took seven stitches.

Barnes never came back to school.

Occasionally, though, he would be waiting for Nipper when school got out at three-thirty. Waiting for him in his car. Barnes had turned seventeen and was lucky enough to get his driver's license on the first try. He had always bragged that he owned a car and worked on it in his father's garage. Nipper had thought it was just another tall tale.

The day Barnes got his license he waited for Nipper at the school gates and brought him down to Gardiner Street, where he proudly showed him an ancient, multicoloured Valiant, which seemed to be constructed almost entirely of polybond.

"Cool," Nipper said.

Barnes grinned. "I know she's not much to look at, but she runs like a clock."

"No, she's great. Listen, you think you could give me a few driving lessons sometime? Mom said it was okay for me to get my learner's permit."

"What are you gonna drive when you get your license?"

"Our car. She said she'd let me take it every now and then as long as I don't crack it up. I hope the frig the third and fourth gears still work. It's not like they ever got much use."

"Okay," Barnes said. "No sweat—I mean, as long as you don't crack up mine, either."

"I'll be careful."

After Barnes had driven around town, they pulled up in front of Madden's Bakery and smoked.

"So you're really not going back?" Nipper said.

"Would you?"

"I don't know. I keep telling myself that it's just another few months and I'll be shed of the bloody place."

"Yeah, well, I don't care how long it is. Fuck 'em all. I'll go to work with the old man. That's probably what I would've ended up doing, anyway."

They stared out at Gardiner Street.

"Listen, Barnes, there's something I got to tell you." Barnes lit another cigarette. Nipper could see the scar running through his eyebrow and curling onto his forehead. He would take that scar to his grave.

"Yeah?"

"He waited."

"What?"

"When Spencer threw the protractor. He *waited*. He saw you turned around talking to Rose, but he waited until you turned face-on again before he threw it."

Barnes shrugged. "So?"

"Don't you get it? He *wanted* to hit you in the face."

Barnes stretched his arms out on the steering wheel. "Is that supposed to surprise me?"

"No. I guess not. But maybe we should *do* something about it. Report him."

"To who? Bannister? He knows all about it. He was the one who drove me to the hospital."

"Fuck Bannister. The police, b'y. We could go to the police and charge him. Assault with a deadly weapon."

"A *protractor*."

"Why not? Jesus, he could've fucking killed you."

"He'd get off," Barnes said. "He's a *Brother*. They wouldn't do nothin' to a Brother. Sure you know what my old man said when I told him what happened? He said Spencer probably didn't mean it. He was probably just trying to scare me. My *old man* said that. Come on, Nipper. Nothing would happen. At worst, they'd give him a warning." Barnes laughed. "Where's Paddy Dunne when you really need him?"

The eight months after Barnes had quit All Angels were the longest of Nipper's school career. It wasn't that Spencer picked on him more than anyone else. After the incident with the protractor, he calmed down considerably. He didn't even adopt a new scapegoat. Perhaps the school board or the Superior General of the Christian Brothers had gotten wind of the episode and advised him that, while it was all right to maintain discipline, he should be careful not to murder any students while he was at it.

The worst thing was that Spencer taught algebra and trigonometry, Nipper's worst subjects, and he was sure he was going to fail both. Whenever he thought that he might have to repeat the year, he nearly threw up.

Nipper couldn't concentrate. When Spencer used the protractor in a demonstration, the equations and graphs blurred into meaningless scrawls.

He saw Spencer's hand creeping across his desk.

The protractor tottering.

Barnes holding the bloody paper towels to his face.

And while Nipper was rerunning those scenes in his mind, he was failing just about every algebra and trigonometry exam.

SIX

42

Nipper walked down Prince Street and saw Barnes's Valiant parked in front of Holy Rosary. Barnes got out and went around to the passenger side. "I hope you're better today than you were the last time," he said.

Nipper grinned and climbed behind the wheel. "That's the reason you take lessons," he said. "I wouldn't need you to teach me to drive if I could already do it, would I? Got a smoke?" As Barnes was taking one out of the pack, Nipper noticed two hand-rolled cigarettes. "I don't mind taking one of the rolls."

Barnes laughed. "I bet you wouldn't."

"I mean it. I roll my own sometimes. It's no odds to me."

Barnes handed him a Rothman's and then cupped his hand over Nipper's ear. "They're not cigarettes," he said in an exaggerated stage whisper. "At least not *regular* cigarettes."

"Then what are they?"

Barnes rolled his eyes. "What do you think, b'y? They're joints."

"Yeah?"

Barnes had told Nipper that he occasionally smoked up with his friends down in Portugal Cove, but Nipper never really believed him.

"Sure last summer I tried something else," he said.

"What?"

Barnes winked. "LSD. California Sunshine."

"You didn't."

"I did."

"Where'd you get it?"

"At the Regatta."

"The *Regatta?*"

"Sure. Me and Brian Hennebury wanted to buy some grass, but this guy he knew was all out. Said all he had was California Sunshine. I'd never heard tell of it, so I asked him what it was. 'Oh, it's the same thing as grass,' he said. 'Just a bit stronger.'"

"You buy it?"

"Me and Brian dropped a hit each."

"So what was it like?"

"Wild, b'y. For one thing, no one told us you were only supposed to take a *half* hit. We probably shouldn't have done it at the Regatta, either. I heard on the radio that there were sixteen thousand people there, and about an hour after I dropped the acid, I thought they were all talkin' to me. I nearly went off me head. Cool though, all the same."

"Listen," Nipper said, "there's a party in Mount Pearl on Saturday night. They want our band to play. Think you could give me and Brigid a drive out? You're invited, too."

"Who's having the party?"

"Charlotte Gosse—she's in Brigid's class. Her parents are out of town for the weekend, and she asked Brigid to stay over. When Charlotte heard about the band, she wondered if we'd play. Peddle's got his old man's car, but he's gonna have to take Scott and the equipment. We'll pay you for the gas."

"Well . . ."

"Charlotte's pretty cute."

"Yeah?" Barnes said. "Okay. Why not?"

Nipper put the car in gear.

When they arrived on Saturday night, the house was already packed. Nipper went downstairs to the rec room to see where they could set up, and there, sitting on the couch with a Jockey

Club beer in his hand, was Paddy Dunne. Nipper hadn't seen him since the day in the gym.

"How's it goin'?" Paddy said, toasting him.

Nipper sat down. "Jesus," he said. "You're a stranger." Paddy's wispy peach fuzz had bloomed into a fiery-red mustache. He had filled out—most of it muscle. Nipper remembered that he worked as a longshoreman.

Paddy reached over and flicked at Nipper's hair. "You're gettin' to be a real hippie. I hear you plays in the band."

"Yeah," Nipper said. "Well, I don't exactly play. I'm the singer."

"Right on. You still at All Angels?"

"It's my last year—if I don't blow it."

"Ah, go on. You'll pass. A smart fella like you." He looked at Nipper coyly. "Crane still there?"

"No, he got transferred to the mainland. Toronto, I think. I don't care where he is as long as it's far from here." Paddy nodded and took a swig of his Jockey. "You know, that was really something the day you decked him." Nipper laughed. "Barnes thought you'd killed him."

Paddy peeled the label off his beer bottle. "The fucker had it coming."

"Did they ever do anything to you? I mean, like charge you for it or anything?"

"Nah. I never heard a word about it. Crane probably thought that if he bitched I'd come back and finish him off. I probably would've too."

"Guys still talk about it at school," Nipper said. "Of course, a lot of 'em thinks we just made it up."

"It's no odds to me." Paddy drained his beer and wiped his mouth on the back of his hand. "You know the only thing I wish? I wish he'd read that composition I wrote—*we* wrote. Not that I wanted to impress him or anything, just to show the son-of-a bitch I could do it." He settled back on the couch. "Anyway, that's ancient history now."

"You still doin' your drawing and stuff?"

"I don't get much chance, b'y. It's kinda busy down at work. By the time I gets home, I'm too baffed out to be at anything like that."

"I know what you mean. My mother says the same thing. Well, I better get the boys."

"Hey, you guys any good, or what?" Paddy asked.

Nipper laughed. "You tell me."

When Nipper got upstairs, Barnes was fishing a beer out of the refrigerator. "Guess who I just saw?"

"Who?"

"Paddy Dunne."

"Yeah? What's he doin' here?"

"Beats me. I suppose he knows Charlotte."

Brigid came over. "Did you say Paddy Dunne is downstairs?"

"Yeah."

"Gee, I should go say hello."

It was a good night for the band. People packed the rec room so tightly Nipper wondered how anyone could move, let alone dance. By eleven they'd run out of songs. "What do we do now?" Nipper asked, as Peddle was tuning his guitar.

"Play 'em all again, I suppose."

They launched into "Light My Fire."

By midnight the band had finished, and most people had gone home. "Hey, Barnes," Nipper said, "don't you think it's time we got a move on?" But Barnes had developed an interest in their host and wasn't in any hurry. Soon, Barnes, Paddy, Nipper and Brigid were the only ones left.

"How's Brendan these days?" Paddy asked, while the others were cleaning up.

"Pretty feeble," Nipper said. "He still goes off on his hikes, but never too far."

"I'm not surprised. How old is he now? Must be at least in his 80s."

"Yeah," Nipper said. "He's gettin' up there, all right. I should go see him more than I do."

"He ever take you out to his special spot?" Paddy asked.

Nipper smiled. "The Lookout? How did you know about that?"

"Followed him one day."

"Yeah," Nipper said. "I've been there. I used to go with him a lot when I was little. He used to teach me the names of things—flowers, constellations, trees, birds—stuff like that. Brendan always wanted to know what something was called. He said it made you see the world better." Nipper paused. "He taught me a lot of things."

"There wasn't too much he didn't know, if you ask me," Paddy said. He leaned forward. "He ever show you his cross?"

"The St. Brigid's Cross?" Nipper nodded. "Yeah, he showed it to me."

"He was dyin' to the world about that cross," Paddy said. "He told me all about it one day. How his uncle or someone had brought it all the way over from Ireland."

"Yeah," Nipper said. "He told me, too. It was his grandfather."

Brigid and Charlotte came up to them.

"Have you looked out the window?" Brigid asked.

"No. Why?"

"You better take a look."

They went upstairs to the living room. Barnes stood at the edge of the picture window; he discreetly pulled back the drapes.

"Get a load of that," he said. Charlotte's house was at the top of a lane about five hundred yards from the main road, and in front of the house, spilling down the lane, were about forty teenagers.

"What do they want?" Nipper asked.

"They're Mount Pearlers," Barnes said.

Charlotte peered out the window. "See that big guy in the green army parka? That's Jackie Simmons. They were at a party, and someone told them there was a bunch of Kildurans over here." Charlotte's face went pale. "Doreen just called and told me."

"Jesus," Nipper said. "Me and Brigid are the only Kildurans here."

"You want to go out and share that bit of information with them?" Barnes said. "Most of 'em are half-crocked."

"I'm a Kilduran, too," Paddy said. "At least I used to be." Nipper peeked out again. There were girls as well as boys. They wrestled and jostled to keep warm.

"Christ," Nipper said. "They're carrying on like they're at a friggin' hockey game or something."

"They're waiting for us to come out," Barnes said. "For the *Kildurans* to come out. And listen—I'm too young to die."

"Take it easy," Paddy said. "We'll hang her down here for a while. It's cold out. They'll give it up and go home out of it soon enough."

An hour later the crowd had shrunk to about half its original size, but those remaining looked like they weren't going anywhere. Cars had pulled into the lane, and people took turns sitting in them to keep warm.

"What are we going to do?" Brigid said.

Charlotte paced around the living room. "I knows that Jackie Simmons. He's a nut case if there ever was one. He'll probably stay out there all night. What if someone calls the police? If Mom finds out I had a party tonight, she'll *murder* me."

"Maybe we should go talk to them," Nipper said.

"Talk?" Barnes said. "You think they know how?"

"Come on," Paddy said. "We can't stay here all night. We're going to get Charlotte in trouble."

They went into the vestibule and put on their boots and coats. Paddy opened the door and went down the front steps. Barnes and Nipper followed. Nipper heard car doors slamming, the click of the screen door. The Mount Pearlers looked at them and fell silent. Barnes was right: they weren't in the mood for talking. They didn't even bother with accusations or insults.

The crowd surged toward them. Nipper suddenly found they were in the centre of a tightening circle.

Jackie Simmons pushed his way through the crowd and stared at them. He dismissed Barnes and Nipper, then looked at Paddy with interest.

The circle closed.

Someone grabbed Nipper by the waist and threw him into the Mount Pearlers across from him. Two guys caught him and threw him back again. They kept it up until Nipper felt like a tennis ball in a volley. Christ, he said to himself. They're not going to beat me up, they're going to shake me to death. But soon they began to punch as well. Nipper tried to time himself: when he was thrown into the circle, he struck out blindly with his fist. A couple of times he actually hit someone. He saw out of the corner of his eye that Barnes was getting the same treatment. Once they nearly crashed into each other.

Suddenly Brigid charged down the steps with her purse in her hand. She began swinging it wildly at the Mount Pearlers. "You get out of here!" she yelled. "Leave them alone!" And soon, almost as if a flock of pigeons had been scattered by a cat, Nipper found that they were alone. The stars in his head dissolved, and he realized he was staring up at the real stars.

Brigid sank down next to him and rocked back and forth on her knees. "Are you all right?"

Nipper sat up and looked around. Barnes staggered over to them. Nipper looked for Paddy, and by the porch light he saw him lying face down in the driveway, his head pushed into a snowbank. Nipper and Brigid ran to him and turned him over. His face was badly swollen, his hair encrusted with snow and blood. He was moaning and cursing.

"Shit," Nipper said. "We got to get him to the hospital."

Charlotte swooped down the front steps and rushed up to them. They helped Paddy to his feet. "Oh, God," Charlotte said. "My parents are going to *kill* me."

"I'll get the car," Barnes said.

"I'm coming, too," Brigid said. "I'll get my coat."

Nipper grabbed her by the arm. "No. We can take care of him. You stay here with Charlotte."

The hospital was only minutes away. While Paddy was with the intern, Barnes and Nipper sat in the waiting room and examined each other's bruises. A raw pink scar ran down the right side of Nipper's neck; Barnes's lower lip was bruised and puffy.

Twenty minutes later, the intern came out with Paddy. "Don't worry," he said. "It's not as bad as it looks."

"Good thing," Barnes said. Paddy's swollen face was an unsettling collage of purple, red and yellow. Barnes said later that looking at Paddy that night reminded him of being stoned on acid. Paddy grinned painfully.

"Be careful with those ribs," the intern said. He turned to go, but then wheeled around and looked back at them. "You know, you guys should grow up before someone really gets hurt."

"Yeah," Nipper said. "I know."

. . .

The next day word got around Kildura that the Mount Pearlers were boasting about how they'd "kicked the shit" out of a bunch of Kildurans. The real Kildura gang was livid. That night they gathered in front of Blake's store. Nipper watched as Dougie Whalen, Turpin, Sinnott and a bunch of other guys pulled chains and tire irons out of their car trunks and piled them into the back seats. When they were finished, Whalen came over to the front step where Nipper was sitting with a Coke. He poked him in the chest.

"You're comin' with us."

"What for?" Nipper said, surprised. "You got enough guys. You don't need me."

Whalen sneered. "I don't want you to *fight*," he said. "I want you to point out those bastards."

"But—"

"Get in the car."

Nipper squeezed into Whalen's green Impala, and the convoy headed off. The car quickly filled with cigarette smoke. Andy Turpin's tire iron stuck painfully into Nipper's ribs. His left leg started to go to sleep, and he shifted uncomfortably. When it came time to jump out, he thought, he'd probably be too stiff to move.

For a long time, no one spoke. Then Whalen looked at Nipper through the rear-view mirror.

"Who else was there besides Jackie Simmons?"

"I don't know. I didn't recognize any of 'em. All I know is that there was a *lot* of 'em."

Whalen stubbed out his cigarette. "Pricks. They knew friggin' well there was no Kildurans at that party. And the gall of 'em, then, to go *braggin'* about it. I mean, we'd never do somethin' like that, would we, Andy?"

"Wouldn't have to," Turpin said. "Anyway, we'll show 'em tonight what the *real* Kildurans can do."

There was a chorus of approval. Whalen turned the car onto the road leading to Mount Pearl. But it soon became clear that no one had formulated a plan. Almost immediately, an argument broke out between Turpin and Sinnott about where the Mount Pearlers hung out. Sinnott said it was Wong's Takeout.

"It *used* to be Wong's," Turpin said, "but that was years ago. Nobody goes there anymore. I don't believe it's even still open."

"Well, where then?" Sinnott said.

"*I* don't know. Whalen, do you know?"

"It makes no odds," Whalen said. "We'll check 'em all." And they did. But it was Sunday night, and they hardly saw a soul. Then, as they were driving by the supermarket, Turpin jabbed his finger at the window. "Look," he said. "There's a bunch of fellas on the steps." Whalen whipped the car into the parking lot and pulled up in front of the main door. Everyone jumped out, brandishing the tire irons and rattling the chains. But the gang turned out to be a bunch of junior high boys sneaking a joint. Their jaws fell open; one of them started to cry. Whalen questioned them for a while, but they said they didn't know anything about Jackie Simmons and his gang.

The Kildurans piled back into their cars. Around midnight, after a lot of cigarettes and tough talk, they headed home.

43

One Saturday morning in June, Nipper packed a lunch and headed up the Old Road with his fishing pole. Ronnie Sheehan had promised to meet him at the South Darning Needle when he got off work at noon. Nipper was in a good mood: he'd passed his driving test the day before. Near Shalloway Pond he saw Brendan staring out over the water. Nipper was struck by how shrunken he looked. His overcoat seemed three sizes too big for him. He turned when he heard Nipper coming and smiled.

"Off to murder a few trout, are you?"

"I guess so."

"Don't mind me. I'm just teasing. Brigid said you got your license."

"Yeah. The test wasn't too bad. He just made me drive up and down the road a few times."

"Well, good for you."

"How you feeling these days?"

"Old, Nicky. I feel old. I never used to, you know. When you were a little fella—and that's not that long ago—I had all the energy in the world. I could beat it in to my lookout and back again in no time. And now I can't get in there at all. I misses it, you know. The ponds and rivers—they're lovely, but there's nothing like the ocean."

"Yeah."

"You know, I can't believe all the walking I used to do. Maybe that's the trouble—I got myself wore out. I've been all over the country up here, oh, a thousand times. There's no one knows more about it than me." Brendan laughed. "Well, except maybe for the fairies."

"You seen any lately?" Nipper said.

Brendan shook his head. "Not a sign. But they're out there. I can still feel 'em." He paused. "You know a funny thing about getting old?"

"What's that?"

"You start remembering things from way back when you were a child. Things you hadn't thought about in sixty or seventy years. I suppose that's all you *can* do when you get older and don't get out much: think about stuff. Anyway, that's what I do these days—think about all the trails and hikes I used to do. At least my memory is still good. I can picture every gully, every flower and shrub."

"What were you thinking about just then?" Nipper asked.

Brendan chuckled. "You'll laugh if I tell you. But if you really want to know, I was thinking about poor old Vincent."

"Who's he?"

"An old cat we had when I was a youngster. I was about, oh, twelve or so. I found him up in the potato field one morning. How he got there or where he came from, I don't know. Maybe he was after deserting from somewhere, like they say our ancestors did. Anyway, he was a pitiful sight hunched down there in the potato plants. And wild? I couldn't get near him for the longest time. Finally I got a-hold to him and brought him home. We had to give him a good wash before we could even tell what kind of a cat he was—I had the scars for weeks—but it turned out he was a tortoiseshell: kind of black and brown and orange all mixed up together.

"He was already an old cat when I found him. You could tell he'd been through the wars: his right ear was just about chewed off. He didn't meow like other cats; he made this little *cack, cack* sound—more like something you'd hear out of a bird. For some reason, Mother was dyin' to the world about him. He liked her, too—used to sleep at the foot of her bed every night.

"Anyway, we had him for years and years. He always had three names. I wanted to call him Vincent, after Vincent van Gogh; you know, that painter fella who chopped his own ear off—sliced it off with a knife. But Mother said Vincent was no name for a cat—that that was a *people* name. So she called him Sim and I called him Vincent and Father just called him Cat. It didn't matter: he'd answer to anything—especially if food was involved. One day—this was in the summer—Mother bawled out the back door to Vincent to come in to his supper, and there he was: gone. No sign of him anywhere. Mother was heartbroken. She sent me out beatin' the woods and fields for him; nothing. Finally, we gave up. Mother figured the fairies took him—although I didn't know what the fairies would be wanting with a skinny old, one-eared cat. I thought a dog was after goin' off with him. And then, about a week and a half after he disappeared, Mother went up to the attic for something, and declare to God, there was Vincent caught in the window! Mother had it open, see, propped up with a stick—you know, where it had been so warm? Poor old Vincent must have been coming or going through the window, and somehow he knocked out the stick. The window came right down on top of him—on his back paw. Trapped him. And of course he couldn't meow properly, so there he was all that time stuck in the window. Mother nearly took a stroke when she saw him. She yelled down the stairs, 'Brendan, get up here!' When I went into the attic, she didn't say a word, just pointed. I saw *something* in the window, but I didn't know what it was. I thought it might have been a rag or an old scarf. You see, poor Vincent was after dryin' right out. I mean, he hadn't had anything to drink for over a week. I lifted up the window and picked him up. Well, he was that light, it was like picking up a feather duster. Now, here's the funny thing. He was almost gone away to nothing. There wasn't the bare sign of a heartbeat, but I knew—I *felt* that he wasn't dead, that his soul was still inside him. Sure enough, one of his eyes flickered, and I said, 'Mom, I believe he's still alive.' Well, her eyes nearly popped out of her head. She took him in her arms and brought him downstairs. Then she got a bowl of milk and stuck his face down in it, but he never had the strength to eat. And do you know what she did? We had this big oil stove, and she opened the door and put him in the oven. She took the bowl of milk and put it next to his head. Then she got a spoon and moistened his lips with the milk, but Vincent could barely open his mouth. We sat there and watched him for a while. And then Father comes into the kitchen and says, 'What's for supper?' Well, he took one look in the oven and didn't say a word. Just turned around and walked right back out again! Then I saw Vincent's mouth open a tiny bit, and his little pink tongue peeked through his teeth. And then it darted out further, like a snake's. He made a lick at the milk bowl. Mother moved it closer to him and started feeding him with the spoon again, and declare to God, but he started coming back to life. In a couple of days, he was up and around—a bit shaky, mind you, but moving. And, my son, what a sight he was—like a walking X-ray with a chewed-off ear. He certainly wasn't the prettiest cat in the world, but Mother didn't care what he looked like.

"We had him for more years after that, him goin' around on three legs because the one the window had fallen on was useless—just used to hang dead-like, not a joog in it. And then one day Vincent got in the front room where none of *us* was allowed, let alone an old cat. Mother went in and caught him sprawled off on her good chair. She smacked her hands together. 'Kiss! Kiss! Get down out of that!' she said. Vincent bolted for the floor. But when Mother looked in the chair, Vincent was after leavin' something behind. It was his old dead leg! Came right off. She told me to take it out in the garden and bury it, but I thought I might keep it for a good-luck piece—you know, like a rabbit's paw. After all, Vincent had been through an awful lot, and he always seemed to survive. But I didn't keep it; it didn't smell too good. So I buried it like she told me.

"Vincent went around with just the three legs for another few years. Then Mother got sick this time, and old Dr. Curtis came to the house to see her. When he went into the kitchen and saw Vincent creepin' across the floor to his milk bowl, he said, 'What in the name of the Blessed Sacred Heart of Jesus is *that*?' He told Mother she was going to have to get him put down; he was probably carrying every disease known to cats and man and probably half a dozen more besides. Mother was heartbroken, didn't want to do it. But if that's what the doctor said, well, you didn't question a doctor. She asked me if I'd do it, but I didn't want any part of it. So she asked Father. He'd never shown much interest in Vincent, but he said, 'No. Not me.' Finally, she asked Phil Hartery—Francis's grandfather. And, well, Phil took Vincent up in the woods and shot him and buried him up there.

"At the time, I thought that was a mortal sin. I mean, the poor creature had been through so much for so long—why not let him go on till he dropped? But I don't know. Maybe it was the best thing. I couldn't imagine then what it must be like to be old, with three legs and a chewed-off ear and every disease known to cats and man and probably half a dozen more besides. When you gets a certain age, maybe it's not such a bad thing if someone takes you up in the woods and puts you out of your misery." Brendan ran his tongue over his teeth and looked at Nipper. "Anyway, enough of that foolishness. How are you gettin' on these days? Finished school yet?"

"End of the month," Nipper said. "If I pass."

"That's right. You and Brigid."

"I don't think *she's* got anything to worry about."

"You're probably right," Brendan said. "She was always smart in school. Still, you never know. I'll say a prayer to St. Brigid for the both of you."

Nipper smiled. "I think I'll say a few myself."

44

*A*nd he did. On the morning Nipper Mooney's final exams started, he went over to Holy Rosary and sat beneath his old friend, the Archangel Michael. He bowed his head. *Oh, please, Michael, oh, please, St. Brigid, just let me pass. I don't want 80s or 90s—just a pass. Just enough so I won't have to go back. Oh, Brigid, ever excellent woman, golden sparkling flame, lead me to the eternal kingdom, the dazzling resplendent sun.*

Lead me out of All Angels.

At first, Nipper thought his prayers might have been answered. His exams went well; even Latin wasn't that bad. But when he looked at the algebra paper, his heart sank. The equations and graphs mesmerized him. He walked out knowing he had failed. Trigonometry was better, but he still didn't complete enough to pass.

Nipper prepared his mother for the worst, but Sharon remained optimistic. The morning his marks came in the mail, she laid the envelope next to his teacup. He looked at it blankly and turned back to his cereal. After a moment, Sharon said, "Do you want me to open it?"

Nipper put down his spoon. "No. I'll do it." He took a bread knife and slit open the envelope. The first thing he saw printed at the bottom was "Pass." Nipper quickly scanned the list of marks, mostly 60s and 70s. Algebra: 62 percent; trigonometry 65 percent. Nipper lay down the transcript. He knew it was a lie. He needed to score at least 80 percent on the algebra final, an exam he'd only completed half of, to get 62.

"Well?" his mother said.

"I passed. Don't ask me how. It must have been St. Brigid."

"What?"

"Never mind."

His mother smiled and hugged him. "I knew you'd pass. All Angels is a good school academically. Everybody knows that."

Nipper stared at the marks and shook his head.

The next evening, on his way down to Brigid's, he met Ronnie Sheehan driving the cows up the road.

"Did you read the paper today?" Ronnie asked.

"What are you talking about? What paper?"

"The newspaper," Ronnie said. "The *Daily News*. There was a story about the public exams. You didn't hear?"

"Hear what?"

"Turns out a whole bunch of people failed the math exams."

"What?"

Ronnie grinned. "Hundreds, according to the paper. But they pushed them through, anyway. Had to."

"Why?"

Ronnie shrugged. "Didn't have anywhere to put 'em if they kept 'em back. People are kickin' up a real stink about it." He laughed. "All that studying you did for nothing."

Brigid was waiting on her front step. "I heard you passed," she said.

Nipper grinned. "God moves in mysterious ways."

"I told Brendan. He said, good for you."

"I think his prayers must have helped—helped a lot of people, apparently."

Brigid smiled. "Yes," she said. "They couldn't have hurt, anyway." She stared down at the ground. "I've made up my mind, Nicky. I'm goin' to go to university in September."

Nipper nodded. "That's what I thought—smart girl like you. Figured out what you're gonna study?"

"Education, I think."

Nipper shook his head. "You just get out of school, and now you're telling me you want to spend the rest of your life in a classroom? It wouldn't be me."

"I think I'd be a good teacher."

"I didn't mean that. I know you will."

Brigid looked up. "I've been talking to Dad," she said. "I'm not going to university here. I'm going to go away."

Something caught in Nipper's throat. He stared at Brigid. "Away? Where?"

"Oh, not far. I want to be able to come home for Christmas and holidays. Probably Nova Scotia."

"Nova Scotia?"

"Yeah. *If* I get accepted." She grinned. "It's what I want to do. Will you miss me?"

"Of course, I will. You know that."

"What are you going to do?"

Nipper shrugged. "Beats me," he said. "I don't have the first clue."

SEVEN

45

On Tuesday, December 16, six months after Nipper had graduated, All Angels burned to the ground. The fire started on the ground floor; the cause was never determined. A mystery. Arson was suspected, but nothing could be proven. Arson wouldn't have surprised Nipper. He had always fantasized that All Angels would go up in smoke. Not, of course, when there was anyone inside—not even Brother Spencer. His fantasy called for a night blaze; no one is hurt, but the place is completely levelled. When he comes down for breakfast the next morning, his mother says, "You can go back to bed. All Angels burned down last night. You don't have to go to school until next year—maybe even longer."

The fire broke out just before the final period in the afternoon. Everyone got out, but there were many close calls. At the last minute, Brother Bannister had gone back in to ensure the building was empty. He immediately rushed out again, pursued by a fireball that licked at the edges of his soutane. The picture in the *Evening Telegram* had been quite dramatic. People called him a hero.

Nipper's favourite story of the fire had to do with its discovery. The only students on the ground floor, a grade five class, were reading quietly, waiting for their teacher. The boy sitting by the door smelled something. He crept out of his desk and peered down the hall, which was rapidly filling with smoke.

"Jesus, b'ys, there's a fire," he said.

"Christ," another boy said. "Go tell someone." But no one would go. They had been trained, under pain of death, to stay

313

put until a teacher showed up, and that's what they were going to do—even if the place was burning down around their ears. A kid named Graham McCarthy ran to the door and looked for himself.

"Shit," he said. "The whole friggin' place is goin' up." One by one the other boys got out of their desks and crowded around the door. But still no one would go for help. Finally, McCarthy sprinted down the hall, bounded up the stairs and knocked on the grade seven door.

He was greeted, to his horror, by none other than Principal Bannister himself. "What are you doing out of your classroom," he demanded.

"Sorry, Burr, but there's a fire."

Bannister glared at him for a moment and then turned to the class. "Memorize the poem 'Autumn Splendour' on page 96." He grabbed McCarthy by the shoulder. "All I can say, Mr. McCarthy, is that, for your sake, there damn well *better* be a fire."

The building was evacuated in quite an orderly fashion. The boys had been trained for that, too.

Nipper had heard about the fire while driving home. He pulled off the road and turned up the radio. Then he put the car in gear and headed back to St. John's.

There was no saving the school. By the time Nipper arrived at four-thirty, the south wing had crumbled into a mound of glowing, smoking ash. The firemen, having given up the school for lost, had turned most of their attention to the surrounding buildings. Six firemen trained snake-like hoses in criss-cross patterns over the monastery.

The smoke ascended, sometimes charcoal-black, sometimes a liquid, greasy grey, in soft spirals heavenward. Surprisingly, there was little actual fire. Even when the west wing collapsed, taking with it the gym with its hardwood floors, the searing, tumbling flames remained remarkably small and self-contained.

Despite the bitter cold, hundreds of people jostled each other for a better look. The police guarded their rope barriers warily, but still some children sneaked beneath them and scampered over hoses and around trucks into the icy schoolyard. One urchin shimmied up the back of the Archangel Gabriel, straddling the neck, his hands grasping Gabriel's forehead, his feet bouncing rhythmically off the angel's stone chest. He lurched forward, pointing excitedly until a cursing constable, slipping and sliding on the ice, plucked him from his perch and dragged him back to the street.

At one point, a woman in hair rollers and house slippers pushed through the crowd. "Did all the children get out?" She looked around wildly and then saw her son hanging over the rope. She grabbed him and cuffed him on the ear. "You get home out of it this very minute!"

Nipper heard more commotion, yells. Suddenly, a half-dozen men ran to the statue of the Virgin Mary, and while flaming two by fours and tarpaper fell around them, they lifted her to safety. The men looked back at the attending angels, but it was too late. They were left to the flames.

In a couple of hours, All Angels had disappeared.

The cold started to drive the spectators away. Nipper pulled his scarf higher around his neck. He was about to leave himself when he saw a tall, gaunt figure huddled inside a thin army parka. A scarf hid his mouth and nose, but Nipper knew who it was: Darrell Wiggins. Their eyes met briefly, but Darrell gave no sign of recognition. He kicked at a piece of jagged ice, then turned and headed out the back entrance of the schoolyard and down Gardiner Street.

46

*B*oth of the schools Nipper had attended were now gone. As soon as he'd arrived on the scene that evening, the first thing that struck him was that, inexplicably, *he* had something to do with the fire. Perhaps the powers-that-be had finally gotten around to his wish and decided to grant it.

Two days later, Nipper drove up Prince Street and parked in front of Holy Rosary. There must have been fifty people milling about. The wind blew hard—harder than usual. Of course, a major windbreak was gone now. Nipper stood on the sidewalk and stared at the wreckage. Bulldozers and Mack trucks were noisily clearing away the debris. It had turned surprisingly warm; the snow was melting into rushing rivulets, exposing the previous year's fossilized garbage.

Nipper stepped into the courtyard and saw Darrell Wiggins standing next to the Archangel Gabriel. His hands were shoved deep into his pockets; he stared at the bulldozers. Nipper looked at Darrell for a moment, then walked up to him. "Hey, Darrell," he called. "Remember me?"

Darrell peered at him myopically and nodded. "Sure. You were in my class."

"Remember my name?"

"Sure I do. It's Nipper."

"Yeah," he said. "Grade eight. Brother Crane. I suppose you remember him?"

Darrell looked up at the concrete steps leading nowhere. "Yeah, I remembers him."

They stood silently for a moment. "So what do you think of the school burning down?"

Darrell shrugged. "I dunno."

"Come on, it must mean *some*thing."

Darrell closed his eyes. Crumbs of yellow crust stuck to his pale lashes. "Brother Crane and all that stuff, I don't . . . I don't like thinking about that." Darrell opened his eyes and looked at Nipper. He chewed his lips and tilted his head toward the ground. "I didn't like going there very much. It wasn't nice." He turned to Nipper, and his voice held a surprising conviction. "I'm *glad* the school burned down."

Nipper looked around the courtyard and listened to the roar of the tractors. Darrell fidgeted with his jacket zipper. "You still living down on Saintsbury Place?"

"Yeah."

"You workin'?"

Darrell nodded. "I works for the *Telegram*—sells it down in front of Woolworth's." He reached into an inside pocket and brought out a pack of DuMauriers. "Want a cigarette?"

Nipper took one. "Thanks. I don't remember you smoking."

"Didn't use to." He grinned, revealing his yellow teeth. "Mom wouldn't let me."

"But she does now?"

He shook his head and stared up at the monastery. "She died."

"Sorry."

Darrell took out a box of matches and lit his cigarette. Then he cupped his hands and, stepping around to guard against the wind, held the flame beneath Nipper's.

"Thanks."

They stood in the quadrangle, smoking, looking on as the

warm wind blew last year's garbage into the sky, and the bulldozers sank their blades into the wet earth.

47

Whenever Nipper saw Brendan up on the Old Road, it was never too far in, usually no farther than Shalloway Pond, sometimes not even that far. When he saw Nipper coming along the road, his first question was always, "How far did you go?" This followed by, "Been to my lookout lately?"

One day Nipper said, "No. I haven't been out there in quite a while."

Brendan nodded. "Well, it is quite a hike. And there's no trout—just ocean. All you minds is the trout."

"I wouldn't say that."

"I remember your poor father, Patrick, coming up here years ago. He was mad for the trout, too."

Nipper looked out over the pond. "Yeah," he said. "He was."

Gradually, Brendan Flynn disappeared entirely from the Old Road. "I heard they're going to put him in a home out in St. John's," Sharon said one night. "It's probably the best thing. Sure, my God, he must be close to ninety. He'll be well looked after out there."

Nipper could not picture Brendan living anywhere other than Kildura—certainly not in an old-age home. "What does Brendan say?" he asked.

"He doesn't say much of anything these days. Just stares out the window, apparently."

"I better go see him before he leaves," Nipper said.

·　　·　　·

The last time Nipper Mooney saw Brendan Flynn, his face had grown chalk-white, dry as ancient parchment. He was as skinny and spindly as the starrigans out on the barrens.

For most of Nipper's visit, Brendan slept, the thin fingers of his right hand clutching his St. Brigid's Cross to his chest. Brigid's mother stood in the doorway. "It's like he's gone back to being a little baby," she said, shaking her head. "Sleeps all the time."

Once, Brendan woke up. He winked at Nipper. "You don't need to worry about me dying just yet, Nicky. I'm not finished yet." He slowly propped himself up on his pillows. "Come here to me," he said. "I got something to ask you." Nipper bent over the bed while Brendan whispered in his ear. Nipper straightened up and nodded. "But don't you be worried," Brendan said. "I still got a bit of time left."

"He's not eating much," Brigid's mother told Nipper in the kitchen. "Not that he was ever a big eater, but now it's just tea and toast, a few Tip Top crackers. He says he never feels hungry. He doesn't even read anymore—not like he used to. Says his eyes are worn out. Well, I can believe that. Sure those books he used to read . . . ruin anyone's eyes, if you ask me." She looked at Nipper curiously. "What did he whisper to you in there?"

Nipper sighed. "He asked me—once he passes on—to say some prayers for the repose of his soul. Prayers to St. Brigid."

On the morning of February 1, 1972, Brendan Flynn went missing from St. Andrew's Mercy Home. He had risen early and dressed in his best clothes. No one saw him leave the building.

It had snowed heavily the day before, and the snow continued into the evening of February 2. The police conducted a search, but no sign of him was found. Brendan, it seemed, had vanished from the face of the earth. "He must have fallen into a snowbank," one policeman told Brigid's father. "Happens sometimes with old people. He might not turn up until the spring thaw."

On the Saturday morning of the 24th of May holiday weekend, Nipper Mooney took his fishing pole and basket and headed up the Old Road. It was drizzling and cold. The road was pocked with potholes filled with water the colour of milky tea. Patches of dirty snow flecked with spruce and fir needles lay in the ditches. When Nipper reached the path to the Damsel's Eye, where he'd planned on trying his luck, he paused briefly and then carried on. It was warmer to just keep walking. Maybe he'd try the Devil's Darning Needles. But he continued past those, too, and he soon realized his true destination.

Nipper stopped occasionally and looked behind him. He felt that someone might be following. But there was never anyone there.

On the way down to Brendan's Lookout, thick, wet branches soaked his jacket and jeans. He slipped repeatedly on the smooth rocks. As he stepped into the clearing, the sun broke through the clouds, which was lucky, he wrote Brigid later, because he might not have seen it.

But Nipper did see it, glinting on a flat boulder. He laid down his fishing pole and picked it up. He looked at it for a long time, cupping it, turning it gently in his hands.

Nipper twirled the chain around his fingers and walked out to the edge of the cliff. A dragonfly zigzagged past his head, then darted into the woods.

Something rustled behind him; he turned to see Paddy Dunne coming down the path. His red hair was slicked back behind his ears. He carried his bamboo, one hand resting lightly on his stained fishing basket.

They looked at each other silently.

"What are you going to do with it?" Paddy said finally.

Nipper looked at the cross again. "It belongs to Brigid now," he said. "Brendan told me once he wanted her to have it. You know, keep it in the family."

Paddy shouldered his bamboo. "So what do you think happened to him?"

Nipper smiled. "Well . . . if you want to know the truth, I think he was stolen by the fairies."

"No," Paddy said, shaking his head. "He went willingly."

Nipper nodded. "You're probably right."

"Yeah," Paddy said. "I think I am." He saluted Nipper with his bamboo, then turned and headed back up the steep path.

Nipper watched Paddy leave. He looked out over the ocean and listened to the breathing waves, the piercing cries of the gulls. A salt wind stirred the juniper and spruce. Nipper held up the cross by its chain and watched as it caught the light, the bright silver reflecting the sun back to heaven.

ACKNOWLEDGEMENTS

The author would like to thank Therese Anctil, Mary Aylward, Rick Boland, Paul Bowdring, Beatrix Brida, Marion Cheeks, Gail Collins, Danny Dodd, Anne Fagan, Bryan Hennessey, Susan Kent, Alison Mews, Dennis Minty, Donna Newhook, Joan Newmann, Kate Newmann, Beth Oberholtzer, Jerry O'Brien, Bert Riggs, Gordon Rodgers, Gerri Rubia, Jack Soucey, Marina Stamp, Michelle Stamp, Julie Temple and Katie Temple.

Special thanks to my editor Carmelita McGrath and to Don Morgan and everyone at Killick Press for their patience and support. Thanks also to Don McKay and my colleagues at UNB who were there at the beginning.

Drafts of parts of this novel have been broadcast on CBC radio.